DARK PEAK

DARK PEAK

GEORGE R. FEHLING

FOUNDERS HOUSE PUBLISHING
www.foundershousepublishing.com

Dark Peak

Published 2015 by Founders House Publishing, LLC
www.foundershousepublishing.com

Cover art © Kjekol/Dreamstime.com
Cover and interior design © 2015 Founders House Publishing, LLC
Paperback Edition: October 2015
ISBN-13: 978-0692554296
ISBN-10: 0692554297

Printed in the United States of America

ACKNOWLEDGMENTS

Sitting down to write one's first novel is a bit like entering the ocean for the first time as an adult. On television and in films, one might have marveled at the vast expanse of water, or in photographs, been entranced by balmy scenes of beautiful women frolicking in the tropical surf. Perhaps one even received idealized postcards from friends, reporting on what a wonderful time they were having by the sea.

But stepping into the ocean for the first time is a completely different experience. The water quickly lets us know who's in charge. It washes over us, sometimes unexpectedly, colder than we might have thought, undercurrents tugging at our legs, trying to pull us deeper, until we're nearly in over our heads.

As I started to write this book in my little studio in Stanfordville, NY, I felt a distinctly cold bucket of water cascade over me as I tried to put down onto paper the story that had been banging around inside my skull for so many years. Then one day, I noticed a small advertisement in a Hudson Valley magazine, and through it, found an instructor and lifeguard in the person of Jeffrey Davis, a former academic turned writing coach, who taught me the basic strokes of the craft, and how to go deep under the waves and survive.

Over the course of five years, it took dozens of friends, teachers, and professionals to help guide me to my destination. I would like to thank every single person who at one point or other listened to me as I drafted one revision after another of this manuscript. Everyone who spared a few moments of their time, or who lent their support in some other way, helped make DARK PEAK a reality.

Most of all, I must thank my wife, Linda, whose patience has been nothing short of saintly. As I spent money on writing conferences, editors, and other necessary pursuits, funds for vacations and other niceties became noticeably absent. Nevertheless, Linda read every version of every chapter, and listened to countless late-night monologues about the goings-on in this fictional world.

I owe a particular debt of gratitude to John Howe, the author of *The End of Fossil Energy*, who was the first person to introduce me to Hubbert's Peak. The editors, contributors and commenters on the popular blog, The Oil Drum, also offered a wealth of facts and inspiration as they debated Peak Oil and the limitations of alternative energy in the mid-2000s.

I'd like to thank my brother, Paul, and my sister Joan, who lent their support in many different ways; Porochista Khakpour and the Taos Summer Writers' Conference, where the novel was incubated; and Rachel Schneider, who taught the Farmer Beginnings' class at Hawthorne Valley Farm and whose introduction to the organic farming community provided inspiration for many aspects of the book.

Friends who provided valuable feedback on early drafts include James Elvin III, Angus Bradley, Jim O'Neill, Danny ten Duis, Katie Corcoran, Christopher Reck, Kay Larson, Jim Roland, David and Jeanne Arner, Tom Turck, and Mike and

Lisa Casey. Additionally, John Michael Greer, Blair Glaser, Delah Brucelli, Dom John, Marc Ostrow, Amy Evans, Dennis Hogarth, Nicole Foss, Charlie Steadman, and Francesca Marina were beacons of light along the way.

A special word of thanks is reserved for my editor, Fiona McLaren, whose expertise, kindness and support helped me explore some of the most important aspects of storytelling, and brought about a level of emotional depth that transformed a rather straightforward peak oil action narrative into something much more intimate and rewarding. And of course, I am sincerely grateful to Shaun and Amanda Kilgore of Founders House Publishing, for bringing DARK PEAK into the wider world.

Finally, I dedicate this book to my mother Sally, whom I miss dearly. She loved stories, and loved to tell them.

DARK PEAK

CHAPTER ONE

Amariah Wales peered through his safety goggles, leaned closer to the lab bench, and struck a long-stemmed wooden match against the side of a metal matchbox. Drawing the matchstick through the air like a magician's wand, he lit the wick of a burner beneath his experiment—an assembly of metal and glass containers arranged neatly on a vertical pole—until an orange flame licked up against the bottom of a transparent beaker. He glanced at a thermometer suspended in the liquid, then stabbed out the match in a small bucket of sand.

Wrapped in the protective cocoon of a fire-resistant lab coat, cap, and gloves, the heir to Pleasant Valley Biofuels, a mature nineteen years old, carefully observed his fifth experiment of the morning. The bulky safety goggles of his own design rested lightly on his patrician nose, shielding his blue and curious eyes from the dangerous environment around him.

The mercury in the thermometer rose as the water in the beaker warmed. He noted the time, picked up his pencil, and made an entry into a small black notebook.

There was a knock at the door. Caleb, one of the support staff, peered at him through the wires of the security window. Amariah reached under the lab bench and pressed a button, activating a buzzer to unlock the door.

"Come on in, but be careful," said Amariah, an eye on the thermometer.

Caleb nodded and silently pushed the door open with a beefy shoulder, drawing behind him a handcart with a single, five-gallon glass jug, solidly wrapped in black cable.

"I've got that ethanol you asked for, Amariah," he said, voice hushed.

"Thanks. Put it over in the corner, please."

Caleb pulled the cart into the room and slid the jar gingerly onto the floor. Wiping his brow in the hook of his arm, he transferred the moisture from his face to the sleeve of his dark shirt, already stained through the back from the heat of the summer outside. "What are you working on today?" he ventured to ask.

The young scientist focused on the flame beneath the beaker. He didn't usually like to chat while he worked, but Caleb was a gentle, simple man, and Amariah always made time to acknowledge the staff.

"I'm trying to find a way to boost the energy of our aviation fuel, so that our planes can travel farther than they do today," said Amariah, eyes on his experiment. "I'm testing each mixture by recording how long it takes to raise the temperature of a beaker of water."

"Oh," said Caleb, squinting at nothing in particular. He adjusted his suspenders with his thumb.

Amariah smiled and continued. "The only other biofuel refinery that we know of is in Albany. That's just about as far as one tank of fuel can take us. In any other direction, we

2

have to turn around when the tank is half empty. I want to go farther than that."

"I get it," said Caleb, brightening. "I guess there's no one else like you out there to make the fuel."

"Something like that," said Amariah, returning to his work.

Caleb grinned and shook his head as he moved the hand-cart closer to the door. "My, my, but that's a lot of alcohol though," he said. "You could have quite a party with that, for sure."

Amariah paused, then purposefully ended the experiment by snuffing out the flame. "Caleb," he said evenly, "the party would be extremely brief and unpleasant. That is laboratory grade ethanol. It's too strong to drink, and it contains methanol that would permanently blind anyone who sipped even the smallest quantity."

"Oh," said Caleb, alarmed. "It said alcohol on the tag, so I just thought—"

"Stick to hemp, Caleb," said Amariah. "You'll get in a lot less trouble that way."

"I didn't mean, oh no, please don't think that I would ever do anything like that," Caleb stammered, his rotund face turning red.

"It's all right," said Amariah. "I'm just kidding."

Amariah was, and he wasn't. The consumption of alcohol was forbidden on the estate—one of his father's hard and fast rules—but people being people, temptation borne out of curiosity would always be there, and many of the chemicals stored in the refinery were deadly.

"That'll be all for now," said the young master.

"Yes, sir," said the man with a slight bow. He still seemed mortified, so just before the door closed, Amariah called out to him.

"Caleb, thank you."

"Yes, sir. I'm … happy to help." He regained his composure and backed away, just as an open palm slapped against the closing door. Caleb's face dropped as he recognized Gareth Covey, the chief engineer.

"What's going on?" asked Gareth. The man had a perpetually surprised look, due in part to a shock of red hair that stood nearly straight up on his head. Amariah and his mother had an ongoing debate whether the man cut his own hair.

"Caleb was just leaving," said Amariah. He nodded and the man scurried away.

Gareth let himself in. As the chief engineer in charge of the biorefinery, he had the keys to every section of the building, including the lab, although Amariah wished he didn't. A thick ring of keys dangled off of a retractable chain attached to his belt, which jangled as he moved about the room.

Gareth eyed the jug of ethanol, then peered over at Amariah's experiment through his large, thick glasses.

"So, what are we working on today?"

Amariah didn't answer. Instead, he struck another match to light the wick that draped into the vessel of experimental fuel.

Gareth ignored the slight and strolled around the table, stealing a glance over Amariah's shoulder. Amariah quickly drew his notebook closer and flipped it shut.

"What do you want, Gareth?"

"From you? Nothing. I just need to make some room in here."

"What do you mean, 'make some room'? For what?"

4

"The Yorkers, of course. You're not going to be the only one in the lab anymore, you know."

Amariah stiffened. "They're going to sit in here?"

"You got someplace else in mind?"

Amariah did have someplace else in mind—Albany, where they belonged. His mouth hung open as he searched for the right words. "My father will be back this afternoon; I want to check this with him."

"Go right ahead," said Gareth. "It's your father's orders. 'The Yorkers are going to need space in the lab.' That's what he told me."

Amariah returned to his work, distracted. The water had already boiled; he had failed to note the time. He cursed and extinguished the flame. He would have to start all over.

Gareth chuckled and moved around the room, making a show of consulting his clipboard. The little micromanager enjoyed irritating the young heir, ever since Amariah had discovered a batch of contaminated fuel and had told his father about it, resulting in the loss of an entire tank of refined biodiesel and a dressing-down of Gareth for his sloppy maintenance.

Something on the lab table caught Amariah's eye. "Hey, Gareth, I think I found a way to boost the energy density of our aviation fuel," he said. "But the mixture keeps separating and I would like your opinion. Why don't you take a look?"

He nodded at an open beaker. It contained a volatile liquid produced by the new biomass processor, which used an enzyme his father had developed to transform waste wood into cellulosic ethanol. The beaker had been sitting open for a few minutes.

Gareth scrutinized Amariah, unsure whether he was being serious. Amariah shrugged and then struck another match as if to relight his experiment. Gareth couldn't help himself, and leaned in for a closer look.

With one quick motion, Amariah tossed the match into the beaker. A fountain of flame erupted over the table. Gareth jumped back and threw his arms up in front of his face, knocking over several items on the table behind him. The flame dissipated as the fumes burned away.

Gareth dropped his arms, realizing he'd been had. "That wasn't very damned funny," he sputtered.

A loud, clanging bell pierced the air. The fire alarm. Gareth stumbled over to a wall panel and inserted a key from his chain. The alarm stopped, but the room continued to hum.

Amariah shut down his experiment and pulled off his lab gear. "Don't touch anything in here, Gareth," he warned.

He stuffed his notebook into his satchel and headed for the door, fuming as he made his way down the corridor. If what Gareth said was true, then this time his father had really gone too far. The lab was a private work space that only he and his father shared. Now, strangers would be sitting in there with them? He would never have any privacy. He would certainly never get any work done. And, on top of it all, they were Yorkers!

He arrived in the biorefinery's main processing area, a cavernous space in the center of the building, where three giant stainless steel mixing tanks dwarfed everything else in the room. Like the rest of the facility, the tanks were functioning relics, installed nearly a century earlier by a long-defunct farmers' cooperative. The Yorkers had a similar refinery in Albany, according to his father, but it was much smaller and not nearly as productive.

At the loading dock, workers shouted as they unloaded oilseed from a line of horse-drawn carts arriving from the surrounding plantations. The oilseed had to be weighed and then dried before storage. The noise made it impossible for him to think.

In the corner, a circular steel staircase led to the roof. He took the metal steps two at a time. At the top, he forced open a heavy metal door and stepped out onto the roof into the open air.

Beautiful, late summer sunshine lit all of Pleasant Valley. Hundreds of acres of canola, soybean, and sunflowers stretched out before him in a multicolored patchwork that reached all the way to the Wales mansion, seated on a rise two miles to the north. A grassy airstrip split the valley down the middle, separating the ramshackle houses of the workers' village to the west, from the red manufacturing and storage sheds to the east.

Amariah reached behind his head and undid the string that held his ponytail, shaking his long brown hair out until it fell over his shoulders. Resting his forearms on the railing, he idly observed the line of wagons lined up at the base of the refinery, the plantation foremen barking orders at their laborers when it was their turn to unload.

The door creaked open behind him. Clarence Hodgkins, Chief of the Wales Guard, stood blinking in the sunlight, the sun glistening off his bald head.

"I thought I'd find you up here," said Hodgkins. "Did you just try to set Gareth on fire?"

Amariah dropped his gaze and shuffled his feet. "He was sticking his nose in my work again, Hodgkins. I just wanted to scare him off."

"Well, you've pissed him off, that's for sure."

"Is that what you came up here to tell me?"

"No, I came up here to ask you to not intentionally set the fire alarms off in the lab. People are jumpy enough as it is."

It was true. Today was the big day. The Yorkers were coming. Amariah's father, the great Kenan Wales, would be hosting a grand affair tonight to celebrate the impending merger of Pleasant Valley Biofuels with American Agrifuels of Albany, New York. All of the neighboring aristocratic families were invited.

"I'm sorry," said Amariah.

Hodgkins shrugged. "Your mother is looking for you. She called on the intercom. She wants you back at the house. The Yorkers will be at the front gate at noon and you're supposed to be dressed and back here in time for the tour."

Amariah turned and regarded the valley, overshadowed by the elephantine hulk of Mount Mansfield, the tallest mountain in Vermont.

"Hodgkins," he said, "do you mind if I ask you a personal question?"

The guardsman drew a slight breath and then ran his hand along his bald head, as if searching for the hair that used to be there. "Sure," he allowed.

"Why do you stay here?" asked Amariah. "You're free to go anywhere you want. Why not go and see the world?"

Hodgkins shrugged. "This is my home. I don't want to go anywhere else."

Amariah pictured the road outside the barrier wall that separated the valley from Jeffersonville, Johnson, and points beyond. He had glimpsed the distant landscape briefly from the air several times during flying lessons with his father, but had never been more than fifty miles from where he was born.

"How far do you think a person could get on their own—without a plane?" asked Amariah.

"Which person specifically? Anyone I know?"

Amariah kept his eyes on the mountain.

"Not very far, even by horseback," conceded Hodgkins. "As I've told you before, there are bandits on the roads. The towns will tax you for passage. By the time you got where you wanted, you would have little left, and that's if you were to arrive there at all. All right? Does that answer your question?"

The sun had only now climbed out from behind the dark peak of Mount Mansfield, which at this hour managed to appear gloomy and ominous even on a hot summer day. But high up near the top, the trees had started to turn, tingeing the green expanse with the hint of yellow and orange.

"Come on, will you? Your mother's waiting!" said Hodgkins. "I'll take you in the wagon."

"I rode Charlemagne over this morning," said Amariah, turning away from the view. "I'll ride him back."

"Suit yourself," said Hodgkins, "but I'll ride along with you, if you don't mind."

Hodgkins held the door open for the young heir and stretched out his arm for Amariah to proceed. The bald security officer took a final look around and then shut the door, locking it from the inside.

CHAPTER TWO

Stone entrance walls marked the boundary between the intensive agriculture of the valley floor and the elevated, manicured grounds of the Wales estate. Several dozen farmhands, crouched over rows of vegetables, ignored Amariah and Hodgkins as they rode through the final acre of cultivated land and up the hill to the family seat.

Arriving at the trim lawn behind the Georgian-style manor house, built by Kenan Wales out of timber, stone, and reclaimed materials from abandoned estates, Hodgkins stopped. "See you at the party," said the guardsman, trying to get Amariah's goat.

"Be careful who you let in," responded Amariah, in kind.

Hodgkins grinned and urged his horse along, disappearing behind the mansion on his way to the main gate. Amariah clicked his tongue and turned Charlemagne right toward the stables, where, to his surprise, the stable master stood already waiting.

The usually jovial man took hold of the bridle as Amariah dismounted. "Your mother is looking for you," he said, apologetically.

"Yes, yes, I know," sighed Amariah. "Thank you, Mr. Tipton."

Amariah stroked his dear horse one final time, then headed off, jogging back up the road and through the garden to an unlocked door on the side of the house. Striding through the spare and elegant halls, decorated by his mother in the neo-Amish style, he encountered servants everywhere—dusting windowsills, carrying trays, and polishing doorknobs. In the grand entrance hall, Jared, the grey underbutler, stood at the top of a tall ladder, replacing lightbulbs in the electric chandelier.

Amariah intoned, "'Let there be light!'"

The elderly man ignored him as he made a final turn of a bulb. Light sprang forth, drawing electricity from the estate's own generator, powered by refined seed oil.

"My job is only to install the bulb, sir," he said, droll as ever.

Amariah laughed. He found it easy to joke with the staff, most of whom he had known since he was a little boy. He gave Jared a wave as he backed away around a corner, and nearly bumped into a housemaid, her eyes downcast as she placed flowers in an earthen vase.

"Excuse me, I'm sorry," said Amariah.

The woman didn't meet his glance, but just mumbled and kept on with her work. Amariah said nothing and kept going. It was well known that her entire family had been killed in the Troubles by a marauding band of Yorkers. Now there she was, tasked with creating a flower arrangement to welcome their former antagonists. He shook his head.

He arrived at the kitchen and pulled open the heavy wooden door. Kitchen staff tended every oven and stovetop. Steam wafted over him, infused with the aroma of roasting meat and boiling potatoes. The Wales' own cooking fuel, processed in the refinery, burned clean.

In the center of the room stood Amariah's mother, an island of calm in an ocean of activity, deep in conversation with the head cook. She wore her hair today in a braid down her slender back. Amariah still thought she was the most beautiful woman he had ever seen.

"Excuse me, sir."

Amariah turned and encountered a pair of striking green eyes under a head of tightly pulled back red hair. The bosomy kitchen maid, newly in service at the estate, held a large harvest basket filled with purple potatoes. While she was only in her mid-twenties, with pale, freckled skin, the girl had a strange, hard look about her, unfortunately all too common among those newly arrived inside the valley's protective walls.

Amariah continued to stare at her, trying not to let his eyes drop to her breasts. She stared right back at him, until he realized he was blocking her way. With a stammer, he excused himself and stepped aside.

Right behind her, coming up the stairs from the basement food stores, huffed Margaret McGrath, the housekeeper. Noticing Amariah, she rolled her eyes, as if she knew exactly what the young man had been thinking.

"If anyone else has forgotten anything, please tell me now," she announced. "I don't want to spend the rest of the day going up and down these stairs." Receiving no response, she swung the gate closed behind her, locking the food storage cellar with a key that never left her person.

"Is there something I can get for you, Amariah?" she asked.

At the mention of his name, his mother looked up and waved him over. "We won't have time to have lunch together today, dear," she said above the noise. "Mrs. McGrath has sent something up to your room."

Amariah came around the table and kissed his mother on the cheek.

"So, here you are at last," she said.

Amariah ignored the rebuke. "What are those?"

On top of a folder on the table lay a stack of small watercolors, painted on cards about five inches high by seven inches wide. The topmost card depicted a beachside scene by the ocean, with a foreground of nesting birds on a grassy dune. His mother had grown up near the sea in Massachusetts and many of her paintings were of seascapes.

"I made one for each table. Each is different. It's part of the table setting." She held it up for him to see.

"Nice work," he said.

"Thank you. Now, go on upstairs and get changed."

"I'll be on time," he said. "They're not expected until noon."

"My dear, the Yorkers are already here—more than an hour early, no less. You need to get changed and get back to the plant to keep them entertained until your father arrives."

"Gareth can do that," he said dejectedly. "I'm sure he would *love* to fill them in."

His mother's eyes darted around the kitchen. "What's the matter with you?" she whispered.

Amariah just shook his head and said nothing.

"Come with me," she said. She spun around and marched off toward a doorway that led out onto a small veranda. The screen door banged shut behind them. As she turned to address her son, a stiffening breeze rustled the upper leaves of the mature rock maples around the house.

"Look," she said, in that lecturing tone he knew so well, "whatever you may feel about this situation, you have a duty to your father and to this household to help things go smoothly today. I want you on your best behavior."

"Did you know that father was going to let the Yorkers into the lab?"

"No. Why? Is that a problem?"

"Everyone thinks this is a mistake."

His mother closed her eyes and sighed. "People have said that many times about your father in the past, and they've been wrong every time."

"Not this time," said Amariah. "You should never have let it get this far."

His mother shrank back and Amariah instantly regretted his remark.

Sarah Wales reached up with her slender hands and adjusted her son's tunic. "Your father believes this is for the best," she said, imploring him with softened eyes. "He believes the time is right, and he wants to give you the opportunity to … to do great things. You are going to be the head of the estate someday, and you are going to have to start to take on more responsibility. And that includes dealing with the Yorkers, whether you like it or not."

"More responsibility!" he exclaimed. "Ever since I was little you have made me feel responsible for everything and everyone around here. For God's sake, I've been a practical employee of this place since I was five!"

"Come on now, that's not fair," said his mother. "This partnership with the Yorkers is an opportunity to start to put things back together again. We all have to put our feelings aside—all of us."

She paused for a moment and took a deep breath. "Your father plans to announce that you will be taking over tonight."

Amariah froze.

"He plans to announce it to everyone," she said again, smiling. "Tonight. To make it official. You're going to be in charge of Pleasant Valley Biofuels. Although, your father will still have a say in how things are done, of course."

"Tonight?" Amariah's world fell in around him, his last chance to leave the valley closing shut. "I thought he was just going to announce the merger with the Yorkers tonight." He tried to keep his voice from sounding like a whine.

"Well, yes, that too," she said, "but he wants everyone to know that you will be the one in charge."

He fought off the tears that threatened to come to his eyes.

"Aren't you pleased?"

He shook his head, afraid to speak, and took a couple of steps to the railing. Far across the valley, near the workers' village, a kite flew in the breeze.

His mother stepped up beside him, and they observed it silently together. "Must be one of the workers' children," she said finally.

The kite dipped and swayed in the breeze, a beautiful sight, and unusual. Few people had time to be flying kites, especially during harvest season.

"It must be nice to be free, like a bird," she said wistfully. "To fly over the walls and go anywhere you want."

Amariah cleared his throat. "I want to see the ocean," he said abruptly. "I want to stand on a beach and look at a hori-

15

zon where there's nothing on the other side. Maybe even go on a ship, and sail to the islands."

"It's too dangerous, you know that."

"I can fly down to the Cape and back. I've got it all figured out."

"As your father has already told you, his plane cannot go that far and back on one tank. You don't know if there's a safe airstrip, and your father doesn't have the time—"

"I want my own plane. I've done the calculations. I can build some extra capacity into the tanks, and then the ocean will be in range, for one person."

"You want your own plane, to fly down to the ocean by yourself?"

"Yes."

"My dear, that's impossible. We need you here. What if something happened? How would we know how to find you?"

"Nothing is going to happen! I can reconnoiter a landing strip from the air."

His mother sighed. "Someday, you'll go off on an adventure. But right now too many people are counting on you. Your father needs you in the lab. Look, you've got your entire life in front of you. Work with the Yorkers and make this merger a success, then maybe someday, you can do, well, whatever you want to do."

Amariah realized it was pointless to discuss this further. His parents wanted him rooted to Pleasant Valley like a tree.

"Get changed now," said his mother. "Look your best. Entertain the Yorkers until your father arrives. And, please, do not be late."

Amariah didn't try to hide his disappointment. Still, he kissed his mother on the cheek and headed back inside to go up to his room.

Before he stepped through the door, he glanced back. His mother had turned to watch the kite again, her dancer's frame silhouetted against a windswept, open sky.

CHAPTER THREE

It took Captain Peck and his troop just over an hour to ride the seven miles from Camp Ethan Allen to the river valley at Underhill Flats—good timing considering the heavy prison wagon that lumbered along behind them. The few people they had passed along the way had kept a wary distance, knowing that the green windowless wagon meant only one thing.

Up ahead in the gloom, the small white farmhouse waited, backed up against thick wooded hillsides that crept down from the mountains. Peck quickened his horse down the dusty road, and his troop kept pace behind him.

Searching the brightening sky, he saw only a few wispy clouds. He turned and glared at his lieutenant. "Where the hell are they?"

Lieutenant Dickins, looking sharp as usual in his crisp green uniform, glanced over each shoulder and shrugged.

Peck turned back to their objective. The farmhouse was one of the few still standing in the long, flat river valley to the southwest of Mount Mansfield. Rebels and bandits were known to lurk among the canola at this time of year, using the high stalks as cover for ambushes, but, with the fields recently harvested, the troop had a clear line of sight all along the river road.

"Keep it tight!" he ordered.

Moving as one, the troop charged the remaining distance up to the house. Coming to a halt with a thunderous clatter, half of the men dismounted, took hold of their rifles and directed them at the two-story wooden farmhouse. All was silent and still, except for the thin gauze curtains that twitched and swayed behind half-open windows.

Peck dismounted with practiced ease, unbuckled a saddlebag and removed a clipboard with a thin collection of papers. He was clean shaven, except for a blonde mustache that he kept well-trimmed. Everything about him projected an aura of calm and professionalism, from the top of his campaign hat down to his shiny black riding boots.

Dickins joined him, his dark-skinned hand resting on his sidearm, and together they strode up onto the porch, boots echoing against the floorboards. The captain rapped on the frame of the screen door and they waited.

Through the dim internal haze, the outline of a young woman emerged, stopping just short of the door on the other side. Dark brown hair extended nearly to her waist. Peck guessed she was around twenty years old. Her brilliant blue eyes widened as she took in the sight of the men with rifles in her front yard.

"Good morning," said Peck, warmly. "Are you the lady of the house?"

"Uhh—"

The two uniformed officers cast an appreciative eye over the girl until a man stomped up and yanked her away from the door. "Stay inside, Hannah," he growled.

Peck recognized Mark Bowman by his thick dark hair and his loose, sun-faded clothing.

"Mr. Bowman?"

"Yes?"

"Mind coming out here for a moment?"

The farmer hesitated and then stepped out onto the porch, trying not to look at the uniformed men in his front yard. Back inside, a woman in a long house dress came forward, wiping her hands on a towel. At the sight of the soldiers, she fumbled with the towel and dropped it.

Captain Peck spoke in a voice loud enough for his men to hear. "Mr. Bowman," he said again, as if to confirm his identity, "it seems that you were a little light on your quota this season."

"Yes, it was a tough year," said the man in his farmer's drawl.

"Yes, it was. Yes, indeed," said Peck, nodding and looking through his paperwork. "You see, though, you are below the quota of most of your neighbors, and we'd like to know why."

Bowman sighed. "You want to know why, Captain? I'm not allowed to rotate my crops, even for a single season, that's why. And, we were given very little fertilizer this year, as you know."

"Well, sir, there's a war on, and times are tough all over. But you're still expected to meet your quota."

"You mean, there *was* a war on," said the woman, chiming in from inside the house. "The war's been over for ten years!"

There was a silence in the air, and the slightest stiffening among the soldiers.

"Sir, why don't you step down here so we can talk privately," said Peck.

The farmer turned to glare at his wife and then did as he was told. Peck accompanied the man down off the porch.

"You see, sir, according to this," he flipped over a page on his clipboard, "you've got nearly forty acres of pretty good bottomland here, and we're just not sure why your yields are down so much."

"Well, we haven't finished taking it all in yet—we've still got some out in the field, as you can see."

Indeed, some of the canola crops still stood behind the house along the edge of the forest.

"Mind if we take a look around?"

Bowman shrugged and said nothing.

The men with the rifles fanned out, eyes darting at the dense, dark woods. The rest of the soldiers dismounted, with the exception of the grizzled old man at the reins of the dark green prison wagon, who sat looking as if he had all day, no matter what was about to happen.

Peck walked with the farmer to the side of the house, where a long white picket fence protected a large vegetable garden—weeded, well tended, and surrounded by a border of colorful flowers.

"Well, well, what have we here?" asked Peck.

"We're allowed to have a small vegetable garden for personal use."

The captain glanced down the nearest row. "Mighty fine vegetables you've got here," he said. "Mighty fine." He fingered a string bean. "Got a green thumb, do we?"

"It's mostly my daughter's doing," said Bowman. "Guess it runs in the family."

"Is that so? I'd love to know your secret."

Bowman blanched. "There is no secret, Captain. We rotate the type of plants each year and use cover crops to give the soil a chance to recover. We can't do that with the oilseed crops, because we're forced to keep all the fields in production all the time. That's why the yields are down."

Peck was barely listening. He walked along the fence with his men until he came around to the other side of the garden closest to the woods, where there lay a long row of piled straw. He lifted his index finger into the air and waved it in a circular motion. His men began removing the straw with their bare hands. Underneath it was a pile of black, moist compost.

He let out a low whistle. "My, my, black gold. Need all of this for a little vegetable garden, do we?"

The farmer said nothing.

"Captain, over here," called a soldier. He stood before the section of the field that had not yet been cut, just beyond the garden, where the stalks of canola were dense and shoulder high.

Within a few steps Peck came into a clearing, cut right into the field, so as to be invisible from the road. The plot was large, nearly a hundred feet wide and twice as long, with deep black soil and row after row of vegetables.

Peck took a good look around. The aerial spotters had done their job well—there was even more here than he imagined.

Satisfied, he gave a signal. Two of his men grabbed the farmer. Peck made a fist and struck him as hard as he could, right in the center of his stomach.

Bowman doubled over and fell to the ground.

The officer grabbed the man's hair and lifted him to his knees. "Little vegetable garden?" he hissed. "There's enough

22

food here to feed a small army. And that's exactly what you're up to, isn't it, *rebel*? Isn't it?"

He slapped him hard across the face, once, twice.

"Father!" The man's daughter ran through a gate in the garden fence and threw herself between the two men. "Stop! Stop it!" she cried, her face twisted. "What's the matter with you?"

Peck straightened up and wiped the back of his hand across his mustache. He gave a command loud enough for everyone to hear.

"Clear this field," he announced. "Take what's ripe and destroy the rest."

He put out his hand for the clipboard and then turned back to the farmer, who was back on the ground, clutching his abdomen.

"Mr. Bowman, you are under arrest," he said, his voice calm. "The charges include failing to meet your quota of oilseed, exceeding your personal quota of homegrown consumable items, black marketeering, and providing aid and comfort to the enemy."

From far away, he heard the unmistakable drone of an airplane engine on approach.

"About time," he muttered.

The drone of the motor grew steadily. Then, over the treetops, a large biplane roared over the crowd, flying in swift and close as it banked around the house. It was uniform green, with a long, narrow fuselage and the three-letter emblem of the Northern Vermont Militia painted on its tail. Peck could see the pilot and copilot seated inside their open cockpits, one behind the other. The plane disappeared behind the treetops as it circled around for another pass.

Peck signaled to a thin, dark-skinned soldier—Sergeant Philips. Moving with purpose, Philips stepped out into a clearing and pulled two flags from a small case. When the plane reappeared, he stood erect, held his arms out straight, and snapped the flags in a precise rhythm. The pilot wagged his wings.

Bowman lay cradled in the arms of his daughter. His wife had run out, too, and now glowered at Peck, her hatred unconcealed.

The captain addressed the two women, his voice pitched low. "I'm going to give you ladies some options to think about," he said. "You tell me everything you know about the rebels, how you communicate with them, and where they're hiding, and you will soon be a family again. If not, your man here will come with us, and then, eventually, he will tell me anyway."

The women said nothing.

Peck shrugged. "Have it your way."

He motioned to his lieutenants. "Take him."

The soldiers lifted the farmer off the ground and dragged him by the armpits along the garden fence toward the waiting wagon. Out in the road, the grizzled old driver stepped down from his perch and went around to the back to open the door.

Peck turned around to watch the soldiers moving through the field, throwing unripened plants on a bonfire. One soldier, slightly chubbier than the rest, had gotten ahead of the others and now carried a big armful of slender orange carrots. He rubbed the dirt off a carrot and took a bite.

Peck nudged his lieutenant and called out to the man. "Hey, you fat bastard, how can you be hungry already? You just ate!"

The other soldiers laughed. The man opened his mouth to protest. Then an arrow flew out of the woods and slammed through the side of his neck, striking just below his ear. The man dropped his bundle and threw his hands up to his neck. He made a horrible gargling sound as blood combined with freshly chewed carrots ran out of his mouth and down his double chin. He dropped to his knees, red-faced and uncomprehending, and then pitched face-first into the dirt.

Instinctively, Peck took a step back. An arrow flew right past his face, the breeze from its tail feathers skimming his forehead.

"Ambush!" he yelled.

From the woods came a hailstorm of arrows. The soldiers scattered, diving behind any shelter they could find. Bowman wrestled free from his captors and ran back into his house. Peck, crouched behind an overturned wheelbarrow, saw the old man leap back onto the wagon and urge the horses away at full gallop.

Peck rose to his knee and fired his handgun into the leafy green forest. In the glare of the sun, his eyes had trouble penetrating the darkness of the woods, but that didn't stop him from unloading his weapon as fast as he could.

Goddamn it!

There were at least two dozen forest commandos up there, Peck estimated—men and women both—pulling arrows out of quivers and firing repeatedly at his panicked soldiers, like goddamned Robin Hoods.

Peck darted from the wheelbarrow and ran along the fence. He was almost at the house when he felt a sharp pain in his right thigh and stumbled to the ground. He twisted his head and saw Bowman in an upstairs window, a rifle in his hands.

25

Peck lurched back to his feet and hobbled to the front of the house where his frightened horse neighed and bucked amidst the tumult. He snatched the lead line off the fence post and threw his arms around the horse's neck, pushing the animal towards the road and throwing his foot over the saddle. Peck clung to its muscled body for dear life as the horse ran down the road.

When he reached a safe distance, he shouted at the horse to stop and dropped clumsily to the ground. At the farmhouse down the road, only Philips still stood, his back against the white picket fence. A handful of rebels had emerged from the woods and were encroaching on him, but Philips held them off with a large-bored gun which he swung back and forth in a wide semi-circle. Abruptly, he lifted his arm straight up into the air and pulled the trigger. A bright red flare exploded out of the gun and arced into the sky.

The plane!

Peck searched the sky. Then he heard it, a sudden shift in the sound of the engine from high above. Apparently, the pilot, who had climbed to a higher altitude after getting the "all clear" signal, had seen the flare. The idiots hadn't heard the gunfire over the sound of the engine.

Now, dark green wings appeared as the plane pitched over into a steep dive. It flew low and fast over the commotion like an angry industrial dragon, passing overhead with a deafening roar, then made a high right turn and barreled down again, guns ablaze.

The rebels scattered. The farmer's wife and daughter ran into the forest, while Bowman stood amidst the chaos in a heated argument with one of the rebels. Gunfire ripped across the ground and the two men darted in opposite directions before dashing into the woods.

The plane circled around again, then again, guns silent. There was nothing left to shoot at; the skirmish was over. Peck watched the biplane hesitate, then pull away and head back towards the airfield. They were probably short on fuel—again.

He ripped his hat off and smashed it with his fist into the dirt. A terrible, hot pain shot up his bleeding leg and he cried out in anguish. Clutching at his thigh, he cursed and drooled through clenched teeth.

His troops lay wounded on the ground, he had been made to look the fool, and the rebels had escaped again under the thick canopy of forest. As the smoke from the bonfire curled into the sky, Peck swore his revenge, knowing that plans were already in motion to ensure his victory.

CHAPTER FOUR

Max, Amariah's closest friend, often hung around the bottom of the hill, chatting up the female farmhands while waiting for the Wales progeny to pass by. Today was no exception.

Moving at a brisk trot, Amariah rode Charlemagne off the grounds of the residence and onto the valley floor, flushing a handful of young women back to their harvest baskets. Max hopped down from his perch on top of the stone wall, ditched his hemp cigarette, and swung up onto his mare. Amariah was fifty yards farther down the road before his friend finally caught up with him.

The sandy-haired boy let out a low whistle. "My, my, look at you," he said, feigning admiration. "You must give me the name of your tailor."

Amariah laughed. He had changed into his fine dress clothes—green velvet breeches, white tunic, matching ivory vest, and shiny dress boots—admittedly a little early in the day to be turned out so sharply, since the banquet wasn't until that evening, but his mother wanted him looking his best for the tour.

"If you must know, her name is Sarah Wales," said Amariah with a grin. "Why don't you give her my name? Maybe she'll give you a discount."

"I have a better idea," said Max. "Why don't we just trade places?"

Max's parents were fallen aristocrats whose farm lay in ruins beyond the protective arm of the Northern Vermont Militia. They lived now in the workers' village, a temporary refuge granted by Kenan and Sarah Wales ten years ago, which had turned into a permanent living arrangement. Their initial gratitude had morphed into silent resentment as their fortunes failed to improve.

Amariah pursed his lips. "Well, for one reason, Max, we hardly look alike, and everyone already knows who you are. Second, I know of at least one girl who is looking rather plump around the middle at the moment, whose parents are none too pleased. And I, for one, have no interest in that."

"Ah, yes, well, that's a tricky situation," said the raccoon-eyed young Romeo, scratching behind his ear.

Max had spent his young life pursuing just about every girl in the valley. Amariah had not. Choosing a wife would be a complicated matter for the heir to Pleasant Valley, likely to involve parents, business, and politics. In any case, he found little to interest him in the proper young women presented to him at society events. Much to the exasperation of their parents, Amariah abstinently refused to pursue any of the attractive young women, even though nearly everyone considered them to be perfectly acceptable potential mates.

The two rode on in silence for a few moments, the noontime sun beating down on the respective riders and horses.

"Hey, why don't we duck out and go for a swim?" Max suggested, changing the subject.

29

Amariah glanced over at his friend, who somehow managed to remain gaunt and pale no matter how much time he spent outdoors. "Can't," he said. "I've got to get back to the plant to give the Yorkers their tour."

"Ah, the Yorkers," said Max. "Your father's new friends."

Amariah winced.

Max leaned in. "With no one left to rape and pillage, they're trying to act respectable now. Nice of your father to put out the welcome mat."

Max's parents blamed the Yorkers for their predicament, claiming that the marauders who had forced them to flee were from the other side of the lake. Although Amariah wondered how they could have been so sure.

"You're a fine one to be leading the tour," continued Max. He lowered his voice in mock seriousness, pretending to be Amariah. "Welcome to Pleasant Valley. See my refinery? Great, now get out."

"Not only that," said Amariah, happy to unburden himself, "but I'm supposed to give them this." He reached around to his saddlebag and produced a white linen envelope.

Max reached across the gap between their horses and plucked it from his hands. Seeing that it was unsealed, he opened it.

"Hey, give that back," said Amariah. Too late, he had forgotten that Max's parents had been left off the guest list.

Max stopped his mare and scanned the embossed invitation, his face falling as he deciphered the script. "Unbelievable," he said. He drooped back into his saddle, the dark circles under his eyes seeming to grow darker.

"Sorry," said Amariah.

30

Max sat upright with a start. "You know what we should do with this?" he said triumphantly, waving the invitation in the air. "Throw it over the wall." The young man glared defiantly at Amariah, thrust out his jaw, then galloped to the east, up the rocky trail that led to the tower beside the secondary gate.

"Max, no!" shouted Amariah. This was no time for fooling around; what was worse, Amariah wasn't sure if he was really fooling.

Clever and quick, Max and his mare raced ahead up the rocky path, teasing Amariah up the twists and turns of the trail, always managing to stay a few paces ahead of Charlemagne. The tall brush, grown wild at the end of the summer, snagged at Amariah's clothes, and although Charlemagne was the stronger horse, the pair could not overtake them.

Max arrived on top of the barrier wall and rode right to the edge, grinning maliciously. He stretched his hand out over the abyss, dangling the invitation above the steep drop. The ground below bristled with sharpened stakes.

"Max, don't," pleaded Amariah. To retrieve the envelope would require the opening of the secondary gate, the involvement of the Wales Guard, and the notification of his parents.

"What's going on down there?" came a booming voice. It was Joshua, the one-armed watchman, calling from the top of his stone tower.

Max's giddiness faded. "We're only fooling around," he answered, haltingly, as he handed the invitation back to Amariah.

"You stupid sow," said Amariah, inspecting the envelope. "My mother would have killed me." He put it carefully back in his saddlebag and then buckled it shut.

Joshua spoke again, his articulation crystal clear despite the distance. "Amariah, aren't you supposed to be at the refinery?"

Amariah peered up at the watchtower, blocking the glare with his hand. Joshua was Amariah's confidante and friend, despite being his father's age. The one-armed watchman knew everything that happened both inside and outside of the wall.

"I'm on my way," said Amariah.

Joshua glanced in the direction of the refinery. "Better hurry."

Amariah gave Max a sharp look and turned away, riding quickly down off the wall, heading south.

"Oh come on, I was just kidding," shouted Max. "Really, enjoy the party!"

But they both knew he didn't mean it.

❧

In their long black suit jackets and matching top hats, the dozen Yorkers resembled members of an undertakers' guild at a funeral for one of their own. Filing out the front doors of the refinery's squat administrative building, they gawked at the towering seed silos, the tallest man-made structures for hundreds of miles around. The eight conjoined towers held nearly all of the canola, soy, and sunflower seeds produced in Northern Vermont for an entire season—a veritable treasure, secured in a concrete castle.

Amariah dismounted, removed the invitation from his saddlebag, and handed Charlemagne's lead to a waiting attendant. He hurried towards the small crowd facing Gareth Covey. Surely he had not missed the tour already?

The Yorkers' drawn, thin faces, tainted black by years of heavy smoking, turned in unison to face him, their stiff white collars concealing the lower half of their flabby necks. They took Amariah in, eyes bulging over droopy mustaches.

"And so," said Gareth, as if he wasn't even there, "when the farmer's cooperative finally abandoned the refinery, Kenan mobilized a group of his neighbors to fend off looters and armed gangs. For nearly two years they took turns sleeping in the administrative building here, and if anyone got too close, they fired warning shots from the top of the silos up there."

The assembled turned and squinted up at the top of the towers.

"Now, we didn't kill anybody as far as we know, but we certainly gave a few looters a scar to remember us by."

Amariah remained off to the side and rolled his eyes. Gareth loved to tell the story of how his father had saved the biorefinery during the Troubles, and each time he told it, he made it sound even more like he had been there himself.

"After the grid went down for good," continued Gareth, "Kenan developed a small batch of biofuel, just enough to get the power back on. Today it's the only biofuel refinery operating in the territory. Without it, the NVM couldn't fly their planes, and the troops up at the border couldn't operate their hardware. That, of course, would make *some* people very happy, which is why we built the barrier wall."

Gareth gestured at the wall that snaked around the valley, appearing less formidable than it did from the outside. "The rebels want to destroy everything we have built here," he said, his voice rising. "We're working every day, trying to bring civilization back from the brink, and they want to drag us all back to the Stone Age! Well, let them go and live in caves like savages. We are restoring mankind to his proper place—masters of the earth, masters of the sky, and someday, if we keep our focus, maybe we'll even go back to the moon!"

One of the Yorkers clapped, and the rest joined in politely, if unenthusiastically.

"Which brings us to our latest addition, our biomass processing facility," said Gareth. He gestured to a brand-new building made of handmade brick that stood several hundred feet away.

"Kenan has discovered, or rediscovered I should say, a process that can efficiently turn trees into cellulosic ethanol," he continued. "This could end the energy shortage once and for all, since we could tap into the forest for an endless supply of liquid fuel. With the extra flying time, the NVM could wipe out the rebels and the rest of us could finally trade our horses for cars."

Amariah shot Gareth a look. His father was adamant that the forest would not be harvested for something as wasteful as automotive fuel, no matter the reason. Trees did not grow back quickly enough to make the process sustainable. He had been very clear about that, even though this had angered their Stakeholders.

Gareth caught Amariah's look and made what seemed to be a painful effort to turn his attention to the young man. "And now may I introduce Kenan's son, Amariah Wales," he said, with an exaggerated flourish. "Glad you could finally join us!"

Some of the men shared sideways glances. Amariah looked down—his vest had been ripped open during his wild ride, with several buttons now hanging loose or missing altogether. Somehow, his sleeves had been smeared with dirt.

He brushed himself off, trying to compose himself, then looked up and scanned the crowd, mustering as much grace as he could manage. "Good afternoon."

A blonde woman stepped out of the group, hand extended. "How delightful! What a pleasure to meet you at last. I'm Madeline Malinger." The hot sun sprang off the woman's red, wide-brimmed hat.

"How do you do?" he said. "It is my pleasure to meet you, Mrs. Malinger. Thank you so much for coming."

"Madeline, please." The woman shook his hand.

He handed the woman the invitation. "Mother asked me to hand-deliver this invitation to you for this evening's event."

The woman took the envelope but did not open it. "Thank you," she said, her brown eyes quickly scanning him up and down. She gestured to a tall young man hovering behind her.

"May I introduce my son—Eric."

"Hey," said the son, his smirk befitting the permanent black stubble that covered his face and chin. Hairy knuckles reached around Mrs. Malinger to shake Amariah's hand.

"Hello," said Amariah. "How was your journey?"

"Just great," said the young Yorker, regarding Amariah's outfit with barely concealed amusement. "I hear we're going to be sitting together. I can't wait to pick your brain."

Amariah managed a faint grin, suddenly uncomfortable in his own clothes. *Fat chance*, he thought.

Mrs. Malinger proceeded to introduce the other men in the group. From their awkward glances, Amariah began to suspect he had some dirt smeared across his cheek.

"Well, now that that's done," said Gareth, "why don't we stroll over to the airstrip? The gentlemen should be landing soon."

"My dear man," said Mrs. Malinger with a laugh. "I do not *stroll* anywhere."

She made a small gesture, and three of the Yorker men peeled away from the group, disappearing around the corner of the administrative building.

Gareth approached him. "What the hell happened to you?"

"I fell off my horse," said Amariah.

"You? You fell?" He made a face.

Out of sight, an engine roared to life, and everyone turned to look. A black car appeared around the corner, shiny as a mirror. Behind it followed two more identical vehicles—a convoy of black metal, glistening chrome, and polished glass. Silver embossed lettering, emblazoned across the front of each of them, spelled out the words, "Range Rover."

"In Albany, we are accustomed to driving, sir," said Mrs. Malinger.

Unlike the open-air summer toys the Stakeholder families played around with, these were real cars, like the ones in the old photographs on the walls of Amariah's room—although decades old and refurbished, of course.

One of the Yorkers moved to open the rear passenger door for Mrs. Malinger, but Gareth leapt in front of him. "Allow me," he offered with a bow.

"Why, thank you," said the woman, pretending to be flattered. Her son hopped into the front passenger seat, and Amariah caught a glimpse of his own disheveled reflection as the car pulled away. Indeed, there was dirt on his face, and on his ivory vest as well. He made an attempt to wipe it off.

Gareth beamed. "Maybe we should get a nice set of cars, like these folks."

"Ask my father, again, if you like," said Amariah.

36

It was a sore spot for Gareth. His father had been firm—their fuel would be used only for aircraft and heavy equipment, period. Neither of these could function without liquid fuel and Kenan forbade the engineer from using any variant for any other purpose, including powering his antique automobile collection, which he kept in a garage at the rear of the refinery.

One of the Yorkers extended his arm at the next car.

"Thanks, but I'll walk," said Amariah.

"Suit yourself," said the Yorker. Gareth climbed in and the cars drove off, leaving Amariah behind in the dust.

He brushed himself off and walked down the dry and dusty road. The midday sun beat down from directly above. He sighed. Principles came at a cost, as his father liked to say.

Faintly, up in the sky, he heard the buzz of an approaching aircraft engine. The crowd down at the hangar craned their necks as the sound grew. A bright yellow biplane soared into view across the top of the barrier wall, made a circle around the silos, and passed right over their heads.

Kenan Wales had arrived.

Amariah could see his father in the rear open cockpit, his long pilot's scarf fluttering in the wind. The plane coasted over the valley like a brilliant golden bird, dipping slightly from side to side, offering a view of the oilseed fields to the passenger up front.

"Kenan's showing him the harvesting equipment at work," said Gareth, to no one in particular.

The Yorkers watched in silence as the plane reached the north end of the valley, turned in a glint of sunlight, and headed back toward the landing strip. It made a graceful approach and touched down neatly on the grass, coming to a stop in front of the hangar. Two mechanics ran to the plane with blocks and ropes. The engine cut and in the abrupt silence Amariah heard his father's booming laugh.

Mrs. Malinger strode to the plane. In the front seat, looking pale and wan, sat her husband, the president of American Agrifuels, Glen Malinger. The mechanics offered to help him down, but his wife shooed them away.

"I'm all right, I'm all right," said Mr. Malinger, although his difficulty in climbing out of the plane suggested otherwise.

Kenan Wales climbed out of the cockpit and pulled off his goggles and cloth helmet. A foot taller than anyone else there, his shock of thick white hair, long and swept back, caught the sun. His massive shoulders had lost little of their strength despite his advancing age.

Kenan patted his passenger gently on the back. "He's fine, Madeline. We hit some turbulence over the lake, that's all. The wind picked up."

Mr. Malinger coughed and mumbled something unintelligible into his handkerchief. Thin strands of black, greasy hair, meant to conceal his bald spot, had blown off his head during the flight and now dangled loosely over his ears. His wife attempted to put the hairs back in place, until one of the crew retrieved a hat from the plane and handed it to her, upon which she pushed it firmly onto her husband's head.

"You should have flown with us," Kenan said, pretending not to notice.

Mrs. Malinger regained her composure and shook her head, feigning horror at the suggestion. "There's no way I would get into one of those things," she said. "I am happy enough to come by car and by boat, thank you. Even though it took us two days to get here." She waved away a fly.

"Yes, we flew over your boat on the way in," said Kenan. "By the size of it, I'm sure you must carry a lot of luggage!"

"Why, Kenan, surely you know that I wanted to look my best for you," she cooed. "And your wife, of course."

Kenan brushed the flirtation aside. "You needn't have bothered," he said. "We're very simple here at the farm."

"Ah, ah, ah," said Madeline, waving a finger. They both laughed.

Amariah thought of his mother, back at the house. His father's apparent affection for the woman made him uncomfortable.

Kenan Wales moved along the line of Yorkers, shaking hands, working the crowd. When he reached Amariah, he called over Mr. Malinger, who blinked twice as he looked Kenan's heir up and down.

His father hesitated as he made the introduction. "May I present my son, Amariah," he said, looking askance at his torn and stained clothing.

Glen Malinger smiled behind his salt-and-pepper goatee, eyebrows raised in curious surprise. He reached out with a short arm, but his small hand made for a clumsy handshake.

"What happened to you?" asked his father.

Amariah repeated his fib about falling off his horse.

"Are you all right?" His gaze bore into his son's eyes.

"Yes."

His father squinted and then turned to the Yorkers and raised his hand. "Everyone, Glen and I made it here from Albany in less than one hour. If our merger is successful, and we can finally achieve this refinery's full capacity, it won't just be people like me and Glen up there, flying alongside the NVM. It will be mail, and commerce, and medicine. The people of the entire Northeast will benefit, and we will have created a brighter future for our children."

The Yorkers clapped. They were already impressed by Kenan, given his wealth and status, but even more so since he could fly a plane; it was a mark of honor and privilege in a world where few people had been up in the air at all.

Amariah noticed the Malingers sharing a few hushed words, their eyes not meeting, their lips barely moving. Madeline appeared surprised, then irritated, before a mask of congeniality returned.

His father gestured at the refinery. "Amariah, did you give our visitors the tour?"

The group didn't move.

"Um, actually, Kenan," said Mrs. Malinger, "Gareth gave us the tour."

Kenan's smile froze. "Oh?"

"Yes, it's my fault, I'm sorry—we got here early. Gareth was very gracious and started showing us around, and, before we knew it, we had made it all the way through. I must say I'm very impressed." She waved her hand in front of her face. "In fact, I find it all a bit overwhelming." She began fanning herself. "Oh, but it's hot here in the sun, isn't it?"

Kenan turned to Gareth, as if looking for an explanation. The engineer just shrugged and grinned.

"Amariah," said his father, "I trust that you were at least able to show our guests the lab and tell them about the new winter fuel mixture you've developed?"

"I, uh," Amariah, flustered, didn't know what to say.

"He was late," said Gareth. "I had to go ahead and explain it all myself."

"Oh …"

There was a gasp as Madeline Malinger collapsed in a heap. The Yorker men rushed in around her.

"Give her some air!" exclaimed her son, pushing one of the dark-suited men back onto his rump.

Mr. Malinger got down on all fours to check on his wife, his short limbs and goatee giving him the appearance of a large rat at a fancy dress party. "It's all right. She just fainted, that's all," he announced, smartly dusting off his hands.

Eric propped his mother up, her red hat askew.

"I'm sorry," she said. "I'm afraid my blood pressure is down."

"Let's get you to the house so you can rest," said Kenan. "We shouldn't have kept you out here in the sun." He hovered around her, seemingly at a loss for what to do.

"That's very kind of you," she said, "but first I need to get my medicine back down at the boat."

"Why not send one of your people down to get it for you?"

"I'm afraid I left it locked in my stateroom, with my personal things, and I don't want anyone going in there besides myself," she said. "I'm terribly sorry, but if I take the car I can be back in time for dinner," she said.

"As you wish," granted Kenan, reluctantly.

Mr. Malinger helped his wife up off the ground and the group walked in a huddle back toward her car. Within moments, she was being driven off toward the main gate.

Mr. Malinger turned to Kenan. "Sorry about that."

"No, not at all. I'm sorry for keeping her out here."

Mr. Malinger gestured to his men and the waiting cars. "Well, I suppose we'll all head over to the house now, if that's okay."

"Yes, of course."

Two stable attendants rode down the road, one on Kenan's white horse Dreamer, the other on Charlemagne. Amariah and his father would be riding back to the house from the airstrip, as was their custom.

"We can drive Gareth back up to the refinery," offered Mr. Malinger.

"No, that won't be necessary," replied Kenan.

Gareth stopped in his tracks.

"I wouldn't want to inconvenience you, Glen," said Kenan. "Please go right on back to the house. Gareth can ride back in the wagon with the other staff, can't you, Gareth?"

Mr. Malinger shrugged and joined the rest of his entourage in the two remaining automobiles, leaving the glowering Gareth behind. The engineer turned and shuffled back toward the refinery.

Amariah and his father mounted their horses and started the ride toward the house. As they trotted beside the electric fence, meant to keep animals and saboteurs out of the oilseed crops, Amariah began to form the words of an explanation as a preamble to complaining about the new seating arrangement in the lab. Depending on how the conversation went, he also planned to bring up the subject of acquiring his own plane.

His father cut him off.

"I expected a lot more from you today," he said.

And with that, he rode on ahead.

42

CHAPTER FIVE

To Christopher Peck, the main entrance to Pleasant Valley Biofuels resembled the gate of a medieval fortress. Spanning the confines of a narrow ravine, it featured tooth-shaped parapets, fieldstone turrets, and massive wooden doors that could be slammed shut at the first sign of trouble. The flag of the Territory of Northern Vermont flew from a pole above the gate, with a smaller flag just below it displaying the Wales' Coat of Arms.

All it's missing is the drawbridge, he thought.

Where the small town of Cambridge once stood, he and his wife Abigail sat in a horse-drawn military carriage, waiting their turn to pass through the security inspection on their way to the banquet. The carriage had jostled quite a bit along the Lamoille River road and now his bandaged leg throbbed under his dress uniform.

NVM troops saluted as the carriage pulled up to the gate. In the faces of his men and women, Peck detected sorrow, but also resolve. The horses stopped in a cobblestoned courtyard inside the first arch.

"Oh look, how nice," said Abigail, pointing with a gloved hand. The courtyard had been festively decorated with colorful flags and flowers.

"Yes, lovely," said Peck.

He knew that in an instant, the confined space could be transformed into a killing pit. But today, it was all dressed up for the Yorkers, just like the Wales Guard, who were neatly turned out in their dress uniforms. The NVM guards at the gate appeared shabby in comparison, and Peck wondered, not for the first time, if Kenan had made it his life's work to make him look bad.

Clarence Hodgkins, Chief of the Wales Guard, approached the carriage and tipped his black top hat. "Good evening, Captain," he said. "Mrs. Peck."

With his shaved face and long green cloak, Hodgkins—the head of security—displayed the welcoming appearance of friendly authority. But he was also a powerful man, crafty in a fight, with hands that could kill.

Hodgkins made small talk with Abigail while two Wales Guardsmen led a bomb-sniffing dog around their carriage. It was standard operating procedure, intended to prevent explosives from getting anywhere near the biorefinery. Far from being insulted, Peck would have been angry if the chief had let any part of the protocol lapse, for the Wales biofuel not only powered Peck's aircraft, but also provided the NVM with its primary source of revenue.

He shifted in his seat. The side mirror provided a view of the Stakeholders' carriages lined up behind him, their wariness of the Yorkers overridden by their apparently limitless greed. They all expected the merger would add to their already significant wealth, but only a few of them knew that, by the end of this evening, Peck expected to have his own reason to celebrate.

"Hodgkins," he said, interrupting his wife's banalities, "I've asked all NVM assigned to Pleasant Valley to join us down here at the barracks tonight. I'll be making a brief announcement, and I'd like everyone to be here, including your people," he said.

Having all of the NVM security troops gather down at the barracks was very unusual, as it would leave the entire perimeter undefended. If Hodgkins was surprised, he didn't show it.

Peck leaned in conspiratorially. "We're going to make a clean sweep of the mountain next week, and drive the rebels out once and for all," he whispered. The statement, while incomplete, wasn't far from the truth.

"I'll see what I can do," said Hodgkins.

Peck smiled. "I like your uniform, Hodgkins, but I'd like even more to see you in one of ours."

Hodgkins returned the smile, but his grey eyes remained as hard as steel. He whistled and rotated a finger in the air. The two massive wooden doors swung open to reveal the valley on the other side.

"Enjoy your evening," said Hodgkins, touching the rim of his hat.

The driver urged the horses forward and Peck slumped back in his seat. As they passed under the interior stone archway, the shape reminded him of a night long ago, below the Lake Champlain Bridge at the outset of the Troubles, and his thoughts went back to one of the pivotal moments of his life.

He and Kenan had been part of a squad of young Vermont National Guardsmen sent out in a small rowboat onto the waters of Lake Champlain. There were rumors of a mass movement of people and military equipment headed for Vermont from the threatened cities along the coast, and all bridges connecting Vermont to New York, New Hampshire, and Massachusetts had been ordered blown. The squad's mission was to destroy the bridge to New York near Crown Point by detonating its center span.

The lake was choppy and the spray cold on that moonless night. Illuminated only by the stars, the young men set out silently into the chop. Peck was a poor swimmer under the best of conditions, and the oars provided little comfort as they creaked and rattled in the stays.

Approaching the casement, the pitching of the boat intensified. Peck grew fearful that the boat would capsize, when, just in time, Kenan, the oldest of the group, leapt out and pulled the bow out of the waves. The young men hauled out the explosives and then climbed like spiders into the superstructure to place the charges.

Peck's job was to cross below the roadbed to the other side without being seen. Several months into the final blackout, the slippery trusses were but dark outlines against the white crests of the lake's churning surface. When he reached the end of the center span, he attached the explosives and connected the wires, his fingers numb in the cold, wet wind. He was nearly done when, out of the corner of his eye, he detected a rowboat approaching from the New York side, a kerosene lantern in the bow.

Turning the rowboat in the waves, the single oarsman shouted above the wind at the troop at the base of the bridge. "Hey! What do you think you're doing?"

"Stay back!" shouted Kenan, rifle in his hands.

The man resumed rowing, his back to Kenan. The squad urged Kenan to fire, but Kenan wasn't the type to shoot a man in the back, even under these circumstances. Peck quickened the pace and finished attaching the wires. Chilled to the bone, he scrambled back toward the other side.

The boatman landed and got out, holding up the lantern to illuminate the scene.

"Get back in your boat!" ordered Kenan, his rifle aimed squarely at the man's chest.

The Yorker watchman scanned the scene, his gaze landing on the empty boxes of explosives. "You idiots! What the hell do you think you're doing?!"

A barefaced boy behind Kenan clutched a plunger detonator. The Yorker strode toward Kenan in a determined effort to get around him. Without another word, Kenan shot the man squarely in the chest. The Yorker died on his feet and fell over backwards, his lifeless body rolling down off the casement into the waves, where it tumbled against the rocks.

Kenan scanned the superstructure. "Hurry up, Chris! Goddammit!"

Peck had come back a different route, and crouched at the top of the arch, looking for a way to get down.

"Jump, dammit!"

Peck lowered his body down until he was holding on only by his fingertips and then dropped the final twenty feet, wind rushing past his ears. A crack, a blinding flash of pain, and he was on his back, shin bone protruding through his torn trouser leg.

Lantern lights scurried across the top of the bridge—Yorker sentries.

Peck screamed in pain as Kenan dragged his friend across the casement by the armpits and heaved him into the boat.

The other young men crowded aboard and began rowing away. From the stern, Kenan held onto the plunger as another Guardsman let out the wire, and just when they had gotten as far as it would allow, he forced the plunger down. A massive explosion lit up the night and the center span dropped as one piece into the water with a tremendous crash. The bridge disappeared into the foam, spawning a giant wave that nearly capsized their small craft. Miraculously, they made it back safely to the shore.

"Christopher!" said Abigail, for the second time.

Peck snapped back to the present. His wife, still plain despite her attempts to appear elegant on this special night, viewed him with concern. "Yes? What is it?

"Are you feeling all right? How's your leg?" She moved to touch it, but he recoiled.

"It's fine."

For months, Peck had languished in an unheated hospital while all of Vermont celebrated Kenan as a hero. He could still remember the pain as the medic set the bone. It was even more painful than getting shot, although that was probably because Bowman only had a .22.

The carriage began the climb up the final hundred yards of the gravel drive. The view, like the main gate, was meant to impress: dozens of acres of food crops lay in neat symmetrical rows, dairy cows and horses grazed in separate pastures, and, off in the distance, the biorefinery, surrounded by hundreds of acres of oilseed crops, let off a plume of white steam.

"Look at the harvest," said Abigail, her voice tinged with awe. "They won't be going hungry this winter."

Christopher took his wife's hand and gave it a squeeze. "And neither will we."

ℬ

"So," said Eric Malinger, through a mouth stuffed with hors d'oeuvres, "I hear you found a way to make fuel that works in winter."

Amariah stood in the center of the ballroom amidst the murmur of a hundred conversations. "Yes," he replied evenly.

"So, how did you do that exactly?"

The heir to Pleasant Valley fingered his glass of fruit juice. On the dais, his father's favorite band of itinerant players dug into their concertina, violin, and drum. They had arrived that morning from their dusty travels, bringing news, gossip, and a rare flamboyance to the stuffy, aristocratic affair.

"The biodiesel turns to jelly once the temperature approaches freezing," said Amariah. "It strangles the engine. We developed an additive that lowers the cloud point so we can operate machinery on all but the coldest nights."

"Yes, I know all that, but how did you do it without petroleum?"

It took all of his upbringing to keep him from telling the greasy Yorker to go to hell.

At the other end of the ballroom, he caught a glimpse of his parents, all smiles as they engaged their guests, displaying the deliberate positivity of hosts drawing out every ounce of their social energy. It dawned on him that, maybe, just maybe, he had been going about things entirely the wrong way. Perhaps he should just do what his mother had told him—make things work with the Yorkers. This jerk wanted his job so badly that maybe he should just let him have it. Perhaps then his parents would get off his back for once in his life.

"I'll tell you what," said Amariah with sudden enthusiasm. "Why don't we get together tomorrow at the lab, and I'll show you around? We can start with the testing apparatus and procedures, and move on from there."

The Yorker's smile faltered. "Sure," he said. "Do you mean—"

"What time—"

The music suddenly stopped. The leader of the musical troupe, a large man whose violin seemed too small for his burly body, raised his bow to the sound of a drumroll and then dropped it like a wand.

Presto! The servants pulled back the screens to reveal the banquet table, resplendent with luscious beef, pork, chicken, and lamb, surrounded on either side with fresh and cooked vegetables selected from their own farm. The blue flame of the Wales' heating fuel flickered beneath the metal trays, warming the buffet. The crowd "oohed" and "aahed" at the sight.

Eric Malinger, surprised by Amariah's sudden camaraderie, uttered a vague excuse and hurried back to his father.

"I see you're making friends," said his mother, appearing at his side. Her braided hair was up in a bun, displaying her graceful and elegant neck, embellished tonight with a simple pearl necklace.

"Just doing my duty, as ordered."

Sarah Wales sighed, "Come on."

She led him over to the clutch of men where his father, finely dressed in a long green cloak, engaged the most senior guests in deep conversation. To his right stood General Barings, tall and regal, a military officer in appearance as well as temperament. To his left hunkered the neckless Bernard Craggs, Chairman of the Board of Stakeholders. Their attention focused on the short, goateed Yorker, Glen Malinger, backed up by his squad of undertakers.

"Glen, how nice to see you!" said his mother.

"How nice to see you again, Sarah," said Malinger, his eyes settling on her like a raptor.

They air-kissed each other. Amariah wondered how she could stand the smell of the stale tobacco that trailed these Yorkers.

"And where is Madeline? Is she feeling better?" asked his mother.

"We expect her at any minute. She had a fainting spell down at the airstrip."

"Yes, I heard—poor thing. Well, do let us know when she arrives."

Malinger, his hair glued to his scalp, made the introductions, while the hostess smiled gracefully as she shook the rest of the Yorkers' hands; a grand performance.

Amariah stood there awkwardly as the conversation turned to business—how many tons of oilseed could the Yorkers ship to the refinery, the locations of the quarries where the Yorkers planned to dump the lye and other waste products of the biodiesel process, and so on.

"Excuse me." The red-haired kitchen maid had worked her way through the crowd with a tray of deviled eggs, Amariah's favorite. As he reached out to help himself, the electric lights sprang on, startling the young woman, who flinched as she encountered the grand chandelier for the first time. General Barings chuckled at her naiveté and headed for his table.

Then something strange happened—the maid stopped and stared directly into Amariah's eyes, cold and unflinching, not subservient at all, like a wild animal. Amariah wanted to say

51

something clever, but once again he was completely tongue-tied in the presence of this girl, so he simply popped one of the eggs into his mouth.

A bell jingled as Jared, the underbutler, called the guests to supper, and the girl swept the tray away.

Nearly two hundred people strolled toward their assigned seats—Stakeholders and their families, NVM officers, and the Yorkers, who had their own table at the foot of the stage. Amariah escorted his mother to their table up on the dais, stopping to welcome Captain Peck, who, on crutches, was being helped along by his wife.

"An ambush; this morning at one of the farms," whispered his mother, as they walked away.

Amariah looked around for his father and saw him detaching himself from one of the Stakeholders, Dotty Labreche, a spinster from Jericho, who had made a beeline for Kenan as soon as she arrived. As his father begged off, the small, plain woman looked after him with a sad expression, made even more pronounced by her brown dress and simple cap.

Everyone always wants something from us, thought Amariah.

He held the chair for his mother as his father strode up the stairs and took a position at the center of the dais. Jared tapped the edge of a knife against a glass and the hubbub died down.

"My dear friends, welcome," said Kenan. "Thank you all for coming. I'd like to begin by acknowledging our special guests, starting with the people you know. Second to my left is of course General Barings, leader of the Northern Vermont Militia, the man responsible for protecting our borders in the north and keeping our territory safe."

Strong applause erupted from the table of military men.

"To the general's left is Captain Christopher Peck, responsible for maintaining law and order in our towns and for helping ensure that our fuel shipments are delivered safely and without interference. Captain Peck is here tonight despite being wounded in an attack on his forces in the Flats this morning, unfortunately with the loss of life. I'm sure we'll be hearing more about this in due course, but I'd like to take this opportunity to thank Captain Peck and his troops for their courage and bravery."

Everyone rose to their feet. Peck sat in the center of the thunderous applause, soaking up the attention, his wife beaming by his side.

"Next to the captain is my wife and partner of many years, Sarah."

His mother rose, smiled, and waved to a roomful of warm applause.

"And our son Amariah."

Amariah felt every eye upon him as he stood and bowed in a fresh set of clothes. Polite, thin applause greeted him. What happened to the announcement? He sat down, embarrassed, trying to conceal his fervent desire to be somewhere, anywhere, far away from Pleasant Valley.

"And finally," said Kenan, "the reason we are all here tonight, from across the Lake, the leader of American Agrifuels and the man who is going to help bring us into the future, Mr. Glen Malinger."

Malinger twisted halfway out of his seat and nodded at the crowd, to brief applause.

Kenan held up his hand. "Now, I know that some of you are not convinced that this merger is the right way forward, so let's address this right away. I'd like to begin by showing you a vision of a world that is not only possible, but necessary. It's a world I believe we could all see in just a few short years. But to get there, we need this partnership with American Agrifuels."

At the back of the room, Eric Malinger wandered back in, apparently late from the bathroom. Rather than come forward and take his seat at the table with the rest of the Yorkers, he meandered over to one of the large windows, framed by decorative curtains that extended from the floor to the ceiling, and produced a rolled cigarette, lighting it with a smoky match. One of the waitstaff swooped down on the younger Malinger, ushering him towards a side door to take his smoke outside. And that's what he did, propping the door open with a chair.

Amariah couldn't help but smirk—so *this* was the type of person his parents so badly wanted in the refinery. *Fine*, he thought. If his parents wanted them here, then so be it. He was tired of fighting. He glanced over at his mother, but she pretended not to notice.

The chandelier dimmed and a bright square appeared on the wall behind his father, followed by a large projection of a photograph of the valley taken from the air. A gasp arose from the audience, most of whom hadn't seen a projected image in decades. The younger members of the audience had probably never seen one at all. Amariah grinned—he had taken the photograph himself, while his father flew the plane, and had processed the image in a darkroom he had built in the lab.

Kenan nodded to Jared at the projector. With a click and a whirr, the slide tray advanced and large white letters flashed onto the image, reading: "A Brighter Future – Pleasant Valley Biofuels and American Agrifuels – Working Together." Kenan nodded again and a new image appeared with a graph.

"Here you can see our annual production over the past five years," he said, pointing with a long wooden wand. "Even with the new fields that have been brought into production, we have never been able to exceed 300,000 gallons a year."

A new slide appeared with different charts.

"Our facility, however, is capable of producing nearly two million gallons a year. Leveraging more of the plant's productive capacity could change our world, but the question has always been 'where will we get the raw materials?' Our soils are already being stretched beyond capacity as it is."

A new image appeared, superimposing additional seed, methanol, and lye onto the Pleasant Valley production chart.

"If we combine the surplus production and raw materials of American Agrifuels with our operation, you can see the result—we can immediately increase our output to one million gallons a year, more than tripling our current production."

A murmur rippled through the crowd.

"And what will we do with all of this extra fuel? Well, as most of you know, my view is that in addition to heat, light, and electricity, we should use the fuel for aviation, the one accomplishment of mankind that is impossible to achieve without liquid fuel. We don't know if anyone else in North America still has the technology for human flight, so this conveys a special responsibility upon us to maintain and propagate this capability."

A new slide displayed a map of the northeast, with an image of Kenan's golden plane flying above it.

"First, we'll restore Air Mail service," he said, "between our region, the coastal towns of New England, the Hudson Valley, and western New York. We can learn what the other communities are doing, leverage specialization of labor, and increase trade."

His enthusiasm rose. "The restoration of rapid communication will mend our social fabric. People will see our planes passing overhead—not searching for rebels or runaway laborers—but carrying cards, letters, parcels, and medicine. But more than that, our planes will carry a message of hope. I believe a better life awaits us all as a result of this merger and that is why the Stakeholder Board believes it is worth putting past differences with our neighbors across the lake aside, in favor of a brighter future. Thank you."

Solid applause. Kenan took a slight bow, acknowledged the crowd, and then motioned to Mr. Malinger.

Amariah noticed the empty chair intended for Madeline. *She must have been really sick*, he thought. Eric still stood at the back of the room by the door, staring at his father like a dog awaiting a command.

Dead silence ensued as the president of American Agrifuels took Kenan's place. Steamy aromas of freshly cooked meat wafted across the stuffy room.

"Okay, it's true that with a million gallons of biofuel a year, you could do a lot more than you can today," Malinger said airily. "But with all respect to our friend Kenan here, I am interested in restoring the civilization of the twenty-first century, not the nineteenth."

Chairs shuffled against the parquet floor. A cough came from the back.

"The people who built this country knew how to take advantage of the resources this land had to offer," he said. "We

56

had cars and trains, we had cruise ships and passenger jets, and we had the Concorde and the Space Shuttle. That's the world I want to live in again, and that's the world I want our children to live in."

"Keep dreaming!" shouted an old man, to mild laughter. His more respectable offspring shushed the old man, who shushed them back.

Malinger, amused, held up his tiny hand. "Sure, sure, a million gallons of biofuel a year won't be enough to restore the world to the way it was. Our country used almost twenty million *barrels* of oil a day at the peak of the Oil Age, not even counting all the coal and natural gas we burned. That's all gone now, of course; however, I'm an optimist. With Kenan's new biomass processor, we could start to get life back the way it used to be. In fact, we could be making millions of gallons of biodiesel and cellulosic ethanol right now. How? Simply by harvesting the forest."

Amariah's mouth fell open. This was not the speech his family had expected Malinger to give.

"Back in Albany, we don't ride around in carriages like Marie Antoinette," said Malinger. "We ride in cars like civilized people. We've even got the lights back on in the streets around the governor's mansion. All of you fine people could have our lifestyle too, merely by harvesting the hillsides around you. I'm sorry to say it, but Kenan has been keeping you in the dark—literally."

There was silence as his father rose slowly to his feet. "Glen," he said, an edge in his deep voice, "it's true that we could be producing more fuel using the biomass processor, but as I've said before, numerous times, to you and the Stakeholders, to use the forest for automotive fuel would be both foolish and dangerous. A hundred-year-old spruce tree

57

will produce only enough fuel to fill an old pickup truck—once! A hundred years! Forests do not regenerate fast enough. And if we did head down that path, the topsoil—"

Malinger cut him off. "Kenan, when a tree falls down in the woods, who does that benefit? Worms? Well, I think people are more important than worms." He turned back to the audience. "Look, folks, I've done the math. Using Kenan's enzyme and the biomass processor at full capacity, along with the oilseed refineries here and in Albany, we could soon be producing *five million gallons* of biodiesel and ethanol a year. You could all be very, very rich. Unfortunately, our friend Kenan here has refused to share the secret of this process with his Stakeholders or his business partners. And I, for one, think you all deserve better."

Many people looked askance at Kenan. This was news to them.

Sarah Wales whispered, "This could be dangerous."

Abruptly, General Barings stood and said, "Everyone, for your own safety, please remain in your seats and do not move."

Through the glass door beside Eric Malinger, a column of men charged into the room carrying automatic weapons. Shrieks and screams erupted as the gunmen dashed up the aisles and took positions facing the crowd. Two men dressed in black stormed up onto the stage and directed their weapons at Amariah and his parents. Amariah stared at the barrel of the gun and pushed back his chair. Where was Hodgkins?

"Amariah, stay put!" barked his father.

"Ladies and gentlemen, please, remain calm," said the general. "These are Glen's men and they are here for your protection."

Amariah scanned the faces in the room. Although many appeared surprised and alarmed, many others did not, including the table of military men.

"Everyone, please, listen." The general was formal and direct. "Every day our men sacrifice themselves to protect our borders and maintain law and order," he said, "but we are not given the fuel we need to finish the job. This morning, Captain Peck's troops were cut down in an ambush, in part because we could not provide the support aircraft with enough fuel to carry out their mission. Well, we've had enough of half measures."

The general turned and addressed Kenan directly. "I'm sorry, Kenan, but it is time that you shared this little secret of yours with the rest of us. And then, my old friend, it's time that you retired."

Amariah looked over at his father, who shook his head and laughed. "Don't be ridiculous. I have no intention of telling you anything. Especially not at gunpoint." Kenan turned and stared at Amariah to ensure he was understood.

Amariah, wide-eyed, nodded in return.

"Have it your own way, Kenan," said the general. "Since that's what you're accustomed to anyway." He gestured to the back of the room. "Gareth knows the process, and he's already on board."

In the back, Gareth stood gloating. Amariah's heart sank. The engineer must have either read his notes or somehow pieced together the formulas on his own.

"So, folks, here's the deal," said Malinger, retaking center stage. "First, you're all going to get very rich. That's if you're with us. Kenan is going into retirement and his family is going with him, right now. We have a nice house reserved for them in Albany, where they will be well treated. They will not be harmed. You have my word on that."

The ratlike Yorker smiled at Sarah Wales, who recoiled in disgust.

Malinger shrugged and then continued. "American Agrifuels is taking over this facility. Gareth will run the plant, your oilseed will continue to be processed, and you will receive your payments on schedule. We will ship seed here from New York for processing. Your payments will increase—in fact, after the next harvest, they will double. Once the rebels are brought under control and the forest is safe, we will start harvesting trees."

Malinger gestured to the general, who addressed Kenan directly. "And now, Kenan, it is time for you to leave," said the general. "You can send for your personal things later. And just so there is no misunderstanding, I will be traveling with you to ensure your safety."

"Get up," said a Yorker militiaman.

Amariah glanced at his parents, and they all rose together. Everything seemed to be happening in slow motion.

His father stepped between his mother and the barrel of the machine gun, and together they shuffled to the end of the dais. Save for the blood thumping in his ears, there wasn't a sound to be heard, as if time itself had skipped a beat. Amariah stepped down onto the polished floor and then the three of them moved down the aisle along the wall, the general close behind. Amariah's face burned as he passed the staring crowd.

At the end of the aisle, Gareth stood by the door, smirking. Amariah turned to avoid his gaze and looked right into the face of the red-haired kitchen maid, who stood with the other servants along the wall. She still held that damned tray.

60

What is she going to do, offer us an hors d'oeuvre on the way out? He shook his head at the absurdity of the thought. But her gaze was on someone behind him.

Gareth called out with a sneer, "Enjoy your life in New—"

A crash and a scream pierced the air. Amariah spun around. The kitchen maid had the general by the hair and stabbed him repeatedly with a knife. Blood poured from the old man's neck as he vainly tried to push the girl off, but she was stronger and had caught him by surprise.

The two guards, who had been focused on Kenan, spun around, taken aback. One fumbled with his weapon as the other tried to pull her off, but she held on tight, turning the knife and ripping out the old man's throat.

In one motion, Amariah's father pulled out a small revolver, pointed it just above Gareth's thick eyeglasses, and shot the traitorous engineer through the forehead. His brains exploded out of the back of his head and he fell in a lump to the floor.

Women screamed. One of the Yorker guards managed to fire a single shot into Kenan's back, sending his father to his knees. Sarah Wales shrieked and threw herself down on her husband, shielding him from further shots.

On the dais, Malinger waved his arms in the air. "Stop shooting!" he cried, to no avail.

Then the room itself seemed to explode. From outside the windows, Hodgkins and the Wales Guard opened fire at the Yorkers, spraying the room with bullets. Amariah threw himself to the floor.

The Yorker militiamen jerked in place like marionettes. One of them pulled the trigger of his machine gun and fired in a wide arc, smashing into the banquet table and the cans of heating fuel. Blue flame coursed down onto the ballroom

61

floor, catching the decorative curtains. With a great whoosh, orange flames swept up to the ceiling, fanned by the wind that poured through the broken windows.

The Stakeholders and their families backed away from the flames and stampeded toward the door. Amariah jumped to his feet and took a stance in front of his parents, until Craggs, the rotund chairman, knocked him aside.

Strong hands grabbed Amariah by the arms and dragged him away: two men in white serving coats whom Amariah did not recognize.

"Let go of me!" he shouted, squirming. He caught a final glimpse of his father, flat on his back, attempting to push his mother toward the door, and his mother refusing, remaining there, her eyes locked on her husband, his face in her hands.

The men pulled Amariah through a servant's door. One of them said, "You're coming with us."

"No!" Amariah struggled, but a blow to the back of his head stopped him cold. The men muscled him down the staff passageway to the rear of the house. He was aware of being heaved into the back of a wagon, where a man tied his hands. The wagon tore away down the dark road toward Joshua's gate.

Flames roared through the ballroom windows like water erupting out of a dam, illuminating the night. People ran from the house in all directions, screaming. Horses and carriages, some without drivers, fled toward the main gate. Amariah thought of his parents, still together in the heart of the inferno and cried out, his voice a strangled moan.

A dark silhouette appeared against the stars of the night sky—Joshua's watchtower. A one-armed man with a lantern jumped into the moving wagon, knelt down and examined

Amariah with concern. Another man barked at him to put out the light.

The wagon lurched forward and gathered speed up the hillside, tossing Amariah from side to side. He feared they would sail off into a ravine. How could the driver possibly see where he was going?

One thing was for certain—the deeper they traveled into the dark woods, the farther he left his home behind.

CHAPTER SIX

Captain Christopher Peck stood in the circular driveway scanning the black smoking ruin of what used to be the Wales mansion. Somewhere in the steaming hole of charred debris lay the remains of the finest home he had ever seen—along with its owners.

The structure's massive timbers had crashed down into the basement in the middle of the night, puncturing and igniting the fuel tanks, renewing the conflagration and nearly killing the bucket brigade. Now, plumes of white smoke curled into the grey damp of morning, ignoring the bare chimneys that stood forlornly off to the side.

He had sent Abigail home before dawn. Soot-smeared and traumatized, she kept asking him how it all could have happened. It was a question he had difficulty answering. In any case, it was a damned shame.

Rubber tires crunched in the gravel drive behind him as a convoy of three Range Rovers slowed to a stop. From the front and rear cars, bodyguards exited and took up defensive positions, warily regarding Peck's uniformed troops. From the middle car, the Malinger family emerged, mouths hanging open, aghast.

Glen Malinger detached himself from his wife and hurried over. "So? Can we salvage anything?"

Peck's response was slow and deliberate. "Once it cools down, we'll go through and extract whatever metal we can find. The heat and the smoke destroyed just about everything else, including the food stores."

The little man stepped aside to dodge a plume of smoke. "What a waste," he clucked. "Are they still in there?"

"Yes, they are."

Peck jerked his head toward a small group of men and women standing on the hillside behind the house, heads bowed. A priest in his garments read from a Bible. "The doctor will examine the remains once we've pulled them out," he said. "Then Kenan, Sarah, and Amariah will be buried together on the hillside. Do you have any instructions for the others?"

Malinger shrugged. "Nah, do what you think is best."

Peck nodded. He would see to it that the general received a proper military funeral, and use it to rally support against the rebels. Gareth and the dead Yorkers would be tossed into an unmarked ditch and forgotten.

Madeline Malinger marched over. "Well, you two really screwed this up," she huffed. "Look at this! This was supposed to be our home!"

Two NVM planes roared overhead, searching for remnants of the Wales Guard. Hodgkins and his men had been tangling with the Yorkers throughout the night as they retreated into the hills. Kenan's head of security had smelled a rat and ruined everything.

Glen Malinger escorted his wife away. "Ah, honey, this is really not the time. Why don't you and Eric head down to refinery and see what you can learn about things down there? I'll join you in a few minutes."

The woman glared at Peck, spun around, and got back into her car. Her son quickly slammed the door and the two cars peeled away down the drive.

Peck poked Malinger in the chest. "Now, you listen to me," he said. "Kenan Wales was a friend of mine and now he's dead. His wife and son are dead. There's blood on our hands because of this. You better see that I get all the fuel I want or they will not be the last bodies to be buried here. You got it?"

The Yorker bodyguards didn't dare to drop their smokes.

"This has been a difficult night for us all," said Malinger, eyes darting about. "Why don't we all take a breather and get together later to discuss next steps?"

"Just get me my fuel."

Malinger and his men got into their cars and left.

Peck motioned to Lieutenant Dickins, whose uniform had somehow remained unstained throughout the ordeal.

"Go over and help the doctor," he said. "And make sure the Wales get a decent burial."

ॐ

A grey fog obscured the dawn as Amariah picked his way through the thick, damp underbrush. Somewhere off in the mist, higher up the mountain, a robin launched into its morning song, its usually cheerful melody sad and foreboding.

Birds sang in the morning to announce they had survived the night. Amariah too had survived, but unlike this creature of the forest, he and his strange companions moved through the woods as quietly as possible.

Tired, thirsty, head throbbing, he tried to focus by identifying passing trees, plants, and rocks, noting landmarks in case he had to find his own way back to the valley. However, the fog and the foliage made it difficult to see more than a few hundred feet in any direction.

He stumbled over an old stone wall, obscured by gnarled roots, vines, and slippery moss. Centuries ago, it had demarcated a wide open field, cleared by the first settlers for grazing sheep. Now it lay at the base of majestic, towering trees, whose dense canopies obscured their crowns, a once-sunny meadow transformed into an uneven obstacle course of decomposing natural debris.

The terrain grew steeper and the trees thinner, until they arrived at a sheer rock face near the top of the mountain. The men made a beeline for a small cave entrance at the foot of the cliff, entering it one by one, deeply hunched over to accommodate their full backpacks. Amariah followed them inside.

In the center of the cave, an oil lamp sat on a rough wooden table. Stacks of empty wooden crates lined the walls. Joshua led Amariah over to a filthy cot in a corner, coated in mice droppings. Amariah didn't even bother to brush them aside, but lay down and passed out.

ʬ

In a dark, restless sleep, Amariah drifted in and out of consciousness, the voices of the men in the cave weaving into his dreams. In one of them, he got up off the cot, walked over to the cave entrance, willed himself into the air, and flew away.

Soaring above the valley, banking and turning through the air as if he was swimming underwater, he wondered why he hadn't been flying like this his entire life—as if he had previously known, but forgotten how.

Over the forested mountainside he flew, down toward Pleasant Valley, passing safely over the sharp pickets that bristled outside of the barrier wall. He circled Joshua's watchtower, kicked past Charlemagne's stable, then headed to the manor house over the roof of the east wing.

Stepping lightly onto the balcony outside his room, he strode to the French doors and pulled them open, then stopped—his room was nothing but a burned shell, the walls and furniture black and charred, his photographs and book-case piled into the center of the room in a smoking heap.

He backed away in a panic and turned to fly away, but then remembered that he really couldn't fly at all. The balcony gave way beneath him, and he fell down into a burning pit, the smell of smoke in his eyes and nose, in his clothes, falling, falling …

He woke with a start, face down on the cot in the cave, mouse droppings sticking to his skin.

At the table in the middle of the room, the men who had led him on the trek up the mountainside chowed down a meal. One of them, with black gaps where his missing teeth should have been, noticed him stir.

"Time to get up, your lordship," he chortled. The other men joined in.

Amariah managed to stand and wobbled over to the table. The piquant aroma of roasted meat reminded him of home.

Then he saw why. The rough table had been covered in a linen tablecloth, set with his parents' fine silverware and monogrammed plates. On a complete table setting stolen from the banquet the men feasted on the food intended for the Stakeholders. Even the tallow candles were lit.

"What the hell?"

One of his mother's watercolor cards lay carelessly on the soiled tablecloth. He reached out to grab it and unintentionally jabbed one of the men in the ear. The man erupted out of his seat, grabbed Amariah by the throat, and pushed him back onto the cot.

"Leave him be!"

It was a familiar voice—Joshua's voice. The one-armed watchman had returned from outside.

The wild man released his grip and sauntered away, grinning at Amariah over his shoulder. "Forgive me, your lordship," he said, and the men laughed again.

"How are you feeling?" asked Joshua.

It was as if he was seeing his old friend for the first time. "You're one of them? A rebel?"

Joshua nodded. "Yup, well, I suppose you could say that."

Amariah lifted his hands to his forehead and scrunched his eyes shut. Joshua, of all people? A rebel spy? God, what had Amariah told him? He knew everything about him! He had even kept the relationship a secret from his parents.

"My parents, are they … did they make it out?"

Joshua shook his head. "No, Amariah, I'm sorry. Your mom and dad perished together in the fire."

Amariah had a vision of his parents as he last saw them, lying together on the floor, the ballroom in flames.

Joshua continued, his voice gentle and genuine. "The stables, the horses, the refinery, the sheds—they're all still there and undamaged. Charlemagne is fine."

The watchman walked over to the table and picked up the watercolor, wiped it off, and handed it to Amariah. It was the same ocean scene that his mother had proudly shown him the day before, now stained with blood from the meat the thieves had bundled into the tablecloth.

Amariah buried his face in his hands and wept. He had left his parents to die. His beautiful mother and accomplished father were now charred skeletons in the smoking ashes of a massive fire pit, and everything he knew was lost forever.

After a few moments, Joshua touched his shoulder.

"Don't touch me!"

Here was a man whom Amariah considered a friend, someone he trusted, someone his father had trusted, and all the while he was one of the rebels, the people most intent on destroying the refinery. Amariah had allowed himself to be lured into a secret friendship with the man, but it was no more than a sham, and he was nothing but a fool.

"I don't know who you are," said Amariah, wiping his eyes with the back of his dirty hand. "Is your name even Joshua, or is that also a lie?"

"That is my name and it always has been my name. I was a friend of your father's and I am still a friend of yours."

"His friend? My father was betrayed by everyone around him, including you!"

"I did no such thing."

"Well then, how did the Yorkers get through the wall? You opened your gate!"

"The NVM let the Yorkers in through the main gate. They assembled down there under some pretense that Peck had set up. They overpowered the Wales Guard and took over. But some of them got away, including Hodgkins, and they shot up the banquet. I only opened my gate so that you and the staff could escape."

"But I didn't want to escape!"

"The important thing is that you're alive," said Joshua, standing. "If you had stayed there, you would now either be dead, or a prisoner of the Yorkers."

The Yorkers, yes. Malinger, and his wife and son. Somehow they had convinced the Stakeholders and Peck to take their side—all for the secret of how to turn trees into liquid fuel. But things hadn't gone quite to plan, had they? Amariah remembered Gareth's surprised look as he fell to the floor, and the panicked look on Malinger's face as the ballroom went up in flames.

"So the assassin—"

"Rebecca."

"Oh, that's her name? She was with you?"

"Yes, she was on a mission."

"Which was what? To burn the house down and kill everyone?"

"To assassinate General Barings. Peck was supposed to be killed in the morning, the general that night. The rest of what happened was not our doing."

Joshua held out his hand to help Amariah off the cot. Amariah let the hand hang there.

"So now what? I'm your prisoner?"

"You are no one's prisoner, but we cannot stay here and you cannot go wandering off your own. Peck will be mounting a big offensive against us, and when he finds out that you weren't killed in the fire, he will also be looking for you. We have to keep moving, unless you would like to be captured by the same people who killed your parents."

Joshua grabbed a hold of the rope and pulled him up with his one arm. As their heads came together, he whispered, "Listen, these men are not your enemies, but they are not

71

your friends. Up here, the world does not revolve around you. Understand?"

Amariah nodded, and Joshua let him go.

"I never told my parents that we were friends," said Amariah.

Joshua picked the ruined watercolor off the floor and put it in his pocket.

"You didn't have to," said the watchman.

CHAPTER SEVEN

High patchy clouds fled across the distant moon as a red-haired rebel tied a thick hemp rope around Amariah's waist. The young man's skeletal face hovered in the shadows as he pulled the knot tight. "Your hands are free to climb, but if you try anything funny, I'll cut your throat," he said with a rotten smile.

The rebel turned and pulled himself up through the rock fall. Amariah followed, holding his breath against the young man's stench while looking for any chance to break free. But the knot was tight, the rocks and tree roots slippery, and soon he was so busy trying not to fall that he didn't have time to think about escape.

Hours later they arrived at a yawning chasm, ancient and forbidding in the thinning moonlight. With dismay, Amariah suddenly realized that he stood before Smuggler's Notch, the gap between Pleasant Valley and the abandoned mountain town of Stowe. He had flown over the Notch a number of times with his father, but had never been up there on foot. It was reputed to be rebel territory and unsafe, and now that he stood there himself, he could confirm that it was, indeed, very much the case.

Still roped to the rebel, Amariah had no choice but to follow the men into the Notch. He did what they did, grasping at roots and rocks, gripping each handhold along the narrow ledge, holding on for dear life. At a large boulder, they stopped. A narrow cleft behind it revealed a dark passageway. The men removed their heavy packs and dragged them inside. Amariah hesitated.

Joshua whispered from close behind. "Just feel your way along, and don't panic."

Heart pounding, Amariah slipped into the crevice, his trousers brushing against the slab. In the darkness, he could hear breathing and movement on either side of him, but could see absolutely nothing, as if he was climbing into his own grave. Fear rose in his chest, and he struggled for air.

The young rebel tugged impatiently on the rope, pulling him along.

"Keep going," urged Joshua.

Amariah slid sideways, feet coming together after each step. At last, he saw a brightening up ahead, a flickering orange light. He grasped at an outstretched hand and was pulled up into a small cave, where an oil lantern cast light against a low domed ceiling.

An armed guard, dressed like the other men, swung the circular wooden door shut and barred it from the inside. Then Amariah was yanked along with the group down a man-made passageway. This opened into a larger, natural tunnel, until all at once, Amariah found himself in a wide open space—an enormous cavern deep inside Mount Mansfield.

Giant stalactites hung from dark heights. Rough walls swirled with colors and textures, like liquid rock that had suddenly hardened. Meandering passageways extended off in every direction, lit by oil lamps that shone from nooks and crannies dripping with white calcite.

The bony young man untied himself from Amariah, coiled the rope like an expert, and walked away without a second look. The rest of the group peeled away in different directions. A thin woman and two small children ran up to hug the grizzled man who had called Amariah "your lordship." The man swung one of the children up into his arms— he was someone's father.

The bizarre, otherworldly scene was more exotic than anything Amariah had ever imagined, something he thought awaited him only in the far-off destinations he had dreamed of, and yet it was here all along, inside the mountain that had loomed over him his entire life. He felt both instantly at home, and utterly homesick.

"How many people live here?" he asked Joshua, who remained by his side.

"Too many."

Amariah quickly made a mental map of his surroundings. It was highly unlikely that the young children had entered the cavern along the treacherous route he had just traveled. There had to be another way out, perhaps down one of the tunnels, or up where the path—

"Well, well," said a woman's voice.

Amariah blinked. A shapely young woman stood before him, hand on one hip. Her wavy red hair draped down over large breasts, concealed beneath a farmer's rough hemp clothing. Amariah recognized the pale skin and haunting green eyes.

"Still in one piece, I see," she said.

Amariah knew her name now—Rebecca.

"You're alive," he said.

"You noticed."

"But you were captured. Right before the fire started."

"Yes."

"But how did you get away?"

"When the fire broke out, the Yorkers loosened their grip, so I did what it says in the rebel instruction manual."

"Rebel instruction manual?"

"Yeah. I kicked them in the balls and then ran like hell."

Joshua chuckled. Had the circumstances been any different, Amariah may have done so as well. Strangely enough, he was happy to see this girl.

"Come on," she said. "It's time for you to meet the boss."

Amariah and Joshua followed the unlikely assassin through the cavern. Grottoes in the walls had been transformed into sleeping spaces, even little bedrooms, with carpets and fabrics. The oil lamps and heaters were the kind that could be found anywhere, but the smell of the burning oil was familiar—the rebels were using Wales biofuel to light and heat the cave.

They came around a stalagmite and Amariah nearly stumbled over a pretty girl with long dark hair. She glanced up as they passed, revealing the bluest pair of eyes he had ever seen, before she quickly turned her attention back to an older woman, who lay weeping on a bed of straw. A man with them stretched on a cot, staring blankly at the ceiling.

They reached the far end of the cavern, where a small staircase had been carved into the rock. Steam and aromas suggested a communal kitchen. At the top of the stairs, leaning against a boulder, a large bearded man glared at Amariah like a statue of some Roman god.

Amariah stood there, not sure what to say to this man. Was this the leader of the rebels? The person who had tormented his family with constant attacks on the refinery, the reason they had spent years constructing a giant wall around the entire valley?

Out of the steam, an older woman appeared. She walked around the burly man and came down the stairs, stocky and fit, her hair cut like a man's.

"So, you must be Amariah Wales," she said. She did not extend her hand.

Amariah nodded.

"My name is Anne. I'm sorry to hear about your parents."

Amariah raised his eyebrows at the big bear of a man, who cocked his head toward the woman and sat down. *She* was the rebel leader?

"You can't be serious," said Amariah.

The woman regarded him with what seemed to be genuine concern. "Your father was a good man, Amariah," she said. "During the Troubles he helped a lot of people in the valley. But then he made some bad choices, and some very poor friends." She folded her arms. "Your mother was very sweet."

Amariah folded his arms as well. Who was this woman to be consoling him? How did she know his parents?

"So," she said, "what do you intend to do with yourself?"

"You're asking *me*?" said Amariah. "I don't know. Apparently I am to be kept here as your prisoner."

"We don't keep prisoners here. But indeed you will be staying with us through the winter. Come spring, you will be given a choice whether to stay or to leave."

"I want to leave now."

"That would be unwise."

The large bearded man spoke up, voice as deep as a drum. "They'll be looking for him. If he wants to leave, let him go."

"He'll be caught. Anyway, he's seen too much now," said the woman.

"I wouldn't have seen anything if you people had just left me alone," said Amariah.

"That certainly was an option," said the woman, scrutinizing him. "We could have left you there to die with your parents. But Joshua has been telling us about you. We felt we had to intervene."

Rebecca interjected. "Even if we let you leave, where would you go? Your home is gone."

"I'll manage," said Amariah.

"Sure you will."

"There's more," said Anne. "Amariah is the only one who knows the process—the enzyme, or whatever it is—that can turn trees into liquid fuel. That's what they want. Isn't that so, Amariah?" She stared into his eyes.

Amariah nodded.

"If they get their hands on you, they'll tear down the entire forest to make the fuel for their planes and tanks," she said. "They'll cut through the woods without a second thought, and keep cutting and cutting until there's nothing left. The soil will wash away and the land will become barren. Your father was right about that at least. So you see, we can't let you go."

Amariah's gaze met the bearded man's. Neither he nor Amariah were happy with the woman's logic, but neither could refute it.

"So, that's settled. But as long as you're going to be with us for a while, you'll have to earn your keep," she said.

"He can chop wood," suggested the man. "Or the latrines could use a cleaning."

"I have a better idea. You can read and write, can't you, Amariah?"

"Yes, of course."

"Well then, you can be our school teacher. We have several children who need to learn. We have a few books here, and every now and then we pick up some more. You could be a big help."

"No, thanks," said Amariah, shaking his head. He didn't want to be a performing monkey for these people. And no sooner had he arrived than someone was giving him something to do. Christ, he couldn't even be a prisoner without someone giving him responsibility.

"Suit yourself," she said, disappointed. "Daniel, get him a bucket and a shovel."

Amariah hesitated. "What about chopping wood?"

"My dear boy," she said. "Do you really think I'm going to give you an axe?"

ॐ

In the lower reaches of the cavern, a tunnel led out into a ravine that tumbled down into a hidden valley. Hiking wearily back into the ravine after a full night of work, Amariah regretted his hasty exchange with the rebel leader. He had just spent the past several hours cleaning latrines with two other men, under the watchful eye of Daniel and another armed guard.

For the two other men, it had obviously been some kind of punishment. Dumping the disgusting contents of the latrines into a hidden pit in the pine forest was obviously a monthly chore. Now Amariah's legs and back ached, and small brown spots had spattered across his boots and fine attire. He had never been as filthy in his entire life.

Two old women poured hot water into a collection of claw foot bathtubs just outside the cave entrance. Above them, the sky lightened with the approach of dawn.

"Hold it," said an old crone, a lifetime of living in her face. "You're not going back in like that. Take off your clothes."

The two other men didn't need prompting, but quickly pulled off their clothes and stepped into the tubs, not at all shy about getting naked in front of the women.

Amariah hesitated, less concerned about being naked than he was about being dirty. He hadn't washed properly since, well, since. Every time he thought about it, he found it hard to believe, but it was all true. His bathroom was now in ashes, just like the rest of his room, his books, his house, his parents, and—

"Come on, come on, get on with it," said the old woman.

Amariah shed his fine clothes, stripped down to his skin and stepped into the tub. The old woman poured hot water at his feet. Amariah immersed himself, and despite the primitive conditions, the bath instantly soothed him. He took a wash towel from the woman, and something that resembled soap, although it certainly didn't look or smell like the soap he was used to. Since there was nothing to shave with, he accepted that he would soon have a full beard like the other men. He lingered only a moment longer than necessary and then got out.

The crone handed him a towel and averted her eyes as Amariah dried himself. She brought over a stack of neatly folded clothes and told him to put them on, which he did. The clothes nearly fit him, although he found the fabric scratchy and uncomfortable.

When they were all dressed, Daniel and the guard led them back through the tunnel to the main cavern. All was quiet. Apparently for the rebels, day and night had been reversed.

Daniel escorted Amariah down a separate passageway to a remote cave drilled out of the stone by someone long ago. An enormous pyramid of old junk filled the center of the space. A cot lay against the wall, a lantern and a small heater beside it.

"You'll sleep here," said Daniel. He tied Amariah's legs and hands to the bedposts. "Give us a reason not to do this and we'll stop doing it."

Daniel left, stopping to consult with a large beefy man who took a seat in a chair just outside.

Amariah lay there on the cold mattress made of straw and gazed at the light flickering in the lantern. The rebels' cavern was lit with fuel from the very refinery they wanted to destroy. The fools.

Amariah wondered which batch it was, and on what happy day he and his father had made it. He pictured the lab, and two of them working side by side, making new discoveries, trying to save the world.

Perhaps his parents lived on somewhere far away. Perhaps their spirits would visit him and guide him through his troubles, or perhaps he too would soon die and join them in some kind of afterlife.

The thought of dying consoled him.

CHAPTER EIGHT

Captain Peck stared at the doctor in disbelief. "Say that again?"

"Amariah is not among the dead," repeated the Wales' personal physician. "All of the bodies have been recovered, and I'm telling you, the boy's not here."

For the past two months the equipment sheds had been used as a makeshift morgue, with the charred remains of the fire victims laid out side by side on the concrete floor. Of the sixteen bodies recovered from the fire, six had been positively identified and buried in Pleasant Valley, including Kenan and Sarah. The general had been interred in Essex Junction with full military honors. Four others had been returned to their Stakeholder families for burial.

The final five corpses, burned and blown apart in the explosion, were proving more difficult to identify; however, according to the doctor, none of the remaining bodies belonged to a nineteen-year-old male.

Peck retrieved his coat. The Wales family may not have been completely wiped out after all. This was very good news.

"Keep this to yourself," he said, heading for the door.

A lot of blame was going around, much of it directed at the Northern Vermont Militia, and Peck in particular. If he could bring Amariah back from the dead, it would do a lot to restore his reputation. Maybe his wife would even pull herself together. She had become a virtual shut-in since the fire, too distraught about his involvement in the fiasco to show her face in public.

Outside in the cold rain, exhaust steam drifted from the tailpipe of the Land Rover that Malinger had given him. Lieutenant Dickins had taught himself to drive, and had left the engine running to keep the car warm.

Peck climbed into the back. The automobile was indeed comfortable, far superior to traveling in a carriage, and a whole lot better than riding a horse in the rain.

"Back to base," he ordered.

The car bullied through the main gate, past his men who stood miserable and wet. Peck saluted through the closed window. Dickins turned onto the river road and headed back to Camp Ethan Allen, where preparations were underway for the assault on the mountain.

"It seems Amariah Wales is not dead after all," said Peck.

"What?" Dickins turned in his seat and nearly drove off the road, his bodybuilder physique unaccustomed to the finesse of powered steering.

Regaining control, his dark brown eyes regarded Peck in the rearview mirror. "Everyone saw him die with his parents. He kept them from being trampled. Several witnesses said so."

"His body isn't there. It's confirmed."

They drove on for a while, windshield wipers ticking away, the trees outside bare and wet.

Finally, Dickins spoke. "Does it matter? Everyone wanted him gone anyway."

"The Stakeholders look like murderers," said Peck. "They're angry. If Amariah were to come back and play nice, it would help."

"So where is he?"

"I don't know. He wanted to run away and see the world. Mommy and Daddy had him so screwed down that he couldn't make a move without them knowing about it. I doubt the kid's ever even been laid."

"Maybe he went to Johnson then," said Dickins with a laugh. The town upriver was home to Madame Daphne's notorious brothel.

"I doubt it, unless he wanted his dick to fall off," said Peck. "No, he wanted to sail the high seas. So he's on his way to Gloucester. Or, maybe he was stupid enough to try to get to Montreal. We'll have to find out."

"What do you mean?"

"Amariah Wales is alive. We bring him back."

"So we're going to look for him?"

"No, *you're* going to look for him. I want you to spread the word, but tell the troops to keep it quiet. Start with the Stakeholders. I want every barn and attic searched. Post men at every estate. Tell them it's for their protection."

"They're not going to like that."

"Screw 'em."

They passed through the Flats, past the site of the Bowmans' former farmhouse. It had burned to the ground after the ambush. He had seen to that.

"Yes, Dickins, the boy genius is out there somewhere," said the captain. "I want you to find him, but be friendly about it—we want him on our side."

84

಄

The cold rain bounced off the wide flat rock, throwing drops of moisture onto the binoculars, obscuring Amariah's view. A rivulet of water coursed off his hat, down his cheek, and into his beard. He brushed the water aside, pulled up his collar, and hunched down, elbows on knees.

Up near the peak of Mount Mansfield, the elements had clashed with geology to create a wide rock ledge, a natural platform with a commanding view of the entire Champlain Valley. Directly in front of the ledge, a cliff plunged a thousand feet straight down. The only way on or off the ledge was through a tunnel door in the rock face behind him, where his guard Cedric sat sheltering from the rain. From his perch, Amariah could keep a distant eye on all of the comings and goings in Pleasant Valley—from the refinery to his left, all the way to the main gate up by the Lamoille River.

Down by the harvester sheds, more than two miles away, a Land Rover had been idling for nearly half an hour, wasting precious fuel, the type of behavior that would have driven his father mad. A man emerged from the sheds and limped to the car—Peck.

Amariah's grip tightened. If he could have, he would have reached down and strangled the bastard with his bare hands. And now the captain had a car; a bribe, no doubt, for his betrayal. He followed the car with his binoculars up to the main gate until it disappeared from view, past the site of his former home and the scorched trunks of the rock maples. No one had bothered to have them felled or trimmed, so there they stood, crippled and burned, their branches raised into the air, as if staring at the site in horror.

On the hillside behind the circular driveway, two white wooden crosses observed the valley, sad and alone. According to Joshua, these were the graves of his parents. On his daily vigils on the ledge, Amariah paid them a long-distance visit. He hoped to earn their forgiveness for his foolishness, for his folly, for his *stupidity* in not recognizing the danger they faced. He had been so preoccupied with his own feelings that he hadn't paid enough attention to what was going on around him.

If only, if only ...

As soon as he could find a way, he would make sure that his parents got proper granite headstones, with inscriptions that would honor their memories. Then, he would stop imagining the hundred different ways he wanted to kill Peck, and actually do it, in the cruelest and most painful way he could devise. But first, he had to get away from the rebels, and get off this goddamned mountain.

ℝ

The inhabitants of Pleasant Valley had always believed Mount Mansfield to be solid rock, never realizing that there was an entire village living inside its dome. It was like a giant ant hill, tunneled out by successive generations of hermits, hippies, survivalists, rebels, and refugees, with hidden entrances all around its slopes. It helped explain why the rebels had a reputation for appearing and disappearing out of nowhere.

Back at the storage cave, Amariah removed his coat and shirt and dried himself with a towel. The space was filled bottom-to-top with junk that the rebels had collected from the surrounding countryside—small engine parts, wiring, cables, plastic sheeting, old skis, gadgets, and tools of all kinds—the types of things that people had been scavenging from abandoned office parks and suburban housing tracks for years.

The rebels didn't know what to do with most of it, but Amariah saw value in just about everything he found.

Soon after he arrived, he had organized everything into piles according to its material composition or function. He took care to hide anything that might be fashioned into a weapon or possible means of escape; however, with the exception of a few blunt objects, sharp fragments of metal, and chemicals, there was nothing that offered an easy solution. Nevertheless, he had put together a small workshop; keeping busy helped take his mind off things, for short periods at least.

Daniel appeared at the entrance. "And how is our Master Wales today?"

"I want to kill Peck."

"Join the club."

"Let me go, and that's what I'll do."

"You'll die trying, I'm certain of that. But it wouldn't matter. Someone else would just take his place. With the Yorkers in charge of the refinery now, nothing would change."

Amariah finished toweling off his hairy head and reached into a small wooden crate. "Here," he said. "For you."

He tossed Daniel a small item wrapped in wax paper.

The burly man caught it in midair, regarded it suspiciously, and then lifted it to his nose. It had the aroma of rose petals.

"What is it?"

"Soap."

Amariah had found some old glycerin in the back of the cave, a byproduct of the refinery's biodiesel process, which the rebels had stolen thinking it was fuel. He had cooked it on the heater and added some old perfume to the mixture.

"You trying to tell me something?"

"Yes, you smell," said Amariah. "But don't take it personally. Everyone in here smells, including me."

"I can't walk around smelling like roses," said Daniel, handing it back.

"Fine, give it to someone else then."

Daniel turned the bar of soap over in his large fingers. "I'm sure the women would love to have some of this, and the children. Why don't you make some more? I don't want to start a riot over one bar of soap."

Amariah flipped open the lid of the crate. It was packed with one hundred bars of soap, each individually wrapped.

Daniel's eyes widened. "Those would make some people very happy."

"Go ahead, take them," said Amariah. "Consider it an early Christmas present."

"Thank you, I'll just do that." Daniel shoved the crate under his huge arm and turned around to leave. "Oh," he said, "I nearly forgot why I came down here. Anne wants you to start eating with everyone else."

Amariah groaned. "Why?"

"She wants you to start integrating so people here get used to you."

Amariah pulled on a blousy shirt and buttoned the cuffs. "Everyone stares at me all the time," he conceded. "I don't like it."

"Can't help you there. Most of these people have never seen an aristocrat before."

"I'd rather not."

Daniel exhaled. "Look, it's not just about you, all right? It's Cedric. Anne wants him to get back to doing something more productive than keeping you company."

88

Amariah raised a quizzical brow and shrugged. "Cedric's tired of keeping me from trying to escape?"

Daniel laughed. "That's rich." He lowered his voice. "You've got it all wrong, Master Wales. Cedric is sitting outside this door to keep you from being beaten up."

&

A few hours later, Amariah found himself in the main cavern, standing in line with about three hundred other people waiting to be served stew ladled from large pots. Most of the refugees were elderly, or mothers with small children.

When it was Amariah's turn, he was handed a metal spoon and a wooden plate. A miniscule portion of stew was ladled onto it, and he did a double-take—the meal consisted of purple potatoes, a specialty of the Wales farm. The rebels must have had stolen them from the cellar when the house caught fire. He shook his head and moved on.

Long wooden tables took up half the cavern. At one, Joshua waved him over, but Amariah ignored him—he no longer knew the man and didn't wish to be in his company.

Anne appeared at his elbow. "We have a seat for you over here, Amariah," said the rebel leader. "Newcomers are seated with other newcomers."

"I see that you're serving our potatoes for dinner," said Amariah, without moving.

"Oh?"

"Yes, purple potatoes are a specialty of our vegetable farmer. I've never seen them anywhere else. How is it that you have them?"

"Amariah, we can't grow food on top of a mountain, you know that. We live off donations. Sometimes we have to take what we need in order to survive."

"What else was in those backpacks? My mother's jewelry?"

"Amariah, we are not thieves, and we have no use for trinkets. Yes, we do take food, and plates and silverware when we can find them. As you can see there are a lot of people up here that we have to take care of, and more are arriving every day. You might ask yourself why."

She led him over to sit at a table with two families. On one side was an old man with a younger woman—his daughter, presumably—and a little boy. On the other side was the family that Amariah had seen when he arrived, the pretty girl with the brilliant blue eyes and her parents. No one was eating. He sat down and picked up his spoon.

The old man gripped his arm. "They want us to say grace first."

From the rock stairs that led to the kitchen, Anne stepped out onto a platform and faced the crowd. The people around Amariah dropped their heads and closed their eyes.

"Lord, thank you for the food we have to eat," Anne intoned. "Let us be grateful for the love of our families. Protect the men and women who are out in the forest tonight keeping us safe. We pray for the day when we can return to our homes and our farms and live the life that you, Lord, had intended for us, to walk in the sun, free from tyranny and slavery."

"Amen," said the crowd.

Amariah pretended not to notice the stares as he dug into his meal. He almost mentioned that the purple potatoes were from his farm, but then thought better of it.

The pretty girl's mother regarded Amariah with disdain. "Well, I'm surprised you can eat at all," she said finally.

"Sorry?"

"I said, I just think it's amazing that you can eat at all, knowing that you are surrounded by all of this suffering that you caused."

"That I caused?"

The old man groaned. "Oh geez, here we go."

The woman's tight brown curls ended at the nape of her flushed red neck. "You are Amariah Wales, aren't you? Of the Wales family of Pleasant Valley? That's who you are, isn't it?"

"Yes."

"And the NVM works for you, right? Forcing people to grow oilseed and then selling the fuel themselves?"

Amariah glanced around the table. Only the sad look of the pretty girl seemed to deserve a serious response.

"The NVM works for the Stakeholders, and for themselves," he replied. "They hold the license to sell our fuel because they have the manpower to distribute it and the means to collect the revenue. But—"

"My husband here knows what it's like to have the NVM come calling to collect. In fact, we all do. It's why we're here in the first place, and not back home on our farms where we belong."

"I think there's been a misunderstanding," said Amariah. "My name is Amariah Wales, and my father is, was, Kenan Wales. We operated the biorefinery and made the fuel that is being used right at this very moment to provide light and to cook the food you're eating. We are not responsible for the NVM, for Captain Peck, or for anything they did. In fact, I hold Peck personally responsible for the death of my parents."

"Well, you only got what you deserved," she said, not about to let anyone else's suffering surpass her own.

91

"Mother, please," said the girl.

The woman shot her daughter a cold stare, and then got up from the table and stormed away.

"I'm sorry," said the girl. "She's upset, we lost our farm—"

"It's okay," said Amariah.

The husband pushed himself out of his chair, but the girl jumped up and said, "No, Father! Eat, please." She took his shoulders and nudged him back down. "Please?"

The girl smiled sadly at Amariah and then went off to find her mother. The father, who had the look of a man who had spent most of his life outdoors, contemplated him somberly.

"I'm sorry about your parents," said the farmer, "but we lost our home too, as have all of these other people, and it's all due to that damn biorefinery of yours."

Amariah recoiled. "Excuse me, but we make fuel for lighting and cooking, and to keep people warm. We powered the military equipment that kept the Canadians out of Vermont. My father was trying to restore aviation, and civilization."

"Restore it, or refashion it into his own utopia?" the farmer shot back. "Your father provided the fuel to the NVM, making him, directly or indirectly, the biggest slave owner of our time."

"Servants," said Amariah. "We had servants on our estate, not slaves."

"No? Were the people free to come and go? It was work on a biofuel plantation like yours as a serf, or live like a slave under Peck and his goons. Even those of us with family farms were forced to put good cropland into oilseed production, just so you rich folks could fly around in your planes.

Your father created an aristocracy, with you Wales at the top!"

Amariah's voice rose. "My father got the refinery working again, after it had been abandoned for years."

"Yes, but then he took it over, which he had no right to do. The refinery belonged to the farmers' cooperative. He enriched himself at everyone else's expense. He even built a wall around it to keep everyone else out!"

Amariah was about to tell this man to go to hell when the little boy spoke. "What's it like to be in an airplane?" he asked.

Amariah took a deep breath. He had forgotten that there was another family at the table. He had nearly lost his temper. It was bad form.

"It's loud. The engine is loud," said Amariah. "But you can see very far. And everyone on the ground looks very small."

"I'd like to go in an airplane someday," said the boy. "Can I, Grandpa?"

"Maybe someday," said the old man.

The farmer lowered his voice. "Look," he said. "I've got nothing against you personally, but all these people here belong back on their farms, growing their crops and raising their children. Instead their farms are occupied, and their soil is being ruined by the NVM. But none of us can leave here because the security forces are out there waiting in their planes, flying over our heads with machine guns, powered by your goddamned fuel."

Amariah was flabbergasted—he had never been spoken to this way.

"No hard feelings, you're a young man, and I know it's not your doing," said the man. He held out his hand. "My name is Bowman. Mark Bowman."

CHAPTER NINE

A barrage of white snowflakes swept past the darkened buildings at the old Burlington Airport, sticking to the corners of the windows where the glass had cracked decades ago. Seated at his desk in the former administrator's office, Captain Peck silently cursed the deepening snowpack that obstructed his runways and the freezing cold temperatures that grounded his planes.

Before the tragedy at Pleasant Valley, Kenan Wales had promised him a new type of winter fuel that would have kept his planes flying on all but the coldest of nights. By now, he had expected to have destroyed the rebels and to have doubled or even tripled his salary through the sale of the extra fuel that Malinger had promised him.

Instead, Malinger and his son were barely able to keep the refinery running at all. Production of the summer fuel had failed—something about the moisture content of the seeds in the silos being too high. So now he wasn't going to have enough heating, lighting, and cooking fuel to get the population through the spring. It was only mid-December, and supplies were already running low.

"Son of a bitch," he groaned.

Lieutenant Dickins inched his head around the door. "Are you all right?"

Peck dismissed him with a wave.

The fall offensive had been a rout, his men retreating back down the mountain with arrows in their backs. The damned rebels wouldn't stand and fight. In the end, the entire effort yielded nothing more than some rumors about caves and fairy tales about the rebels being able to appear and disappear out of nowhere. "Gods of the hills" they called them. How absurd.

He got out of his chair, opened a cabinet, and took out a bottle of whiskey. He would sleep in his office again tonight. Abigail had been having recurring nightmares about Amariah being lost in the mountains. He had thought the news about the boy would have snapped her out of her depression; instead she awoke every morning in tears, begging him to find Kenan and Sarah's son.

He swirled the whiskey in his glass and gazed at the distant peak of Mount Mansfield, white and dim under heavy grey skies. Malinger and his son obviously needed some encouragement. What was needed was some action.

"Dickins!"

The lieutenant's light brown face appeared at the door. "Yes, Captain?"

"I want you to get a troop together. We're going up to Pleasant Valley."

"Today?" The lieutenant looked askance at the snowstorm outside the window.

Peck wondered why his kind had ever moved to Vermont in the first place. "Yes, today. What did I just say?"

Dickins retreated back out the door.

They would have to travel by covered sleigh, since the Land Rover would be sitting idle in the hangar, along with all of his planes, until the temperature climbed above freezing again. Depending on the roads, he could be up at the refinery by tomorrow afternoon. That would mean a stop along the way.

The whiskey warmed his gut as he contemplated where he would spend the night. The Stakeholders had gotten a lot less accommodating since the fire. The Labreche sisters would probably put him up, as long as he gave them some fuel in return. The old broads were mercantile.

He took a final look out the window, scrutinizing every line of the dark peak of the distant mountain, willing it to reveal its secrets. No answers came.

❧

Just after dark, the convoy of covered sleighs arrived at the Labreche estate in Jericho. Two NVM guards, posted out front, waved them through.

The Victorian mansion adjoined several hundred acres of rolling farmland. A special dispensation meant that members of the Stakeholder Board could devote far less land to oilseed than the rest of the population, a perk the women exploited. Most of their farm was devoted to root vegetables and meat, which they sold to hungry villagers through the winter for a tidy profit.

Although their visit was unannounced, the sisters welcomed Peck and his men enthusiastically, rushing their servants through the house to accommodate their guests. Rooms that were still habitable, and not packed with antique clothing and other objects rescued from abandoned estates, were freshened for the night.

Peck dropped his bag on the bed, washed his face in a basin, and then joined the women and Lieutenant Dickins for dinner. Dotty and Betty had changed out of their housedresses into more formal attire, reeking of mothballs. Talk turned quickly to business.

"We haven't had a fuel delivery since September," said Dotty between bites. "Can we be expecting one soon?"

Peck took a sip of his blueberry wine before answering. "The Yorkers have been having some problems. We've brought along some extra fuel for you both, just so you don't run low."

Betty, the younger of the two spinsters, nodded and refilled his glass. The wine tasted odd, more like fruit juice than real wine, but it was still better than cold water, which is what the rest of his men were getting in the servants' quarters.

"Thank you so much, Captain," said Dotty, dabbing at the corners of her mouth with a faded linen napkin. "Has *anyone* been getting their supplies?"

Chewed food slipped from Peck's mouth into his glass, so he downed its contents to cover the blunder. He smacked his lips. "Kenan always kept a reserve supply of all of his fuels for emergencies. We were able to distribute those supplies until a few weeks ago, but then Malinger never produced a new batch. The biodiesel reserves spoiled and now we barely have enough left for ourselves."

"I thought that the Yorkers were going to *increase* production," said Betty, blinking behind her thick glasses.

Dickins spoke through a mouthful of food. "Didn't we all."

Peck shot him a look, and Dotty put her fork down. "Captain, if I may be so bold, the Board is becoming extremely

98

concerned. We have not received payment from you for the past two months."

"I can't charge for fuel I don't have," he replied evenly. "Obviously, I can't make payments to the Board if I don't have any money coming in."

"Well, I certainly hope that you can get Malinger back on track."

The captain examined his empty glass. "You know, Dotty, we could pay a lot more attention to Malinger if we weren't always fighting off rebel ambushes. They're stealing fuel and making life difficult for us all."

"How awful," said Dotty. "What gives them the right to steal fuel from hard-working people? It's not fair to us. Those people should be ashamed of themselves."

"I know you hear things, so can I ask you a favor? If you ever hear about anyone helping the rebels, with food or supplies, I need to know about it. It would make things much easier for everyone."

"Of course," she said. "You will be the first to know. More wine?"

"Thank you," said Peck. He sat back. The lamb had been delicious.

"Now," said Dotty, "enough talk of business. Why don't we go into the parlor? Betty has just learned some new songs on the piano."

Peck and Dickins rose and followed the pair into another room, rejoining the lower-ranking men. Together, surrounded by mismatched antiques and striped wallpaper, they all sat politely through an hour's performance of off-key musical tunes that Peck had never heard before, and hoped never to hear again.

The next morning, the convoy arrived at the main gate to Pleasant Valley. Peck's NVM guards, caught unawares, loitered outside the darkened gatehouse, kicking among scattered refuse, animal bones, and the circular black stains of burned-out bonfires. Kenan would have been appalled. From the window of the sleigh, Peck ordered the place cleaned up.

The situation down at the refinery was even worse. An enormous pile of discarded oilseed, several stories high, lay beside the refinery in the snow. The entire season's supply, worth a small fortune, had been left outside to rot.

Peck marched inside. The place was eerily quiet, a far cry from the productive hum that characterized the place when Kenan was alive. What's more, the power seemed to be off.

A Yorker guard went to retrieve Glen Malinger, who arrived in the lobby unshaven and unkempt.

"Hey, Chris. This is a surprise," said the little man. "Come on back to my office."

Peck left Dickins and his men at the door and followed Malinger farther into the deserted building. Once inside Gareth's old office, Peck slammed the door and backed the Yorker against the desk. "Don't you ever speak that way to me in front of my men again, do you understand?"

"Wha …?" Malinger fumbled for words. "Oh sure. Captain, right? You prefer to be called Captain. Sure, no problem. Sorry."

Pcck plopped down in a chair. Malinger pulled a drawer out of an old filing cabinet and retrieved a bottle of potato vodka, along with an antique shot glass with the word "NASCAR" painted on the side. He poured the captain a drink.

"A little too early for me," said the Yorker, giggling.

Peck downed the contents and slammed the glass back onto the desk. Malinger stared and then poured him another shot.

Peck took the glass and toyed with it. "Where's my fuel?"

"Right, well, we've got it, got it right back there in the tanks." Malinger settled back in his oversized chair. "But our trucks can't run because of the cold, as you know. Once the weather warms up we'll have it to you. No problem."

Peck downed the vodka and wiped his mouth with his sleeve. "No problem, huh? You ruined the entire season's oilseed supply. I've got people sitting in the dark and cold because of you. They don't pay me, and I don't pay the Stakeholders, and everybody is up my ass because of you."

"Now, Chris, er … Captain, hah," he said, making a show of correcting himself. "It's true we had some problems. I put it down to a learning curve. This facility is much bigger than the one we have in Albany. Plus we lost the chief engineer." He opened his palms wide as if to say that none of this was his fault. "This wasn't expected and it wasn't part of the plan."

"What about the biomass processor? Use some wood."

"Gareth didn't write anything down. Most of the staff ran away, and no one knows how to recreate the enzyme. Without that to break down the lignin in the biodigester, it doesn't work."

Peck reached for the bottle and poured himself another shot.

"Now, I'm not blaming anyone, don't get me wrong," said Malinger, eying the draining bottle, "but our agreement was based on us taking over a fully operational plant with all of the staff. Not—well, er, not what happened."

Peck wanted to knock the little greaseball to the floor, but without him there would be no chance of having any fuel, and that would mean chaos. He downed the rest of his glass and regarded the bristled Yorker coldly.

"Let me be absolutely clear, Glen. I want as much fuel as possible loaded aboard horse-drawn wagons tomorrow morning, just like the Wales used to do, so I can start making deliveries. Furthermore, I want you to figure out how to get that biomass processor working, because if we can't replace the lost oilseed, we might not get through the winter with our heads attached. While you're at it, I want you to figure out how Kenan planned to give me fuel that could work in the winter. In short, I want everything I was promised. I want my planes in the air. I want my airfield plowed and my equipment running, I want my goddamned *car* working, and I will not accept any more excuses!" He was halfway across the desk.

Malinger nodded, his eyes wide.

"Of course you do, Captain," said Malinger. "I understand. You want all of those things. That's only natural. But as I said, we don't have either of those formulas. If Amariah had written them down, the notes were destroyed in the fire. Gareth never wrote anything down, and he's dead. But we're working on it. In fact, I have my son working on both of these things right now, in the lab."

Peck dropped back into the chair. "He won't figure it out. We need to find Amariah Wales."

"Amariah is long gone by now. I heard he got on a ship."

"Maybe. Maybe not."

"Well, he's not hiding with the Stakeholders. We would have seen some sign of him by now. I heard he went to Montreal."

"He didn't go to Canada."

"How do you know?"

Peck recalled the docks in Montreal. They were tough. Amariah Wales, the aristocrat, wouldn't stand a chance, even if he had escaped with any money, which he hadn't. Peck's men had opened the safe in the ruins of the mansion after the fire. The paper money had burned to ashes, and Peck had confiscated all of the gold coins for safekeeping.

"We have troops holding back the Canadians on the Richelieu River, we have guards at all of the border crossings, and we have spies in all of the border towns. No one has seen anyone matching his description."

"You see? There's very little we can do."

Peck pushed himself up out of the chair and strolled over to the wall. Gareth's old photographs had faded with age. Half a century ago, cars, speedboats, and jet planes were commonplace. Now most of them were trash in an enormous garbage dump somewhere.

In one photograph, a helmeted fighter pilot, face obscured behind a respirator, gave a thumbs-up.

"Let's offer a reward," said Peck. "You put up the money and I'll put the word out."

"You want me to put up the money? I don't have any money. It's all tied up in my wife's property."

"Look, Glen, I'm going to give you a month to get it together. Then I want to see a demonstration. For starters, I want to see one of those cars of yours driving around outside in the snow. Kenan said that he could make the biodiesel work in winter by using isopropyl alcohol. He said they made it using pine trees. So cut down some goddamned pine trees. I want to see proof that you two geniuses are going to be able to come through for me. You got it?"

He opened the door. "And don't plan on going anywhere until you have it figured out. I'm going to leave a squad here to help you."

He left Malinger at his desk and walked back through the empty plant. His men were not going to like staying up here for the next month, but they could take over the barracks, down by the gate, and he would make it worth their while.

"You're all staying," he said to Dickins, waiting at the door.

"We are?" The lieutenant's beefy shoulders sagged.

"I want this place cleaned up and everything working again. Take what you need. Crack the whip."

Dickins nodded, crestfallen.

"And cheer up. I'll send you all something to play with."

He slapped Dickins on the back and headed out the door, telling the driver to head to Johnson. He would pay a visit to Madame Daphne. After all, he had to sleep somewhere, and she just might have some new girls to offer.

He settled back into the seat of the covered sleigh and watched the valley slip by, deep in snow. As he passed the site of the former Wales mansion, he looked away, not wanting to encounter the two crosses up on the hill.

Here, in the land of the living, he would take care of himself and his men. It was one of the perks of being alive. He would eat, drink, and get laid, and then arrange the same for his men. And he would use one of Kenan's gold pieces to pay for it.

∽

"Emily, pay attention please," said Hannah.

The aspiring young teacher stood in front of the make-shift slate blackboard, on which she had just written the words "Happy New Year!" roughly in white chalk. Two little girls giggled in the front row.

Emily's mother, the mousy young widow Ella, came forward and told the little conspirators to settle down, which they did. Hannah smiled at the class and continued.

"Today," she said, "we are joined by Amariah Wales, who has agreed to help me with tutoring in math and reading. If it's your turn to read one of our books, and you need some help, you can come to either Amariah or myself, and we will help you."

All heads turned to look at him. Most of the children smiled, as did some of the adults.

Amariah grinned. His popularity had soared after Daniel had distributed the soap, and he now knew many of the people in the cavern by name.

Two of those in the class, however, weren't smiling: Miriam Bowman gave him the withering look she always had at the ready, and he also received a cold stare from Ira, the young man to whom he had been tied on the trek up the mountain. Ira had broken his arm during the NVM's recent assault, and was now on leave from duty, his arm in a cast. Ira was clearly infatuated with Hannah and hung around her like a dog.

Hannah resumed the lesson, turning to write the words "cat" and "bat" and "hat" on the slate. The adults paid just as much attention as the children, squinting to see what she had written. Amariah didn't know whether it was due to their lack of eyeglasses, or from the dim light of the oil lamps, but from the back row he had trouble seeing the board himself.

"What other words sound like 'bat'?" Hannah asked the class.

105

The children chimed in, and so did Ira, his voice deeper and out of place among the little ones.

Amariah gave Hannah a lot of credit for having the courage to stand up in front of the crowd. While her lesson wasn't as refined as those of his own childhood tutor, there was apparently a lot more to being a teacher than simply helping children to learn. It didn't help that there wasn't any paper or writing instruments other than the broken nub of chalk.

"Who wants to practice writing on the board?" asked Hannah.

Ira's hand shot up. Hannah chose little Emily instead. Ella caught Amariah's expression and gave him a smile.

Amariah dropped his gaze. He didn't want to make an enemy out of Ira. As creepy as he was, the young fighter had a lot of friends, and Amariah had to be careful when they were in the cavern and not out in their tree stands. Without Cedric as a bodyguard, he didn't want to end up having an unfortunate "accident" when no one else was around.

Later that night, the fallen heir was busy at his workbench making wax when little Emily appeared at the door, a book in her hands. Her mother Ella held back, leaning against the wall.

Amariah turned down the flame beneath the pot, and then flipped a tarp to conceal his latest project. He wiped his hands with an old rag and got down from his stool.

"Hi," he said.

"Amariah," said the little girl, "could you read me a story?" She stood there with a hopeful expression, the book too big for her little body.

"Sure."

He took the book. It was old, of course, and yellowed—they all were—but the print was still legible. An illustration embellished the cover: *Why the Right is Wrong*, a book written decades ago, back when the subject mattered to the person who wrote it. Someone now long dead.

"This isn't a book for a little girl," he said. "What other books to do you have?"

Emily dashed off, leaving Amariah alone with the short-haired widow.

"So, how did you get here?" he asked. It was the standard way to open a conversation in the cave.

"The Yorkers came to the workers' village," she said, sauntering over to observe the boiling wax. "They told us we would be working for them. But we weren't going to work for any damned Yorkers. We gave them more of a fight than they bargained for."

"That's where you lived? The workers' village?" His ears picked up. "Do you know what happened to Max Colpe and his parents?"

"Oh, them. They were the first to run. But eventually our street was taken, and we had to run too. Emily and I escaped through Joshua's gate." She turned and regarded him, just a few inches away. The pale, plain woman was perhaps just a year or two older than himself.

"Where are you from?" he asked.

"Vergennes."

Amariah frowned. There had been a lot of fighting in the lake towns during the Troubles. Most of Vergennes had burned to the ground.

"I'm sorry."

Ella continued to inspect his workbench, glancing at the stolen fuel cans that contained the glycerin he used to make the soap. The lettering was still stenciled to the side: "Property of Pleasant Valley Biofuels."

"Oh, I remember those," said Ella, brushing against him. "That's your fuel, right? What the NVM delivered?"

"Those are our cans, yes."

"We used to use your fuel to light our lanterns. Until my husband died. Then we had no money. Fortunately the NVM accepted more than money. Then we were back in business."

"I'm sorry, what?"

She laughed and stood before him, smelling of rose petals.

"You know. We used to call it 'getting Waled,'" she whispered.

Amariah took a step back. "I had no idea," he stammered. "Oh—"

Little Emily ran back in with several books in her hands, a welcome intrusion. Amariah turned to the girl, face warm, and took the first book, a slender volume with the grand title *The History of the World* written across its old plastic cover. The old electronic book's grey screen had been dead for decades, its contents beyond retrieval. He tossed it aside, avoiding Ella's gaze.

He flipped through several more paper books, some in better condition than others: a couple of novels, a book about managing in one minute—whatever that meant—and a book on hang gliding. At the bottom of the pile there was a colorful, horizontal book that was different from the rest. *Where the Wild Things Are.*

He picked it up and flipped through it. The pictures had retained their color.

"This will do." He sat down on his cot and patted the blanket.

Emily climbed up beside him and Amariah read her a story about a mischievous little boy who was sent to his room, which turned into a wild and strange place filled with monstrous creatures. At the end, the little boy smelled his dinner and returned to his home, leaving the wild things behind in their wild world.

Amariah closed the book. Emily smiled.

"I want to go back to my room too," she said. She looked up at Amariah as if he could do something about it. "When can we go back home? I want to go back to *my* room."

Ella reached for her daughter's hand. "Shush now. Amariah doesn't own the village anymore ... or do you?"

Amariah shook his head.

"Well, thank you, in any case," she said. She took her daughter off the bed, letting the fingers of her other hand slide across his shoulders. As she leaned over to pick up the books, her blouse hung open, exposing her breasts.

Amariah looked away.

Ella stood back up, took the girl by one hand and the pitiful collection of books in the other, and sidled toward the exit.

"Thank you, again," she sighed, lingering for a moment.

Amariah remained seated. "Good night," he said finally.

The sad pair walked away.

Amariah fell back on his bed. His parents would have been shocked to know that their name was being bastardized that way. Or would they? Perhaps they knew about the NVM's abuses and had turned a blind eye. The thought of his parents being complicit in the suffering outside the valley seemed impossible, and yet each person here seemed to have a story that was completely at odds with the world Amariah thought he knew. What if these people were right and he was actually responsible for their plight?

He turned over and faced the lantern's flickering light. Down the tunnel, coughs echoed from the dim cavern.

Despite the politics outside the barrier wall, he was certain his mother would have been appalled at the conditions in the cave and would have tried her best to do something about it. He could picture her moving among the grottos, checking on everyone's well-being, with the courage to take matters into her own hands.

Perhaps he could do something to make amends. Although he lacked his mother's healing touch, he was still a Wales.

A thought occurred to him. He got back out of bed, put on his moccasins, and turned the lamp up to its brightest. He carried it around to the far side of the pile and began searching for some old engine parts.

There was indeed something he could do to help improve conditions in the cave. Something that would benefit everyone.

He pulled together what he needed and then got to work, determined to show these people the best of what the Wales family once represented.

It would be his parting gift.

CHAPTER TEN

A bedraggled crowd gathered in the snowy street in front of the old Town Hall in Jeffersonville as Captain Peck nailed a poster to the announcement board:

WANT ALIVE
Amariah Wales

For Questioning in Relation
to the Events Involving
the Fire and Fatalities the Night
of September 17th

$100 in Gold

A bespectacled old man in a tattered beret read the poster aloud for the benefit of the others, causing a stir. The amount was equivalent to an entire year's income for a free trades-man. Peck scanned the faces of the two dozen bundled-up townspeople, waiting for a tipster to come forward, trying to

detect any reaction that would indicate someone had information about Amariah's whereabouts. But all he observed
was some eagerness about the money and a scratching of
covered heads.

A month had passed since he had last visited Malinger at
the biorefinery. Now he was back, in the deep freeze of February, making a show of his presence in the largest and closest town to Pleasant Valley. Jeffersonville was the gateway to
the mountain road, and the nearest settlement to rebel territory, so he made sure to display his authority to remind them
all who was in charge.

From the direction of the river road, a fine covered sleigh
approached, led by two brown horses. This would be Isaac,
the last of the Stakeholders arriving for the meeting in the old
Town Hall. Peck had called a meeting with the eleven most
powerful people in the territory, most of whom already waited inside. Isaac was the oldest of the bunch and always the
last to arrive.

The driver pulled the horses to a stop and then sprang out
to pull open the sleigh door. The old man emerged, tipped his
hat to the crowd, and hurried into the building, surrounded by
NVM guards. Peck gave the mangy pack one last scan, disappointed that the promised money had failed to provide an
immediate result. Then he followed Isaac inside, leaving four
guards posted out in front.

The red brick building was originally a church and then a
Town Hall, in which the common man had made his voice
heard, voting in the presence of his neighbors. There was
none of that nonsense anymore. Now the Stakeholders called
the shots, the NVM did the dirty work, and everyone else
knew their place, or else.

At the center of the room, the elderly Stakeholders had gathered around a large conference table, murmuring amongst themselves. At the far end sat Bernard Craggs, the Board's crusty old chairman. The other Stakeholders—all from established Vermont families—grew silent. Peck strode through the room and sat in a heavy chair at the far end. No one greeted him.

Craggs looked up. "Okay, we all know why we're here," he said, gruffly. "Obviously there have been some issues up at the plant. This has caused us all a lot of problems."

A murmur of "hear, hear" went around the table.

"So, Captain," said Craggs, "why don't we begin with you? Perhaps you can explain just what the hell is going on up there."

Peck took his time; it was important to remain cool with these characters. "Mr. Chairman, as you know, our friend Malinger and his son put a large quantity of oilseed into the silos before it had been properly dried. That contaminated the rest of the oilseed, causing all of it to rot in the silos. The fuel supply for an entire season has been ruined. We are running low on heating, lighting, and cooking fuel, as well as bio-diesel, and we're rationing supplies. Our customers are getting nervous, as they should be, as we are going to run out of fuel before the next harvest is in. Or, should I say, *they* will run out of fuel. No one at this table will end up sitting in the cold and the dark, I'm sure of that." Peck smiled.

The Stakeholders held their poker faces. Each one of them had tanks full of basic biofuel stored away on their estates to keep their generators running and their lanterns lit. Biodiesel, however, was another matter, since it would only be a few months until it all went bad.

"How are you planning on handling the public?" asked Craggs.

"We'll make examples of fuel thieves and wood poachers with public hangings. That always keeps them quiet. But I wouldn't want to be riding around in a fancy carriage without extra security until the fuel starts flowing again, I can tell you that much."

There was shuffling around the table. Good. Peck wanted the Stakeholders to be afraid. Like it or not, they would need him all the more.

"Now, there may be a solution for our little problem," said the captain. "You'll recall the biomass processor up at Pleasant Valley. I know some of you assumed that it was useless, since, well, since we lost Kenan."

Some eyes went to where Kenan had always sat, first chair to Craggs's right, when he was the twelfth member of the Board.

"However, the boy Amariah knows how the thing works and we can be reasonably certain that he knows the formula for that enzyme as well. So in fact, there is a very simple solution to all of our problems, and that is for the person who knows where Amariah is hiding to tell us all where he is. Right now."

Peck scanned their faces. They all stared directly back at him, shocked. Peck didn't actually think that someone hiding Amariah would deliver him on the spot. What he was trying to do was to get someone to reveal they knew something, or even better, for two people to look at the person who may be hiding the boy.

But there was no coordinated look, no revealing glance, only confusion. If someone was hiding Amariah, they weren't giving it away.

114

Dotty Labreche spoke up. He hadn't seen her since the night he had spent at her home. The spinster wore an old brooch for the occasion, along with an old dress reeking of mothballs.

"Captain, if Amariah Wales had any sense, he would be far away from here by now," she said. "I doubt that anyone is going to take that reward. They'd never be able to spend the money. And why is he suddenly 'Wanted' anyway? He didn't do anything."

"I want him—so that means he's wanted."

No one laughed. Peck cleared his throat.

"We should all be very interested in getting that young man back in the refinery where he belongs," he continued. "Not only does he hold the key to that biomass processor, he's also the one who figured out how to keep the biodiesel from freezing in winter. This could extend the reach of our air power throughout the year. This would be very helpful right now, as we'll need to keep the rebels at bay before we can start any major timber harvesting."

"With the boy back, we could get rid of the Yorkers," suggested Craggs.

"Perhaps we could," acknowledged Peck. "Now, whatever you may feel about Malinger, until we find Amariah, he is our best chance of getting that facility back in operation. If the boy is dead somewhere, Malinger is the only one who can get things back to normal once the harvest is in. And the sooner things get back to normal, the sooner you'll get paid."

He gestured to a pile of papers on the conference table, an assortment of letters and copies of unpaid bills, tied neatly into a bundle. He didn't touch it.

115

"I have a summary of all of your accounts here. I also have all of your letters, some of which were rather less than polite, I must say." He looked pointedly at Isaac.

"Here's the bottom line: Once I get my fuel, the people will pay me, I will pay my men, and you will all get paid for your oilseed. Then, and only then, Malinger will get paid. It's that simple. Now, who has anything to say?"

Isaac was the first to speak up, as always. "Captain Peck, there seems to be a misunderstanding. We are not here to talk about next year's payments, but about last year's. We delivered tons of oilseed for which we have not been paid. That product represents a significant investment."

Peck answered slowly and carefully. "Isaac," he said, "you're a businessman. I'm sure that you understand when I say that I am not going to pay for fuel that I never received. It costs us a lot of money to keep troops at the refinery and on your farms for your protection. I have to ship food and supplies here every week. In fact, I will be sending down a very large shipment of food from Enosburg in the middle of March—three wagons full of food and other supplies to support the garrison at Pleasant Valley. Now, I am happy to do what I can, Isaac, but the NVM is not a charity."

Wynant, the lumber miller, came to the old man's aid. "What Isaac is saying, Captain, is that you promised us we would receive our payments on schedule. This was an implied guarantee you would honor our contracts. In fact, I recall being told we would all be rich. From what we hear, however, not only was last year's crop ruined, but in fact Malinger doesn't have the slightest idea what he's doing. We can't afford another year of mistakes."

Peck noted the lack of any dissent or any looks over in Wynant's direction. Since Peck's spies hadn't reported any

116

group meetings, they must have been communicating in secret. He would have to find out how.

Wynant went on. "We expect to be paid for what we delivered last season. These bills are already six months past due. Not only that, we expect to be paid in advance before we plant this next season, or we will consider growing other crops instead."

Peck leaned back in his chair and chuckled. "Okay, Wynant, and exactly who do you plan to sell those crops to? That's something I'd be very interested to learn."

Wynant fumbled for some words, then backed down.

Smart man, thought Peck. The NVM controlled all of the roads and river access in the territory. Crops and livestock were easy targets for diversion, confiscation, or, if necessary, sabotage.

Peck adopted a conciliatory tone. "Look, folks, I didn't come here to quarrel. You'll get your money when I get my fuel. I'm making every effort to ensure that Malinger is getting back on schedule, including providing my own personal supervision. We are also offering incentives to bring back some of the more skilled engineers, including a rather large incentive for Amariah, I might add."

"Maybe *too* large," said Craggs.

Peck ignored the quip. "A month ago I left a squad with Malinger to make sure that things got back on track. After this meeting I will be going up for a demonstration of the winter fuel we were promised by Kenan. With that fuel, we can protect ourselves as we harvest timber, with the expectation that the biomass processor will soon be back in working order. The rebels won't have the benefit of tree cover, and they won't be expecting an attack from the air. We can do some very serious damage, and maybe even wipe them out once and for all."

The Stakeholders all banged on the table in agreement, except for Isaac. "I hear that Amariah has gone to Canada," said the old man. "They say he plans to come back down here with an army to kick your ass."

The Stakeholders laughed.

Peck rose abruptly, knocking over his chair. "Isaac! You of all people should know better than to joke about that. Amariah Wales is the key to solving this. If he dies out there, we're all screwed. Help me find him, for God's sake."

He scanned the chastened, fossilized faces and then headed for the door, leaving their correspondence behind on the tabletop.

As he donned his coat, Peck addressed the aristocrats one last time. "I'm going up to knock some sense into Malinger. But don't forget, chums, in times like these, it's the people who have the most to lose who should be the most afraid."

၈၁

Smartly turned out in their winter uniforms, Peck's troops saluted as he arrived at the main gate. The inspection of his sleigh proceeded swiftly and professionally and his men waved him through.

Down at the refinery, the pile of rotting oilseed was gone. In its place a small motor course had been fashioned for the demonstration. A snowman even held a racing flag—one of the antiques from Gareth's office, no doubt. A bit of fun born of cabin fever, but a promising sign nonetheless.

Lieutenant Dickins opened the door, his dark nose reddish from the cold. Peck got out and strode inside, finding the welcome area neat, tidy, and polished with Wales Wax.

"Looking good, Lieutenant," he said. "Let's hope Malinger made as much progress as you did."

His men followed as he entered the cavernous processing room. Malinger and his son, surrounded by the Yorker engineers, waited before the giant steel mixing tanks. They had cleaned themselves up; the kid was even wearing a white lab coat.

"Welcome back, Captain," said Malinger.

The Yorker engineers, watched closely by Peck's men, all stiffened to attention.

Peck glanced over at Dickins, who grinned. Apparently, a little intimidation went a long way.

"Thank you," said Peck. "So, what have you got to show me?"

"Well, I think you'll be impressed," said Malinger.

"I certainly hope so."

"We've made quite a bit of progress on the fuel mixture," said the kid, Eric. He held a glass jug filled with pale brown fuel. "We'd like to show you the result."

Malinger extended his arm toward the back door, and they all went into the mud room where the Yorkers put on their winter coats, hats, scarves, and gloves. The group stepped outside, ice and snow crunching beneath their feet. Despite the bright sunshine, the air hung frigid and still. Frosted beards glistened with little beads of ice.

Dickins gave a signal, and somewhere an engine revved to life. Around the corner of the administrative building came Malinger's Range Rover. It worked!

The driver of the car proceeded into the makeshift track, driving between the little orange flags stuck into the snow. Upon completing the course, the car pulled up in front of the group and came to a stop.

119

"Care to take a ride, Captain?" said Malinger, beaming.

"Sure. Why don't you join me?"

Malinger went over and tapped on the window. The driver got out and Malinger took the wheel. Peck got in the front passenger seat and the kid hopped into the back. Malinger put the car in gear and drove around the makeshift course.

"So, it seems that you got it all figured out," said Peck.

"Yes, Captain, we do," said the kid.

"So what was the secret?"

"Well, it's rather complicated," said Malinger.

"And it is?" said Peck, again.

"The pine trees need to be fermented in a certain way to create the isopropyl alcohol," said Malinger.

"And which way is that?"

"Well, as I said, it's rather complicated."

"I want a full report, in writing, by tomorrow," said Peck.

Malinger blanched.

Peck continued, "You've got the car running, that's what I wanted to see. Congratulations. This means our planes will fly too, right?"

Malinger made a turn around an obstacle in the snow course. "Yes," he said, drawing out the word to indicate "maybe."

"Good. So I'll take ten thousand gallons to start," said Peck. "I want it delivered by next week. I think you know our address."

"Uh, Captain, we were able to synthesize an amount of fuel that worked in the winter for this demonstration, as you asked, as a proof-of-concept. However, building up the process into a production environment will take some time."

Peck exploded. "Goddammit, Malinger!" he said, pounding on the dashboard. "I want my planes in the air. We need

120

to start harvesting trees. Entire hillsides need to be cut. We need air cover now. The rebels won't be expecting planes in the winter. Once the leaves grow in it will be too late!"

"Yes, I understand that, Captain," said Malinger, deliberately calm. "But even Amariah didn't have a full production process worked out. Eric is working very hard to ramp up production, but it will take some time."

Peck reached up with his left hand and spun the rearview mirror so he could see the kid in the back. "How much time, Eric?"

"Uh, well, we're certainly working on it." The kid's eyes kept darting over at his father.

Malinger reached up and returned the rearview mirror to its proper orientation. "Captain," he said. "We've done what you asked. We have the car running in winter. The fuel is working. Give us some time and we'll get the plant into production capacity. We're going to do everything we can to help you get your planes in the air."

He spun the car around another obstacle. "But if you want the biomass processor back in operation, then find Amariah Wales. Get him back here at the plant and back to work. Or at least, get him to tell us what he knows, because, honestly, we don't have the enzyme figured out yet. Without that, you won't need to start clear-cutting anything."

Malinger brought the car to a stop back in front of the plant. Peck got out and walked over to his men.

"So, what's the secret of the winter fuel?" he asked Dickins.

"Damned if I know," said his lieutenant. "Eric worked for a month mixing things together, then one morning he announced he had it solved."

Peck looked up and scrutinized the mountain. Somewhere up there, the rebels who shot him, killed General Barings, ruined his chance for riches, and pitched his wife into a full nervous breakdown, waited for his revenge. He imagined himself flying over the peak and through the mountain passes, catching them exposed in the snow and ripping them apart with his guns. And after he followed their tracks to their hideout, he would rid himself of these "gods of the hills" once and for all.

୬

Deep inside Mount Mansfield, Amariah sat hunched over his worktable, scrubbing corroded electrical parts recovered from the junk pile.

"Hi," said a female voice.

Amariah looked up. It was Hannah, and she was alone.

"Hi there."

"Mind if I come in?"

"Not at all."

She made a cursory inspection of the small metal parts strewn across his workbench. "What are you doing?"

"It's a surprise."

Hannah shrugged, then strolled around the room in her distinctly indifferent way, idly observing the items Amariah had finally organized into neat, high piles. In addition to the old engine parts, sheets of plastic, glass containers, and old plastic jugs filled with chemicals, there were large rings of cable, coiled and stacked to the ceiling. A narrow passageway wound through it all, and Hannah drifted slowly from one item to the next.

"Wow. So this is where the mad scientist works," she said.

"Yes. Don't touch anything dangerous."

She laughed. "*Oooh*, I won't."

She came around the bend, stopping at two saw horses covered in a tarp and lifted the edge. There was nothing there—Amariah had hidden his most recent project deep within the pile.

"Is there something in particular you're looking for?"

"I need more things to use to teach the children," she said. "Do you have any books down here?"

"No, you've got them all. But I'm sure I could pull out something for show and tell."

She regarded him coyly. "Oh really?"

Amariah laughed and gestured across the room. "There are a lot of things here that I could explain to the kids."

"What would you tell them? Here's a piece of junk that once used to be part of something important? This is how the world once was and no longer is?"

She picked up an old electric lamp timer, the kind used to turn lights on and off when someone wasn't home. She turned it over, apparently unsure what it was, then placed it back down on the pile.

"No," he said. "I would tell them, 'Here are some raw materials that were once made into something useful, and can once again be useful, if you understand science.'"

"My, my," she said, "an optimist, living in a cave. How unusual. Maybe we should use you for show and tell."

Amariah smiled despite himself. He had always been suspicious of girls when they flirted with him, perhaps because his mother had warned him of young women seeking to elevate their status. But Hannah was smart and very pretty indeed—her dark hair today was tied in a ponytail that went all the way down her back, and he liked her blue eyes.

"My father once told me it was pointless to cry over things you've lost," said Amariah. "That one should learn one's lesson and then move on. That's what I'm trying to do. Although it hasn't been easy."

She grew still. "Amariah—" she began, but then she stopped, her eyes cast over Amariah's shoulder. He turned. Miriam Bowman stood there, watching them.

"So, here you are," she said.

Amariah was glad he had remained in his chair.

"Let's go, Hannah," said the woman, glaring at them both.

Hannah rolled her eyes and moved to leave, but as she did, she turned and smiled at him. "Why don't you pick something and bring it up to show the kids?" she suggested.

"I'm working on something right now that might brighten their day," he said with a smile. He kept the smile for Miriam, but it was not returned.

∞

Anchoring an electrical cable next to a stalactite was more challenging than Amariah had anticipated.

Teetering on top of a tall ladder in a high, far corner of the main cavern, he hammered another piton into the stone beside the slippery rock, being careful not to crack the formation and send it smashing onto the heads of his helpers below. He twisted a piece of wire to secure the cable, then connected its two exposed ends to a refurbished light fixture, tightening the screws with a small screwdriver he lifted from his work belt.

Wire was one thing not in short supply in the caves. The countryside was littered with it—electrical cable, telephone wire, old Internet cable—synthetic black strands lay in the weeds beside every roadside. It had become a ubiquitous building material, used for lashing things together, protecting bottles from breaking, and many other uses, but this was probably the first time in a while that someone was using it for the purpose for which it was intended.

From the light fixture, the wire snaked down along the wall and into a tunnel, eventually extending all the way to the lower reaches of the cavern, where an underground stream coursed through a dark channel. There, with help from his team, Amariah had installed a jerry-rigged, micro-hydro generator.

Tom, one of the team of old men helping out, waited at the bottom of the ladder, holding the box of lightbulbs. "It's the last one, so don't break it," announced the man, too nearsighted and frail to be out in the woods on patrol.

Amariah reached the bottom of the ladder. "Thanks, Tom," he said. He took the lightbulb and carefully placed it into a cloth sack attached to his belt, then climbed back to the top to screw it in.

The bulbs were handmade by a glass blower in Johnson, the same man who had made the bulbs for the Wales mansion and the other fine estates. Amariah had asked Daniel to pay a secret visit to the man on his next supply run, and, without naming names, to get a dozen bulbs. Amariah wasn't sure what he had used to pay for them all, but Daniel had come through.

He climbed down and, with the help of the men, took down the ladder and placed it alongside the wall. "Come on, gentlemen, let's see how we did."

The group walked together into the center of the main cavern, the usual murmur of dinnertime activity punctuated by the occasional cries of children. Anne motioned for

Amariah to join her on the platform. She called for every-one's attention and took his hand.

"Tonight we have a special treat for you," she said. "You've all seen Amariah working on his latest project, and he has promised me that it is going to be something special. Amariah?"

The crowd fell silent as Amariah walked over to a knife switch fastened to the wall near the kitchen. He tried to think of something profound to say. Perhaps something about Prometheus?

"I hope this works," was all he could manage. He held his breath as he threw the big switch down.

The cavern exploded with light and the people gasped. Most had never seen a single electric light, let alone an entire lighting display. Amariah examined his handiwork. All of the bulbs burned brightly; the cavern radiated with varying hues of colored light. For the first time, he could see the full extent of the enormous cavern, from the floor where they stood, to the small grottoes people called home, up the piles of fallen rock and into the narrow passages that spidered off into the giant anthill of a mountain.

The lights grew brighter as the bulbs warmed up and a few people shielded their eyes. Having not been outside for months, they had grown accustomed to the dimness of oil lamps in near-darkness. The bulbs grew brighter still and some people shrieked.

Amariah quickly turned down the dimmer. "Sorry," he said.

Those who had covered their faces now peered out at the sight and the "oohs" and "aahs" began. The stalactites and stalagmites, merely dark and ominous shadows before, basked in the glow of deep reds, yellows, and blues. He had designed the lighting both for function as well as ambiance, and it gave the cavern warmth and depth. The crowd burst into spontaneous applause. Amariah called his team of older men onto the platform and they all took a bow.

"Come on, everyone, eat your soup before it gets cold!" said Amariah.

A final cheer rolled into hundreds of separate conversations, the loudest cacophony of voices he had heard since the night of the banquet. He retrieved a bowl of soup and took his usual seat. Hannah beamed at him, and even her parents seemed pleased with him for once. He sat down and accepted their compliments gracefully, praising the men who worked with him on the project.

The little boy couldn't take his eyes off the ceiling. "It's wonderful, Grandpa," he said.

"I can finally see what I'm eating!" said the boy's mother.

The others at the table agreed and examined the contents of their bowls. The old man looked down into his own bowl and made a face.

"There's a bug in my soup," he said.

CHAPTER ELEVEN

Amariah pulled on the handle with all his might, but the door wouldn't budge.

"It's frozen shut," he said.

"Here, let me try," said Hannah.

"Be my guest."

Hannah spit into her cupped hands, rubbed them together, then gently pulled on the handle with the tips of two fingers.

"Nope," she said. "It's stuck."

Amariah laughed. He picked up a stone and tapped along the doorframe, trying to break the icy bonds. Then, with all his might, he pulled again and the door sprang open. Snow and ice fell inside, Amariah tumbled to the floor, and Hannah laughed.

They were in the upper cave just inside the ledge. Deep snow completely filled the doorway, glowing an icy blue, backlit by the sun.

"Wow, it's pretty," said Hannah. She reached out and brushed the translucent crust with her gloved fingertips.

"Put your sunglasses on," said Amariah.

"Oh right." Hannah pulled out a pair of sunglasses and put them on. They were an ancient pair of pink Minnie

Mouse sunglasses, a throwaway gift for a little girl a long time ago. The more sturdy pairs of sunglasses were being worn by the fighters out in the snow to prevent snow-blindness. These were the only pair that Daniel had left, but they were better than nothing.

"Stand back." Amariah broke into the crust with a shovel and dug out a space big enough for them to stand outside. This was the very same ledge where Amariah had spent so many days when he had first arrived, grieving over the loss of his parents. Six months later, he was back again, having been up there only once since, to install some additional cable along the passageway—preparation, he told his team, for the arrival of some additional lightbulbs. Now, he was here to show Hannah the view. Or at least, that's what he told her.

"Ladies first."

She stepped outside. "Wow."

On this bright winter afternoon, the cloudless sky was a deep blue, the sun a brilliant star, and the reflection off the snow glaringly bright. Amariah pulled on a pair of scratched old ski goggles he had found in the pile.

"Keep yours on," he said.

Hannah squinted. "Don't worry."

Amariah decided to dig out a little farther. "Here, back up," he said. "Make sure you don't close the door."

He dug a short path so they could move all the way out onto the ledge. "We don't want to go any farther. I can't remember exactly where the edge is."

"Yikes," said Hannah. "This is far enough for me."

Amariah pitched the shovel into the deep snow. He reached into his jacket and pulled out the binoculars Daniel had lent him. "Close your eyes and leave them closed."

"What are you going to do?"

129

"Don't worry."

She laughed. "Okay, here goes." She closed her eyes and Amariah lifted the sunglasses off her face.

"Don't throw me off!"

He draped the strap of the binoculars around her neck and put the lenses up to her eyes. "Okay, now open your eyes again."

Hannah flinched for a second until she realized what Amariah was holding up against her face. Then her eyes adjusted and she leaned forward.

"Wow!"

He put his arm around her neck to help her hold on to the binoculars, while adjusting a knob with the other. "Here, you focus them on top, like this." He had never been this close to her before. The smell of roses in her hair reminded him of summer.

"Now I can see better," she said. "Wow. I never used one of these. You can see all the way to the other side of the lake."

"Yup," Amariah grunted. The expanse was indeed a remarkable sight, especially after being in the cave for so long.

"The lake's still frozen," said Hannah. "I wouldn't want to be out there today."

"Nope."

"When my mother was alive we had a little camp in Colchester," she said, scanning the shore. "We even had a little sailboat. My father used to take us out. I've never gone so fast! That was freedom, out on the big waves, with the wind. It was like being on the ocean."

"Your mother?"

"Yeah. Miriam's my step mother. My real mother died of the flu."

"I'm sorry," said Amariah, strangely relieved.

They stood in silence for a few moments.

"You know, this all used to be part of the ocean," he said, changing the subject.

"Yeah, right."

"It's true," he said. "After the last Ice Age, the ground was so depressed from the weight of the ice that it remained that way for a long time. It was lower than the sea, so the ocean came all the way down the St. Lawrence and into the valley, all the way up to the base of the mountain here. They used to find whale bones buried down by the lake."

"Are you serious?"

"Yes, absolutely. Then, over time, the earth rebounded, the ocean waters drained back into the sea, and this became a freshwater lake."

"Wow," she said, again. "I'd love to see the ocean."

"That was once a dream of mine too."

"You mean you've never seen it either?"

"Nope."

"But you had a plane, right? Freedom. Why didn't you just fly down there? Land on the beach, go swimming, and fly back? I would have."

"Well," he said, "you need a full tank to get down there and a full tank to get back. There's nowhere down there that has a refinery that can make the fuel, so it would be a one-way trip. The only other place that has a refinery with compatible fuel is in Albany, and, well—"

"No ocean there," she said.

"Nope."

She turned the binoculars inland. "Hey, I can see my farm, I think." She searched for a few moments. "The house must be behind the hill; I can't see it." She searched for a few moments more. Then her shoulders sank. "Here, take these. Give me my sunglasses back."

They made the switch.

"How far is the ocean?" she asked.

"More than two hundred miles from here. Massachusetts."

"Let's go," she said.

"What?"

"Let's go and see the ocean."

"Right, let's just do that."

"No, I'm serious."

"It's easier said than done."

"Well, where there's a will there's a way, right?"

"Not always," said Amariah. "You'd need a good team of horses, enough food for them, and some heavily armed guards. It would take at least a week to get there, if you didn't get robbed on the roads. Then you'd have to make your way all the way back up. The road is long and steep. Most of the towns have barricades. You'd need to pay them off, and you need someone to watch your back."

"We could go together, you and me. We could watch one another's backs."

Amariah began to think she was serious. "What about the kids? Your teaching?"

"Well, there is that," she said, with a faraway look. "I love the kids, but I don't expect to spend the rest of my life living in a cave. I want to get out of here. You too. You need to get out of here, too."

Amariah said nothing.

She put her arm around his shoulder. "Let's run away together. Let's do it."

He tilted his head and smiled a half-smile, as if to say he'd think about it. Then she kissed him—her warm, full lips on his, the tip of her tongue flicking into his mouth.

Before he knew it, they were making out. Tongues deep in each other's mouths, hands over each other's bodies, and neither one cared if anyone saw.

ॐ

At dinner that night, Hannah touched his foot with hers under the table, while keeping a straight face and talking to her parents about teaching. Amariah noted the ease with which she carried off her deception, but resisted the urge to pull his foot away.

Later, they left the table separately. Hannah's face revealed nothing out of the ordinary, although earlier, she had suggested they meet in the lower tunnel that led to the underground stream where Amariah had set the generator. Despite a number of misgivings, he went. He waited a good long while before she finally arrived. They whispered a greeting, slipped into a dark recess where they couldn't be seen, and put their hands on each other, picking right up where they had left off.

Their embrace grew heated and passionate, and just as things were about to go too far, Hannah said, "I think I'd better go now. My father will be looking for me."

Amariah let her go. "All right," he said. They tucked in their shirts and put themselves into a presentable form.

"Come on, I'll walk you back," he said.

They headed back up the tunnel, came around a corner, and stopped—Ira and two of his friends stood blocking the way.

"Hey, pretty boy, we're going to mess you up," said Ira, slapping his hand against his cast. All three of them reeked of alcohol.

His two friends leapt against Amariah and pushed him up against the wall.

"Let go of him!" screamed Hannah.

Ira punched Amariah in the face, glancing off his nose. Amariah kicked at Ira, knocking him back. Unfazed, Ira whirled around and struck him in the gut with his casted right hand. Amariah doubled over.

Hannah shrieked and dashed away up the tunnel. Amariah tried his best to defend himself, but he wasn't a trained fighter like these boys, and it was three against one. He fell into a crouch, and they began kicking him, hard, laughing as they did.

"Hey you!"

A shadowy figure grabbed Ira by the ponytail and yanked him back. A punch to the mouth sent him sprawling onto the floor. The two boys looked up, surprised. Standing there with his fists in the air was Mark Bowman, Hannah behind him.

"Get back!" said Bowman.

The boys ran off down the tunnel.

Bowman stepped hard on Ira's bad arm, pinning him to the ground. "Don't move!"

The noise and commotion attracted people from the main cavern, and a small crowd came running, including Anne and Rebecca.

"What's going on?" asked Anne, breathless.

"Ira and his friends were beating Amariah," said Bowman. "It was three against one."

"Amariah, are you all right?"

"Not really," said Amariah. His ribs hurt and his nose bled.

"Ira! Get up!" shouted Rebecca.

Ira was slow to get to his feet, wobbly from the punch in the face and the moonshine. Rebecca twisted his arm and pushed him against the wall.

"Explain yourself!" demanded Anne.

Ira didn't make eye contact and slurred his words. "Why is he here? Huh? What is he doing here? We're out in the trees, freezing our asses off, and he's in here sleeping in a bed! Why?"

"All of us came here for our own reasons, Ira," said Anne. "None of which are your business. This is entirely unacceptable."

Ira's eyes were red and blood seeped around his stained teeth. "Can't you see? We have them on the ropes. They're running out of fuel. Soon we can stand and fight. That's unless *he* gets away. He'll make more fuel and then lead them right to us!" He tried to lunge at Amariah, but Rebecca held him back.

"Calm down!" shouted Anne. "Whether Amariah stays or leaves is not your decision."

"He's not one of us."

"Yes, Ira, he is one of us," said Anne.

"No, he isn't. He's one of them."

"No, Ira, he is one of us."

"How can you say that?"

"Because, Ira, Amariah is my nephew."

Rebecca gasped and put her hand up to her mouth. "He's what?"

"Amariah is my nephew," said Anne. "Kenan Wales was my brother."

❧

Rebecca and Anne led Amariah to Anne's private room, a high grotto overlooking the main cavern. Rebecca helped him over to a couch.

"Come and sit down," said Anne.

The couch was soft and comfortable. Amariah realized that he hadn't sat on one in more than six months. Anne came back with a towel, sat down beside him, and moistened it in a bowl of water. Rebecca took a seat in an armchair, her attention on Anne, smoldering.

"Where'd you get the couch?" he asked.

Anne dabbed at his nose. "I didn't always live in a cave, you know. I brought it along when we took shelter here. I had a house in Stowe. Or, I should say, I have a house in Stowe."

"Oh," he said. He didn't know that.

"Amariah, there are things that I haven't told you. I did this for a reason, to give you a chance to make up your own mind about us."

"Oh?"

Anne handed him the towel, then went over to a chest in the corner and unlocked it. She took out an old photo album, sat back down, and held it in her lap. "I want you to prepare yourself, Amariah. There are pictures of your parents in here."

Amariah's heart nearly stopped. He hadn't seen anything of his parents since the firc.

She opened the book to the first page. It was a photo of a house, in the summertime. A color photograph, still in good condition.

"This is my house in Stowe. From what I'm told, it's still standing. I plan to go back to it someday. We had a special

136

breed of rosebushes out front that could withstand the long winters. I'm hoping they're still alive."

She flipped the page. "Here's a picture of a barbecue, on the Fourth of July, thirty years ago."

It was indeed a picture of a barbecue, with a large group of people lounging on a front porch, after the war, but before the Troubles. The group of friends appeared relaxed and happy. A young woman sat in a rocking chair with a drink in her hand.

Amariah examined the photo. The woman was his mother. His father stood nearby, his arm around a short woman with shoulder-length hair.

"That's your father," said Anne. "And that's me."

It was unmistakably Anne.

"Your father was my older brother. I'm your aunt."

Amariah glanced down at the book, and then back at Anne. His head whirled. "I don't understand," he said. "Why didn't anyone tell me?"

"Your father and I had a falling out. We didn't see eye to eye …" she glanced over at Rebecca, "… on a lot of things. The Troubles turned many people against one another, including families. For many of us, the wounds were too deep. There was no going back."

She took the towel and rinsed out the blood in the bowl.

"At first your father sold his fuel to farmers, for tractors and whatnot. He flew his plane. That caught the attention of the military and the police. He started selling them fuel, and of course they wanted more. Soon they had taken over distribution and had everyone by the throat. I warned him we were becoming a police state—that the emergency powers after the Troubles would never be lifted. He didn't want to hear it; he was getting rich. Then he broke contact."

She handed him back the towel.

"Things got worse for the people around here. A group of us knew there was only one way to put a stop to it—to destroy the refinery so the police couldn't control the sky."

Amariah stared at the photographs, his gaze coursing over every inch of his beloved mother and father. What a deep and dark place he had been in since their deaths. He had missed them so much. Yet even though they smiled at him through these fading photographs from the past, the knowledge of their grisly fates cast a shadow over any happiness he might have felt from this reunion, transforming the still images from an innocent moment long ago into the worst kind of horror show imaginable.

Sarah and Kenan had been more than just his parents; they had been his best friends. And yet they had kept so much from him, their only child. So many secrets. He hadn't really known them at all. His entire life had been a lie. He buried his face in the bloody towel and wept.

After a while, Anne put her hand on his knee. The only family he had left sat on the couch beside him.

"You see, Amariah," she said gently, "that's why you're here. The refinery must be destroyed, and you have to be the one to destroy it."

CHAPTER TWELVE

Hannah had let her hair down, shielding her face from view. She knew he was there, of course; the abrupt way she spun her head was always a dead giveaway.

Sitting alone at an empty table on the other side of the moodily lit main cavern, Amariah fixed his eyes on the farmer's daughter as she made her way back from the food line. But try as he might, she refused to meet his gaze.

Mark Bowman had forbidden Amariah from speaking to Hannah, or even approaching her. It wasn't an easy thing to do in their little underground universe, yet somehow Hannah managed to honor her father's wishes, steering clear of Amariah as if she had a sixth sense. Lately, she had even taken to sitting with her back towards him during dinner, leaving him to wither in the full glare of her curly haired stepmother.

Amariah picked up his spoon and dully stirred his watery bowl, wondering for the hundredth time what type of meat he was eating. The cooks refused to say; which, he had to admit, was probably for the best.

From behind him, Anne swept into view and slid onto the opposite bench. "So, here you are."

"Of course I'm here. Where else would I be?"

"You tell me. We've been looking all over for you."

"I was checking on the generator," he said, daring to take a spoonful.

"Oh really? We must have just missed you then."

Amariah swallowed and grimaced. "I've also been running cable to the upper chamber. So I might have been up there."

One of the female cooks approached and placed a bowl of the thin mixture in front of his aunt, who accepted it with a silent nod. The cook glanced coldly at both of them and then walked away.

It wasn't the first brush-off of the rebel leader Amariah had witnessed lately. Anne's revelation had come at a cost. To some people, her estrangement from his father was proof of her integrity; to others, the relationship itself was cause for suspicion. Even Rebecca had distanced herself, moving out of the grotto the two of them shared. Or so he had heard.

"Have you given any thought to what we talked about?" asked his aunt, casually. For the first time Amariah noticed that she held her spoon just as his father used to, between her fingers.

"Yes, I have."

"And? Any ideas?"

"Well, you've got the high ground. Why don't you try firing shells at it?"

"We don't have any cannons, Amariah, you know that. Or shells."

"What about mortars?"

"We've tried that too. The refinery is concrete, the storage tanks are reinforced, and we don't have a clear view of the pumps. We've tried hurling boulders at it, but we give our position away as soon as we cut loose the trebuchet."

Amariah knew all of this, of course. His father and the Wales Guard had taken every precaution against these very things. He concealed a grin by pretending to inspect his long beard.

"We need to get inside the gates," said Anne, stirring the bowl. "We can send in a sabotage team, but we need to find a way in."

"Rebecca found a way in."

Anne hesitated. "The only people in the valley now are Yorker engineers and NVM paramilitaries. There's no way to get a saboteur in now."

"Well, I'll try to think of something."

"Think harder," she said, tossing her spoon on the table.

Amariah groaned. The refinery was the only source of liquid fuel in the entire region. Destroying it would deprive everyone of lighting, cooking and heating oil, and render all motorized equipment useless. Even if his parents had been on the wrong side of things, he couldn't bring himself to think seriously about destroying the people's only chance for a better future.

He glanced over at Hannah, wishing he could be with her, somewhere far away.

Anne regarded her nephew with a level gaze. "You know, Amariah, the sooner the refinery is destroyed, the sooner everyone can get out of here. Then everyone can get on with their lives, and do whatever they want to. No matter what other people might think." She raised an eyebrow, just like his father used to do. "That's something worth working towards, wouldn't you think?"

Amariah pushed his bowl away in disgust. The rat meat stew, or whatever it was, tasted awful tonight.

"Yes, I agree," he said. "And the sooner the better."

இ

Two weeks later, as a March blizzard blasted away at Mount Mansfield, Amariah lay under his bed covers, listening to the steady drip-drip-drip of meltwater falling into pans on the floor of the storage cave.

Anne had been persistent, probing him for flaws in the structure of the barrier and the processes the Wales Guard had used to secure it. "The refinery must be destroyed," she kept saying. But Amariah still wasn't sure. Without mechanized agriculture, people would be reduced to subsistence-level living conditions, always just one bad summer away from starvation. The former heir to Pleasant Valley Biofuels would forever be known for destroying the last chance many people had for a civilized life.

One thing was certain, however; Anne had lied to him. Or at least, she had misled him. He wanted out. And now, with a howling storm upon them, it was time for him to go.

He got out of bed, already fully dressed, and padded over to the junk pile, removing two freshly waxed skis along with a handmade pair of ski boots and two poles he had fashioned out of old wood. He stuffed the skis and gear into a long duffle bag, the kind he had been using during his lighting project, put on a backpack, and left the storage cave. He followed the tunnel only partway, then cut up a path through the rock fall, avoiding the main passageways.

When he reached the corridor that led to the upper chamber, he stopped to unfasten the as-yet unconnected electrical wire from its piton, and then dragged it along behind him, a hundred yards of un-spliced, heavy-duty cable. It would have been impossible to carry it during his escape attempt, which is why he had enlisted the old men to help him install this extra section.

Arriving at the upper chamber, he checked the firmly anchored piton near the door and rehearsed his plan: open the door, lower the duffel bag over the edge, and then rappel several hundred feet down the cliff until he reached the snowy slope. After donning the ski equipment, he would make his way down the mountain, avoiding the rebels' tree stands, and be at the bottom of the mountain before anyone knew he was gone. The storm would cover his tracks. He would emerge onto the road near Johnson, and then keep going until he reached his destination: Gloucester, Massachusetts, with its docks, its ships, and the promise of new life, far away.

He addressed the door he and Hannah had opened together. At the time, he had told her he wanted to show her the view. That was true. However, he didn't tell her he also wanted to get the door open without anyone being suspicious. What had happened afterwards between them was unexpected.

Hannah. His first real love. How ironic; after years of being pursued by rich and lovely aristocratic girls, the first girl he actually wanted had dropped him cold, apparently without a second thought.

Perhaps someday he would come back again and find her when they were older. But for now, he had no intention of being manipulated into destroying the refinery. He certainly wasn't going to be responsible for sending people back to the Stone Age, and he wasn't going to stay in this cave for one minute longer.

He threw back the upper bolt. Looser than he expected, it slammed against its bracket with a clang. He winced. Just then a scream echoed up from the lower chamber, followed by shouts for help. He hesitated; everything was set, all he had to do was unbolt the other latch and open the door. More shouts and cries for help. Damn. Had he been discovered?

He quickly removed his jacket and pushed the kit into a dark corner. He ruffled his clothes, wanting to appear as if he had just gotten out of bed. Hurrying down the passageway, he warily followed the shouts all the way down to the lower entrance by the ravine.

Daniel and the supply team, returning after a long absence, stood caked in snow and ice. Usually, they would be carrying heavy packs. This time, the packs were light. They had come back from their supply run frozen and empty-handed.

Women ran past Amariah with dry clothes. Others knelt down to help the men out of their snowshoes. Soon, others emerged from the tunnel and gathered around, fretting around the men. Nurse Isabelle warned that frostbite was a serious concern and called for cold water.

Anne arrived, disheveled in her robe. "What happened?"

Daniel's icy beard hardly moved as he spoke. "The NVM are everywhere," he croaked. "On the farms, and in Jeffersonville. We couldn't get near our sources, or the town. We've got nothing."

As the women struggled to remove the frozen straps of his empty backpack, Daniel explained how they had snowshoed to the outskirts of Johnson to the house of a family sympathetic to the rebel cause. They didn't dare return until the storm hit.

"Why all the soldiers now?" asked Nurse Isabelle, removing Daniel's frozen snowshoes. It was unusual for there to be a big troop presence until spring.

Daniel reached into his jacket with a swollen red hand and pulled out a piece of paper. He handed it to Anne. "This is why."

In the dim light, Anne held up a Wanted poster, with Amariah's name printed in large letters, above a reward of $100 in gold.

Amariah beheld the poster, aghast.

"Someone down there really wants to find you, my friend," said Daniel.

"It was only a matter of time," said Anne.

"The Yorkers ruined the seed," said Daniel. "There's no fuel anywhere. People are desperate."

Amariah reread the poster twice. "He's blaming me for the fire?"

Anne shrugged. The refugees around him, thin and pale in their tattered robes, paid him no attention, instead tending to the frozen men who lay grimacing beside their empty packs. Empty, because of him.

Rebecca, nearby, put her hand on his shoulder. "Don't worry," she said, "we won't give you up."

"They want me to formulate the enzyme," he stammered. "They can make up for the oilseed by harvesting trees to run through the biomass processor. Once they start that, there'll be no stopping them. They can use the fuel to power big equipment to cut down even more trees. They'll strip the entire forest."

"Then we'll have to get you out of here," said Anne, "and get you far away where they won't find you."

145

Daniel made a face. It was the very suggestion he had made when Amariah had first arrived.

At the edge of the crowd, Amariah caught a glimpse of long dark hair. Hannah hovered just inside the circle of light, shielded by her parents. Only this time, she didn't look away; her attention was fully on him, her eyes red and her face streaked with tears.

Amariah faltered. He had been within seconds of running off, leaving everyone in the cavern to starve to death under a festive lighting display. He crumpled the Wanted poster in his hands.

"I'm not going anywhere," said Amariah. "I'm staying here."

"Well, how nice," said Daniel. "We can all starve together."

Anne considered the empty packs. "We need more food. We'll never make it to summer."

"If we can't get to the farms, then we can't get donations," said Daniel, wearily. "It's too risky to buy supplies in the towns. And we're not going to steal food from starving farmers."

"So that leaves only one option," said Anne. "We have to take it from the NVM."

That got everyone's attention.

"Peck has increased his shipments to the garrison at Pleasant Valley," she said. "There's a big one coming down from Enosburg within the next couple of weeks. We can ambush it on the road."

There was silence as the implications sank in. No one relished the idea of mounting an ambush in the deep snows of winter, even if the planes were still grounded.

"This is all my fault," said Amariah. "I'd like to help, somehow."

Daniel shook his head. "You would just get in the way, and if you got caught, they would come after us stronger than ever. Besides, we need you to keep the lights on." He gave him a wan smile.

Anne put a stop to the conversation. "Get these men up into the cavern and get them warm. We'll talk about this later."

Amariah looked for Hannah, but she was gone.

He didn't linger. Daniel had just saved him from making a terrible mistake. If skiing down the mountain during a white-out hadn't killed him, he surely would have been captured at a roadblock.

He scurried up to the upper cave and replaced the wire along the wall. Retrieving his kit, he snuck back to the storage cave and shoved the skis back in their hiding place.

He stole a glimpse outside the entrance to his cave and exhaled. Fortunately, no one had discovered his escape attempt, or that he had nearly abandoned them all in their greatest hour of need.

‡

The rebels planned their attacks in a secluded section of the cavern, where small boulders formed a circular basin around a large pit of sand. In the center of the sandy patch, someone had placed a small model of a covered bridge amidst carefully molded hills. Ropes snaked through the model landscape, representing rivers, streams, and brooks. Amariah realized he was looking at the bridge near Jeffersonville that connected the town to the farms of the north. It had been there in one form or another for more than two hundred years.

147

The hardest of the fighters, male and female, sat around the model, their faces serious. The meeting was by invitation only, and for the first time, Anne had asked Amariah to join. He edged in beside Rebecca, who sat rigid and focused.

Anne took a stance in the sandy patch, holding a long, tapered stick. Her tone with the fighters was tough.

"These next few weeks are critical," she said. "Amariah is devising a way for us to get into the valley so we can sabotage the refinery."

All heads turned to face him. Amariah held still, praying she wouldn't ask him to discuss his plan, since honestly, he didn't have one. Mercifully, she moved on.

"But we'll never make it if we run out of food, and we have very little left." Anne went on to describe how her sources, whom she did not name, assured her that a food convoy would be passing over the river within the next week. The crossing northeast of Jeffersonville was an ideal place for an ambush.

"We'll attack the convoy as it crosses the bridge," she said, "but getting back up here with the supplies intact will be critical. Therefore, this operation will be a hijack. We need a team to take out the soldiers and hijack the wagons. Then we'll rendezvous with a larger group to take everything up at once."

Amariah's heart raced. He had never participated in the planning of a murder before. He twisted his beard in his fingers until Rebecca turned and gave him a withering look. Fidgeting with his beard was an irritating new habit, even to him. He sat on his hand.

"We can't wound the horses," Anne continued. "If we do, we're stuck. So we can't use our bows, and we can't shoot."

"Great," said Daniel. It had taken him nearly a week to recover from his ordeal, but he was back to his usual self.

"I will lead the attack," said Anne. "Daniel, pick your team. Once we confirm their approach, we'll have to get down there fast and undetected. So we'll be taking the express."

"Oh no," said Daniel.

"Oh yes," said Anne, "so pick people who aren't afraid of heights. There will only be five of us on the hijack team. At the rendezvous point we'll need at least a dozen people, maybe more. They'll need sleds and strong legs to haul everything back up here."

Amariah didn't know what Anne was talking about. An express? What was that?

"We know this shipment will be a big one," said Anne. "It's worth the risk. Let's get on with it."

The group began to disperse. Amariah approached his aunt.

"Anne," he said, "what if I just turned myself in, but refused to help them?"

"That's out of the question, Amariah, forget it. Look, we need some explosives to take out the guard station. Is that something you can help us with?"

Amariah hesitated. He had built lots of rockets and explosives in his youth, experimenting with chemicals and fooling around, but he had never built an actual weapon to hurt people.

"Well, we have plenty of combustible material—"

"Great. See? You're just the man for the job. Work with Rebecca on the details."

Amariah walked away, conflicted. He was about to build weapons to help the rebels fight the NVM. It was quite pos-

149

sible that his explosives would hurt or kill someone, possibly even someone he knew. He was in over his head. He stroked his beard as he waited for Rebecca to finish consulting with the fighters, then caught up with her.

"So, what's the express service, anyway?" he asked.

"It's a fast way to get from here down into the valley, but it's a one-way trip," she said. "Come with me, and I'll tell you what we need so you can get started."

Amariah trailed along behind his friend, the rebel assassin, consulting his doubts.

"Come on, let's go!" she said.

They went a few more steps down the passageway, then abruptly she swung around and confronted him, hands on hips. Amariah's heart nearly stopped.

She looked him squarely in the face. "And will you trim that beard, for heaven's sake? You're starting to look like a crazy person."

∞

A week later, a breathless messenger brought word of the shipment. The wagons were following the expected route and would cross the river the next morning.

"How do we know what's in this shipment?" Amariah had asked Anne.

"We know," was all she said.

Daniel had picked three men for the assault: two Latino farmers, the brothers Francisco and Antonio, and Ira, whose arm had healed. Ira had been forced to apologize to Amariah, and was being given a chance to redeem himself. Anne had also asked that Amariah go along, as a way to ease the grumbling among the fighters. He would be going only part of the way, carrying the explosives he had fabricated. Rebecca would join them as well, and travel back together with him for safety.

Once the packs had been double-checked and the team assembled, the seven of them left the main cavern through a locked tunnel Amariah had not been in before. Daniel carried an oil lantern to light the way. Deeper and deeper they went, at one point startling a colony of bats huddling in a dark recess. Eventually, they arrived at a small wooden door, which Daniel unlatched and pulled open.

Fresh air swept over them, and one by one they entered a small cave from the rear, the ceiling too low to stand upright, the floor too slippery with guano to sit.

"Where are we?" asked Amariah.

"The Notch," said Francisco. "Get your snowshoes on."

The group moved closer to the cave opening, over which meltwater dripped like raindrops, and put on their gear. As they moved outside, a large dollop of cold water fell down Amariah's neck and trickled down to his lower back. Fine mist obscured the deep ravine, where bare rocks and trees clung to the steep hillsides, wet.

"Be careful," said Antonio. "The snow is still deep, but underneath it, it's all ice. Don't get too close to the edge."

They filed out of the cave, Francisco and Antonio in the lead. Far in the distance, the Lamoille River Valley spread out like a white and brown quilt that had been left out in the afternoon fog. Amariah realized then that the mist he was in was actually a cloud; they were that high.

He hadn't been this far away from the main cavern in months. While all winter he had longed to be outside, he now found the experience disorienting. The Notch seemed perilously deep, the slopes steep and treacherous. He took deep breaths.

151

Agoraphobia, he told himself.

He trudged forward, cursing his own clumsiness, his pack seemingly loose and off-balance. The stark shadows played tricks with his vision, making him jolt backwards more than once. He reached out and grabbed a tree branch to steady himself.

"Come on," hissed Rebecca, gaining distance ahead of him.

Sweat dripped from his forehead, and not just from the exertion. He stopped for a moment to catch his breath, and held on to tree root.

Ira, behind him, grew impatient. "Move over. I'm passing you."

The eager young fighter tramped around Amariah nearer to the edge. He gained ground in front, stamping his feet to make a point of his progress. As he threw a disdainful look over his shoulder, the entire section of snow beneath him gave way, and his feet swept out from under him. For a moment, Ira dangled above the abyss, clinging to a rotten birch trunk with one hand, but then the trunk crumbled, and he fell out of sight with a terrified scream. Amariah held on to the root with both hands as the snow slipped out from beneath him.

Rebecca shouted, "Shit!"

The slide stopped. No one moved. There was now bare ground between Amariah and the rest of the team. A large and slippery rock. Black ice.

"Keep coming!" Anne said in a loud hush.

"Can you make it?" asked Daniel.

Amariah nodded. It was go forward or go over the cliff. He held onto rocks and tree roots and crossed the spot where the snow had slid away, using every ounce of energy to get across the exposed outcrop.

Daniel grabbed him by the arm and lifted him toward flat ground, where Amariah hunched over, hands on knees, desperate to catch his breath.

Daniel lay down flat on his belly and crawled to the edge. He shook his head. "There's nothing we can do."

Amariah moved closer to Rebecca to get a better look. Amid the dark, jagged rocks lay Ira's lifeless body, twisted gruesomely at the bottom of a crevasse.

"We have to keep going," urged Anne.

Ira's hand twitched, and Amariah looked up, alarmed. "We're just going to leave him?"

"We have to. We'll come back for him later, if we can."

Amariah looked again at Ira's broken, bloody body, waiting for another sign of movement. Had Ira not passed him by, it could very well have been him down there. Would Anne have abandoned him just as easily?

"Amariah!" barked Anne. "We've got hundreds more people relying on us. Move it."

Unhappily, they continued on, stepping even more carefully as they began to descend. Finally, they reached the floor of the Notch, where the ruins of an old ranger station lay buried deep beneath the snow. The building had collapsed onto itself years ago. The only thing visible now were the tops of the visitor signs poking out of rusty holes in the snow, all bent over and brown.

As they began the climb up the other side, Amariah wondered what Anne was going to do without Ira. He was supposed to use the explosives to take out the guard station and kill the NVM stationed there. Without that part of the plan, the team could be captured as they drove the hijacked wagons up the mountain road. But the group was already moving on, and it took everything he had just to keep up.

They passed a frozen pond and arrived at a collection of derelict buildings. Rusted towers still stood at what used to be the top of an old ski lift.

Amariah scanned the scene. Surely the ski lifts no longer worked—the old cable car was in its station, doors open, insides rusted out, and the chairlifts rotted away. Besides, there was no electricity, and hadn't been for more than forty years.

Anne and the others pressed on to the base of the highest tower, which still held the cables for the cable car. Anne motioned for Amariah and Rebecca to remove their backpacks. Amariah's contained the explosives and the delivery mechanism, Rebecca's five sets of straps, harnesses, and a metal assembly of wheels.

The cables passed through a clear channel in the treetops, all the way down to the bottom of the mountain. It finally dawned on Amariah what these people were about to do. He was glad he wasn't going.

"Amariah, we're going to need your help," said Anne. It was very matter of fact, as if she was asking him to take out the trash. "You made the grenades, and you know how to use them. You'll take Ira's place."

"Who, me?"

Rebecca interjected. "What are you talking about? I'll go."

Anne pulled her friend aside and the two of them had a hushed and hurried conversation. Rebecca seemed unusually upset, until she finally pressed her lips against Anne's, a passionate kiss on the mouth.

Seeing Amariah's look of surprise, Anne broke off the embrace and said, "Come on, I'll explain when we get down to the bottom. Put a harness on, and do what we do."

Amariah wasn't sure exactly what she would be explaining, but he went ahead and put on his harness. "How far down do these lines go?" he asked Daniel.

"There's a network; they all connect. In the summer we can move around under the tree canopy."

Yet another way the rebels were able to appear seemingly out of nowhere, Amariah realized. Gliding silently through the forest, they could travel miles over the rocky terrain and gorges, completely hidden from view.

"We'll hide the harnesses in the usual spot," Anne said to Rebecca. "Send Joshua."

Daniel stretched out his arms, twisting his torso back and forth. "Who's first?" he asked.

But Anne was already climbing the old metal ladder that led up to the top of the tower. Stepping out onto a little platform, she hooked the wheel assembly over the top of the cable and pulled it tight with a click. Now little more than a silhouette against the fading sky, she gave the team a thumbs-up, and then stepped into the void. The wheels made a low-pitched whirring sound as she zipped over the bare trees, and in a fast but controlled fall, she disappeared into the gloom.

Francisco quickly climbed up behind her and did the same.

Daniel made a show of allowing Francisco's brother, Antonio, to go ahead of him.

"Oh no, you don't," said Antonio.

Daniel looked apprehensively down the long line. "All right, let's get this over with."

He climbed up the tower, his large frame moving slowly. After stepping into his harness, he closed his eyes, then stepped off the platform, the cable dipping from his weight. He zipped down, the sound of the whirring wheels fading away, until he too vanished from view.

"Okay, your turn," said Rebecca. "Just click this over the wire, and then squeeze this to slow down before you hit the next tower. Then unhitch yourself and do the same thing on the other side."

"Okay."

"Don't slow down too much or you'll get stuck between towers. Then you'll have to release yourself and jump."

"Oh."

Amariah climbed up the tower, rung after rung, the wind whistling in his ears. By the time he got to the top, he was shivering, either from the cold of the fog or the fear. Nevertheless, he forced himself to do what the others had done, took a deep breath, and stepped off the platform. The harness caught his weight; he swung out into the open air and gathered speed. Afraid to test the brakes and get stuck, he sped down to the next tower, waiting until the last moment to brake, wheels screeching, nearly knocking Daniel off the platform.

"Jesus Christ!" exclaimed the burly man.

He settled Amariah on the platform and helped him get hitched on the other side. "You go ahead of me this time. Just keep doing the same thing each time you come to a tower. Anne will be waiting for you down below. And use your brakes, dammit!"

Amariah hesitated; it was nearly dark.

"Don't worry," said Daniel. "By this time tomorrow, you'll be riding back up the mountain on top of a nice, cushy wagon."

CHAPTER THIRTEEN

The three supply wagons rocked back and forth over the rutted road as they made their way down the embankment toward the covered bridge. A grizzled old man sat atop the lead wagon, controlling four horses, while the armed soldier beside him scanned the brown and dormant shrubbery along the riverbanks.

Amariah lay on a small hill above the bridge, face pressed into his sleeve, one eye on the green NVM wagons. Since before dawn he had lain there, his thighs cold and numb, chest wet from the snowmelt that seeped into his clothes. By the position of the hazy sun, he judged it was past noon. He hadn't eaten in nearly twenty-four hours.

Fighting the urge to raise his head, he listened until he heard the clump-clump of hooves on wooden floorboards. When the third set of hooves entered the rickety structure, he looked up just in time to see Anne and Francisco drop into the road and pull a large net across the exit. On the far side of the river, Daniel and Antonio did the same, securing the net with hooks, sealing the wagons inside.

Horses whinnied and men shouted. A shotgun blast took out a corner of the bridge above Anne's head.

The rebel leader crouched down and set fire to a large torch, emitting thick black smoke.

"All we want are the wagons!" she screamed with a startling ferocity. "We have fuel! Do not resist or we will set fire to this bridge right now with you on it! Surrender or be burned alive!"

The diminutive woman whose moderate tone managed the crowd in the cave was not the Anne who stood at the bridge, torch in one hand, can of fuel in the other, breathing fire.

Amariah fretted. *Would she actually ignite the fuel? There were twelve horses in there!*

After a long silence, a soldier's rifle passed through the net, butt-end first, followed by several handguns. Francisco collected the guns, and Anne hurled the torch into the river. Amariah finally caught his breath, relieved he hadn't just participated in a massacre of both men and animals.

Anne undid the hooks and the soldiers walked off the bridge, hands in the air. Behind them Daniel and Antonio followed, holding pistols at their prisoners' backs. Amariah finally sat up, his limbs and joints aching. The shortage of food and lack of exercise over the winter had left him thinner and weaker than he had ever been before.

"Remove your coats and hats and gloves and turn around and put your hands behind you," Anne commanded. The grizzled old man began to do as he was told. "Not you," she said.

The other men removed their outer clothing and handed it over.

"Turn around!"

Antonio roped the men together while Daniel and Francisco donned the uniforms and retrieved the wagons. Amariah got to his feet.

"You're driving," Anne told the old man. "Get up there." She had a small revolver which she shoved into his belly. The old man complied, and Anne climbed up next to him. The rest of the ambush team clambered aboard the trailing wagons and hid their backpacks under the seats.

"We have snipers on the hills," Anne announced. "Do not attempt to untie yourselves for at least fifteen minutes." She checked in with Daniel, at the reins of the second wagon, then sat.

She turned to the glum and chastened men. "This will all be over one day. We know what you've done, who you are, and where you live. We will be watching each of you from this day forward. Remember, judgment day is coming!"

With that, she pulled on a soldier's hat and motioned to Amariah, who limped down the hill, carrying two packs.

"Pick him up," Anne said to the driver. The wagon moved forward, and Amariah climbed aboard, cold, hungry, and stiff. He threw himself on top and lay flat as Anne had told him to do. The three wagons pulled away from the bridge, gained speed, and charged down the road as fast as the muddy potholes would allow, rattling Amariah's bones and teeth. A few minutes later, shivering in the wind, he caught a glimpse of the church tower in Jeffersonville.

"Slow down," said Anne to the driver, pulling the hat down over her eyes. "Head high."

The old man turned onto Church Street and led the convoy at a brisk clip down the middle of the street. Amariah hoped that no one observing from a second-story window would see him splayed out on top, so he tried to make himself as small as possible. The wagons passed over the slight rise at the crossroads and headed up the mountain road toward the guard house that marked the beginning of rebel territory.

"Get ready," said Anne to Amariah, pointedly not mentioning his name.

The former heir to Pleasant Valley, who grew up sheltered behind lines of NVM troops, got to his knees, unfastened one pack, and withdrew a meter-long section of PVC pipe wrapped in black cable. From the other pack he withdrew a handmade, rocket-propelled grenade. He inserted it into his homemade bazooka, then lay back down, aiming the contraption forward.

The old driver's face dropped. "Now just a minute—"

"Quiet!" Anne hissed. "Take it nice and easy."

Amariah's heart beat faster as they approached the guard station, the soldiers scrambling to their feet at the unexpected sight, unsure how to react.

Anne ducked aside. "Now!"

Amariah winced and pulled the trigger, igniting the propellant. The grenade rocketed out of the bazooka to the guard house and exploded on impact, blasting the small structure to pieces. The shockwave rippled over him, seeming to pull the air out of his chest. He quickly loaded another rocket and fired it at the gate that crossed the road, aiming at the structure, not the men.

"This is where you get off!" said Anne to the old soldier. She kicked the man off the wagon, sending him tumbling into a snowbank, and grabbed the reins. A rebel whoop leapt from her throat as she raced the horses up the road toward the mountain.

160

Amariah turned to see the damage. A cloud of black smoke poured from the guardhouse. Daniel gave Amariah a big smile and let loose a rebel yell. "Whoo-hoo!"

The horses galloped ahead, and Amariah was thrown off balance. He dropped the bazooka, grabbed the rails, and lay back down flat, acutely aware of the jagged boulders passing in the riverbed below. His body rattled like a bag of bones with each bump in the road.

After nearly two miles, they approached an abandoned church, neglected and forlorn on a rise near the base of the mountain. Anne slowed the horses and pulled the lead wagon around behind the vacant building, bringing it to a stop by the edge the bare, snowy woods. The other two wagons pulled in close behind. Anne jumped to her feet and scanned the perimeter, pistol in her hand.

The mission was a success—they had made it up to the rendezvous point with the hijacked shipment. Amariah glanced at the trees on the ridge of the hill, expecting a small crowd to appear at any moment to help sled the contents up to the nearest cave entrance. It wouldn't be long before NVM troops arrived.

"Nice shooting," said Anne.

"Thanks," he said, relieved that he hadn't killed anyone. "I hope there's some food that's ready to eat. I'm starving."

Anne grinned and called out to Francisco. "Open her up!"

The solidly built Latino farmer reached behind Daniel and pulled out a pair of bolt cutters. He approached the rear of the lead wagon, ready to snap through the padlock.

He lifted the tool, then hesitated, squinting. "Hey, this lock is made of paper."

Anne gasped. "Don't open it!"

The rear doors burst open and Francisco stumbled back. A deafening blast erupted from within, and Francisco fell over, shot point-blank shot in the chest. Uniformed NVM troops piled out of all three wagons, guns drawn.

The air around Amariah erupted in gunfire. Anne fired off two rounds from her pistol, hitting two men, but a soldier with a rifle blasted at her and knocked her off the wagon. Daniel spun awkwardly and fell to the ground, also shot. Amariah dropped and cringed, waiting for the pain of a bullet to pierce his flesh.

A man shouted, "Hold your fire, dammit!"

Amariah's heart sank as he recognized the voice. Captain Peck. He had been hiding in the wagon the entire time. A trap.

"Raise your hands!" shouted a soldier, standing where Anne had been just a few moments before.

Amariah lifted his head, sick to his stomach. The end of a rifle barrel pointed in his face. He raised his hands and dropped his gaze. He hoped Peck wouldn't recognize him; he had lost a lot of weight, and was hidden behind a long beard.

"Get down," snarled the soldier.

Amariah turned his back to Peck and crawled down the ladder, ears ringing from the cacophony. Soldiers gripped him by the arms and hurled him to the ground beside Anne and Daniel. Francisco and Antonio followed; both dead. Antonio's blank gaze fixed on Amariah. Blood oozed from his mouth.

Amariah looked away, scanning the snowy hillside, hoping the rendezvous party would see what had happened and retreat without being discovered.

Peck scrutinized his captives. "Well, well. Look what we have here." The captain leaned in to peer at Daniel's wound-

162

ed leg, then stamped on it with the heel of his dirty boot. Daniel cried out in pain. The soldiers laughed.

"Stop the bleeding," Peck said. "Throw them in a wagon and lock it tight. We're going to have some fun tonight."

The aide stood there, mouth open, as if trying to speak. Then he tottered forward against Peck, fingers clutching at the captain's shirt. Peck, startled, spun the man around, revealing an arrow in his back. He let the soldier drop to the ground.

Arrows and gunfire spit out of the church, striking the NVM men beside Peck. The rendezvous team was already here!

Amariah had only a second to act. He sprang forward and tackled Peck's bad leg, ramming his shoulder into it as hard as he could. The leg buckled, and Peck collapsed to the ground with a shout. Amariah dropped down onto the startled man's chest and pummeled him in the eyes, again and again with both fists, his fury unrestrained.

A soldier dove against Amariah, knocking him off. Together they rolled over the ground, each trying to get a firm grip on the other. They came face to face, and the shock of recognition appeared in the soldier's eyes. "It's you!"

Max, his childhood friend, wore an NVM uniform.

"Max!"

His friend's eyes grew more determined. He tightened his grip and straddled Amariah, pinning his arms.

"Captain! It's—" But then his head was knocked to one side as a bullet penetrated his brain.

Amariah recoiled and cried out, squirming out from under his friend's body as fast as he could. He backed away on the ground, revolted by the sight.

Anne grabbed his arm and gestured to the rendezvous team, struggling to escape through the deep snow of the woods.

"Get them out of here, now!" she gasped. "Run! Run!"

Amariah did as he was told, staying low and hurrying after the panicked withdrawal. Broken snowshoes lay amid deep footprints.

Up ahead, Amariah saw Joshua struggling to help a young woman, so he raised his knees as high as he could until he reached the pair, and lifted the girl up under his arm.

"Hannah!"

His former lover trembled.

"Keep moving!" he pleaded.

Joshua took up a position behind them but fell immediately to the ground, shot in the back by a bullet that would have struck Amariah. The one-armed watchman tried to push himself up as soldiers approached, but the snow was too deep, and he sank to his shoulder.

There was no way for Amariah to help both Joshua and Hannah. He heard Anne shouting "Run!" So in a snap decision he grabbed Hannah as tightly as he could and used of all his strength to drag her over the hill, shielding them both from gunfire behind the tree trunks.

ℝ

Peck rolled over onto all fours, dazed, his vision blurred. He staggered to his feet, standing on one leg, his old wound throbbing. Bodies lay around him in the snow, including that of Max Campo, the new recruit. He took the boy's gun, lifted it toward the trees and fired repeatedly at the fleeing rebels until he had emptied the chamber.

Not this time, he told himself.

The lieutenant fired behind the shelter of the second wagon.

"Dickins! Get the prisoners out of here!"

Peck swung up on top of the lead wagon, grabbed the reins, and urged the horses around the church, charging down the mountain road toward Jeffersonville, trying desperately to maintain speed while keeping the wagon from flying off the cliff. He passed the smoking guardhouse and nearly ran over the crowd that had gathered in the street.

"Out of the way!"

He raced the horses to the river road, made a sharp left and headed to the main gate at Pleasant Valley, where his troops warily anticipated his wild approach.

"Open the gate, goddammit!"

His men scrambled, and the iron gate rose. Peck ducked his head as the wagon tore through the courtyard and down the muddy road toward the airfield. He whipped the horses without mercy until he arrived in front of the hangar. As he climbed down, the terrorized horses lurched forward, and he hit the ground at an angle, twisting his leg and sending a sharp hot pain up his spine.

Peck clutched his leg in agony. The rebel with the long beard had reopened his old wound, and now a bloody stain seeped through his trousers.

He hobbled toward the hangar and burst through the door. A handful of pilots and mechanics sat beside a wood stove playing cards. Kenan's plane sat in one corner, covered in canvas. The other two planes were his, left there since the night of the fire, serviced and repainted.

"You!" he said to a pilot. "Can those planes fly?"

"Yes, Captain, but it's still too cold."

"We'll see about that," said Peck. "Get them ready for takeoff, and make sure they have plenty of ammunition!"

Peck burst outside. The horses had run off with the carriage. He limped toward the refinery, growing angrier with each step.

Finally, he stumbled through the door. "Where's Malinger?" he asked the guard.

The young man saluted and pointed toward the back office. Peck hurried through the corridor past the giant steel mixing tanks, then burst in on Malinger, dozing in his chair. He knocked the Yorker's feet off the desk and spun him around.

"What is it? What's the matter?" said Malinger, blinking. "Wha—what happened to your eyes?"

Peck touched his face, his eyes swollen from the rebel's punches. It didn't matter. "I need two planes up in the air right now."

"You what? It's still too cold. The fuel will gel—"

"Malinger! Give me the fuel that you used to run the car. You said you made a whole batch. I only need enough for two planes for one flight!"

"I'm not sure we have enough!"

Peck pulled out his revolver and pointed it at Malinger's head. "Glen, fill up those two planes right now or I will blow your brains out." He cocked the hammer of his revolver.

"Okay, fine. Fine, have it your way."

Malinger's son burst in, frantic. His father motioned to him. "Eric, let's go and get the captain some fuel for his planes." He pulled the boy along by the arm.

Dickins and his men gathered outside the office. Peck snapped his fingers. "Go with them and watch what they do," he said. "Bring the fuel out front and do it fast."

He limped back outside. His men had retrieved the carriage and he climbed aboard. After a few tortuous minutes, Malinger and his son cautiously exited the front of the building, each carrying a jerrican filled with fuel, followed by Dickins hustling two more cans, which he handed up to Peck.

Malinger handed his can over. "For what it's worth, keep your altitude low and don't fly after sunset."

Peck ignored the little man, ordering his men to drive down to the hangar, where the attendants prepared the planes for flight. Peck rode along, observing the patches of snow still clinging to the dormant brown grass of the runway.

He hurried over to the lead plane and climbed into the cockpit. "I'm flying this one myself," he said to the startled mechanic. He pulled on the cloth helmet and goggles, and pointed at the more experienced pilot. "You! Let's go!"

The pilot looked up at the cold grey sky and hesitated.

"It's the winter fuel," urged Peck. "Move!"

"Where are we going?"

"Just follow my lead, and shoot to kill, do you understand?"

The pilot grinned. After months of sitting around, he would finally be seeing some action.

The ground crew took hold of Peck's propeller and cranked it down. After a few tries, the engine caught, belched smoke, and roared to life. Peck brought the engine up to full power, then released the brake and headed down the runway.

The plane bounced along the wet, patchy ground, gaining speed, the engine rough. He pulled back on the stick and was airborne, the cold wind screaming around him. Throwing the stick hard to the right, he flew toward the ridge, gaining altitude as the other plane fell in behind him.

After months of being grounded, traveling no faster than a horse-driven winter sleigh, the vibration of the motor invigorated him. He settled behind the controls, extending his senses into the aircraft: its engine, wings, flaps, and guns. He powered over the treetops like a god, free at last from the tyranny of gravity.

And now, he would slaughter the rebels from the sky.

&

The rendezvous team struggled up the cold and darkening trail, heading for the lowest cave entrance, still almost half a mile away. The higher they went, the deeper the snow. The sky had turned a deep, rippled red, with bright stars appearing between the clouds. A chill wind blew down on them as the temperature plummeted.

"Hannah, what were you doing down here?" asked Amariah, between breaths.

"I wanted to help," she said wearily. "You were."

"You could have been killed. I can't believe your parents—"

Amariah stopped and cocked his head. Then heard it again—the unmistakable sound of aircraft.

"No, it can't be."

At first a distant rumble, the noise grew like thunder until two planes charged over the ridge and swept over their heads. Dark green, heavily armed NVM planes turned to attack the retreating column.

"Oh my God!" screamed Hannah.

Amariah stood open-mouthed. The Yorkers had recreated his winter fuel formula, but how? He hadn't shared it with anyone except his father.

Amid screams and shouts, the rendezvous team scattered. With no leaf cover, the civilians were helplessly exposed on the surface of the white snow.

The pitch of the engines rose, the planes banked into a steep turn, lined up for a strafing run, and dove toward them.

"Get behind the trees!" shouted Amariah. "Quick!"

He yanked Hannah behind the widest trunk nearby and held her tight. Machine-gun bullets ripped into the trees and snow. Several people around them fell to the ground.

The planes pulled up high, engines roaring like a swarm of ten thousand hornets, then banked around tightly for another run.

Some of the uninjured ran. Some stopped to tend to the wounded. Others stood in the deepening chill of the shadow of the ridge, clutching each other, waiting for the inevitable.

"Keep moving!" yelled Amariah.

He ran farther up the slope, pulling Hannah toward a cluster of boulders at the base of a cliff.

"Look out!" Hannah screamed. Bullets ricocheted all around them, chipping rock fragments into their skin. The grinding of the planes and the machine guns reverberated against the rocky hills, catching them all in the echo of a droning, mechanized well of death.

The cave entrance lay just ahead, a shadow in the deepening twilight. "We've got to keep moving!" he cried. But Hannah's face and hands were bloodied, and she curled into a ball, sobbing.

The planes continued their attack, picking off the few who ran, or who clustered together seeking shelter. Amariah pulled Hannah another few yards, then threw himself over her, pressing them both into a narrow cleft in the rocks.

169

The plane spat fire, then stopped, engine sputtering. It seemed to lose power for a moment, then the engine grudgingly reengaged.

Amariah risked a look. Engine trouble!

The pilot broke off the attack and pulled the plane around, heading west, its engine alternately revving and dying, the pilot in his open cockpit struggling to gain altitude. The plane nearly made it to the ridge when the engine died completely, the plane flipped over and smashed into the mountain.

The other plane now experienced the same problem, although its pilot managed to keep it airborne. Slowly it climbed, barely making it up and over the ridge before it disappeared from view.

Amariah led Hannah the final few yards and lay her inside the shelter of the cave, safe. On impulse, he kissed her, then hurried back to help the others. Bodies lay sprawled on the ground, some twitching, some still. Blood coated everything—the snow, the trees, and the faces and hands of the survivors who knelt weeping with the dead.

It was Amariah who had developed the winter fuel. These people never would have been out in the woods if they had known the planes would be able to ambush them under exposed conditions. Unbelievably, his father had wanted him to make even more of the fuel. To what end? For what possible good?

He carried several wounded civilians back to the cave, but each time he went back, he saw more bodies lying facedown in the snow, and survivors rocking back and forth, moaning and crying.

That the fuel had failed was of little comfort. Amariah had had enough. Whatever benefit the biofuel refinery provided, it wasn't worth the suffering and death it caused in the hands of the NVM.

Anne was right. The refinery and biomass processor both had to be destroyed, and he would be the one to do it.

CHAPTER FOURTEEN

Peck held onto the control stick for dear life, the engine gasping, desperate for fuel. Up ahead, he watched the other plane fall out of the sky and smash into the mountain.

He willed his aircraft up, the wheels brushing the tips of the snowy treetops, and barely crested the ridge.

Teeth chattering, he wrestled the biplane down toward the darkened landing strip. Then the engine died completely, sending him into a steep glide. With all his might, he pulled into an approach and braced himself for a crash. He hit the ground hard, thrown against his restraints, managing to remain upright as the plane bounced to a stop at the far end of the runway.

The dark woods were just off the nose of the propeller. A few feet more and he would have crashed into the trees. He unfastened the restraints, cursing, and lifted himself out of the open cockpit and down onto solid ground.

From across the field, two lanterns approached: the two hangar attendants on horseback. "Are you all right, Captain?" asked one, astonished.

Peck spat on the ground. "The fuel was bad!" He ripped off the cloth helmet and threw it into the plane. "We're going to need a recovery team on the other side of the ridge. Get a crew together."

They would salvage what they could of the fallen plane, but it was probably a total loss. If the pilot had survived, he would have to make it through the night alone. Most likely, they would find him in the morning, beheaded by the rebels. He cursed again. It took nearly a year to build a plane from scratch, and scavenged engine parts were getting harder to find.

"Get off," he said to the nearest rider.

He mounted the man's horse and bolted back to the refinery, each jolt reminding him of his wound. As the shock of the accident wore off, he grew angrier by the minute, until he finally reached the refinery, enraged.

He stormed through the building, heading directly to the kitchen in the living quarters, where the Yorkers sat, eating. When Malinger spotted him, he stopped chewing, dropped his spoon, and glanced around for somewhere to run.

"The fuel was no good!" shouted Peck. "I just lost a man up there! And a plane!"

"I warned you," said Malinger, backing away. "I told you not to fly too high or after dark. The fuel must have gelled in the fuel line. I warned you!"

"You drove that car around in the middle of February! It was colder than it is now, even at altitude!"

He spun around and bore into Dickins. "What did they do?"

Dickins's light brown skin darkened. "They took some fuel out of a tank in the lab, then they added some other fuel to it," said the lieutenant, nervously.

"We didn't have enough of the winter fuel!" said Malinger. "We had to cut it with the summer fuel. You should have listened to me!"

"You said you made an entire batch for the demonstration. So where is it?"

Malinger's mouth moved up and down, but no words came.

Peck scanned the table of frightened Yorkers, and then strode over to Malinger's son. He grabbed the young man by the collar and pointed the gun in his face. "Start talking, junior."

The boy winced and shrank his face away from the gun barrel. "We found some of the winter fuel mixture left over in the lab," he whined. "Amariah must have made it."

"Shut up, Eric!" said his father.

"That's what we used when you drove the car around," said Eric, nearly crying. "We couldn't figure it out. You didn't give us enough time."

"You mean to tell me the fuel you used in the car was made by Amariah?"

"Yes!"

The older Malinger intervened. "Put the gun down, Captain! We thought we would have all summer to figure it out. We didn't know you were going to come up here today and want to fly planes!"

Peck pushed the blubbering boy back in his seat. "I ought to kill you both right now!"

"Do that and you'll have nothing. Nothing!" shouted Malinger. "Nothing to sell, nothing to protect your men, nothing for the troops up at the border; you'll be powerless. Look, it's not our fault!"

For a moment, Peck considered executing the father and son on the spot. Then he thought better of it.

"Our deal is off, Glen," he said, uncocking the pistol. "From now on you're working for me."

He turned to Dickins. "Do not let either of these two out of your sight. When they take a shit, I want you there handing them the corn cob. Got it?"

Dickins's nostrils flared as he sized up each Yorker. He, too, had been deceived.

Peck grabbed Malinger's plate and threw it at him. "Get it together, Glen, and you may just live to see your wife again," he said finally. "If you don't, I may just pay her a visit myself."

He limped out of the building, got on the horse, and rode down to the garrison under the light of a crescent moon. The blood from the reopened wound had seeped through his pants leg into his boot. With each bounce, a fresh pain shot through his leg.

His prisoners should have arrived by now. If Amariah was the only one who could make the fuel, then Amariah was the one he needed. He would torture the prisoners until they told him where he was, and if they didn't know, then they would die with his name on their lips.

&

Despair raced through the cavern like a torrent. None were spared the horror of what had occurred, nor the dawning realization of their own vulnerability. Some gathered around lost loved ones' bodies and wailed. Others mourned that their strongest and most capable leaders were now at the mercy of the sadistic Captain Peck. Not even the youngest of children were spared the collective expression of grief and fear.

Amariah held a compress against a male teenager's tattered belly, assisting Nurse Isabelle. The wounds were beyond her abilities, and the young man died on the floor in front of them.

Now ten were dead, and at least a dozen wounded. Anne, Daniel, and Joshua had been taken prisoner and were almost certainly being tortured. The surviving NVM pilot, whoever he was, had seen the cave entrance before disappearing over the ridge. Leaderless and hungry, they were far worse off than before.

With each broken, bloody body the rebels sledded into the cavern, Amariah's hatred for Peck and the Yorkers burned stronger, matched only by his anger at himself—a spoiled rich kid blinkered to the realities of this terrible world by his own blind stupidity and pampered selfishness. He had worked with his father in the laboratory thinking that he was doing good for humanity, keeping liquid fuel flowing to retain at least a fragment of the world's great scientific accomplishments of the Oil Age. But here, on the floor in front of him, a young boy's fluttering, fading, heartbeat was the actual dismal, fatal outcome of everything he and his father had strived to achieve.

A frantic Rebecca darted from one patient to the next, hands twitching, increasingly distraught. Finally, she marched over to the sandy section of the cave where the ill-fated ambush had been planned, the little bridge and blocks of wood representing the wagons still there. She kicked them away with a guttural scream.

"Anne, Daniel, and Joshua are still alive down there. I'm going down to rescue them," she announced, her eyes wild. "I need a team. Who's with me?"

Voices erupted. Some pointed out the risks involved: the prisoners were being interrogated in the barracks behind the wall; the barrier could not be breached; the gate was a death-trap. Even if they made it through the first heavy door, there was an entire troop stationed there. A frontal assault would be a bloodbath.

Amariah parted company with the dead boy, his hands sticky with blood. "It'll be suicide if you attack the gate head-on," he confirmed. "It was built to counter just such an attack."

"We'll use explosives," she said. "You can make some."

"If you could get close enough to the gate, you might get through the first door. But you'll never make it through the inner courtyard. You'll be slaughtered like bears in a pit."

"What about the other gates?"

"The secondary gates are all next to guard towers, and those are manned by the Yorkers and the NVM. You'll get caught in the spikes and shot in no-man's-land before you even get close."

"Well, we can't just sit up here and do nothing," said Rebecca, her voice edging towards hysterical.

"I'm not saying that," said Amariah. "But if you try to attack the gate head-on you'll get killed, and what good will you be then?"

One of the fighters spoke up. "There isn't anything we can do," he said. "We have to accept it and move on. Once the trees grow back in we can move around again. We've held the NVM off for years—we can go on doing so."

Rebecca glared at him. "Whoever was in that plane saw us heading for an entrance. As soon as they can move, they'll have soldiers down there breaking in the door. We only have days, if that. I'm not going to sit here and do nothing. Anyone who wants to join me, come now!"

Amariah couldn't believe what Rebecca was proposing. He scanned the faces of the distraught people in the cave, paralyzed by indecision and infighting. Someone needed to take a stand.

"Rebecca! Look around you!" he said, rising to his full height. "What happens if you get killed? Who's going to take care of these people? The children? Use your head! Do you know what the NVM will do if they get their hands on these people?"

Amariah saw Ella hovering nearby with little Emily in her arms, frightened. He turned his back and lowered his voice. "I want to rescue them, too," he whispered. "For God's sake, Anne is the only family I've got. But we have to find a better way."

℘

Peck's men lounged against the walls in the back room of the barracks, the air stuffy and close. On a table in the center of the room, Peck gloated over the great bear of a man who was now his captive, spread-eagled on a tabletop, his wrists and ankles bound to the table legs.

Despite his dire condition, the rebel refused to speak.

"Where is Amariah Wales?" Peck asked again. "Where can I find him?"

The man stared at the ceiling, silent.

Peck stuck his finger into his captive's bloody wound and dug it around, causing the man to cry out. Peck held up his bloody index finger and pretended to inspect it. "Gee, this doesn't look too good," he said. "You'd better get a doctor or you're going to lose this leg."

His men chuckled as Peck wiped his bloody finger on the man's clothing.

Peck's own leg throbbed, but he was trying hard to hide the pain. He had changed his pants and tied a bandage around the wound to stop the bleeding, nevertheless he felt warm and slightly nauseous. A fever. He had sent for the doctor, but the jackoff had gone AWOL. He wiped the sweat out of his eyes with the back of his hand.

"You know, I had a visitor this morning," he said to the rebel. "A man who's soon going to be one hundred dollars richer. And what that man told me is that Amariah is hiding with you rebels. Now this man, he had good reason for his suspicions. But before I give him the reward, I told him I was going to need proof."

Peck had indeed been paid a visit. The glass blower from Johnson had told Peck that he used to make specialty items for the Wales mansion, including lightbulbs. He had recently received a request for a dozen bulbs. The customer wasn't a regular, and this raised his suspicions. Who would need a dozen lightbulbs? Some of the Stakeholders had electricity, from generators powered by oilseed on their own estates. But no house had more than a handful of electric lights.

It turned out that the glassblower had never been paid after the fire. No one, not even the Stakeholders, would honor the Wales' debts. He had been stiffed and wanted his money. Peck gave him one paper dollar, and told him that he would get the rest once he had confirmed his story.

"So, how about it?" he said to the rebel on the table. "Is he with you or not?"

The man grimaced, but said nothing.

"I'm not going to play games with you," said Peck. "The truth is that you may not be with us for very much longer.

179

Yes, that's right. And I'm sure you'd like to die that way, too. A hero, carrying your rebel secrets to the grave. But unfortunately for you, it's not going to be that simple."

His men looked at him. They knew Peck could get creative with his interrogations, and wondered what he had planned for this man.

"Lieutenant," said Peck. "Bring in that nice young boy, the son of the rebel we picked up a couple of months ago."

His men glanced at one another. The boy's father had died in captivity a few months before, and the little blonde orphan had been put to work cutting wood. He was quiet and did what he was told. The men liked that. Dickins hesitantly left the room.

"You see," said Peck, turning his attention back to the man on the table. "I know all about you do-or-die types, bravely meeting your end. You're an honorable man and I respect that. We all do. But once you die, there will be an entire new generation of rebels that I'll have to deal with, and this is getting tiresome. I mean, these bows and arrows, all of this Robin Hood bullshit. You've hurt a lot of my men that way."

Peck snatched the man's right hand, and held up his index and middle finger.

"These two fingers are what you use to pull back on your bow, correct?" said Peck. "It would be awfully hard to shoot at us without these two fingers, wouldn't it? So I'm going to give you a demonstration of how we're going to protect ourselves in the future against you people."

Peck removed the hunting knife from his belt and put it on the table. "Bring in the boy."

His men shifted uncomfortably, and the rebel finally turned his head, his lips curled back in a snarl.

180

That got his attention.

"This young man that we found," said Peck, "well, his father was a rebel, and I suspect that he'll grow up to be one too. You know, the apple doesn't fall very far from the tree."

The door opened and Dickins brought in the boy, stiff and nervous, no more than ten years old. He scanned the faces of the soldiers, their worried expressions giving him pause.

Peck continued speaking. "You see, once you're dead, we can put your body on display in the town. Someone will recognize you, and then we'll know who you are, or rather, who you were. It will then be a rather simple matter to find your relatives. And once we do, the boys and girls in your family are going to be rebel-proofed. Like this one. Come over here, son."

The boy complied. Peck put his arm around the boy and held him close.

"Now, I don't understand what the big fuss is about," said Peck. "I'm just trying to find Amariah Wales. I'm not going to hurt him—in fact, I'm just trying to give him a job. But I've already wasted far too much time looking for him. I need him back in the refinery now. So I'm going to ask you this simple question, just one … last … time."

Peck grabbed the boy's wrist and splayed out the fingers of his right hand on the tabletop beside the rebel's face. The boy cried out in surprise and terror. Peck picked up his hunting knife and slammed the butt of the knife onto the tabletop. He lifted the handle over the boy's index finger, the blade poised as if to slice through a carrot.

"Is Amariah Wales hiding in your camp, or isn't he?"

The rebel considered the determined look on Peck's face. "You're not going to do that," said the rebel, his voice coarse and broken.

"Try me."

"Captain, could I speak to you for a moment?" said Dickins.

"If you don't like it get out."

The rebel spoke. "Yes."

Everyone froze. Peck's grip did not ease one bit.

"Go on," said Peck.

"He's been with us since the night of the fire," said the rebel. "He's in our camp." The man licked his dry lips.

"Proof?"

"I know he has some information you want," said the rebel. "Something about an enzyme, and he knows how to make biodiesel work in winter."

Peck smiled. Now he was getting somewhere.

"But he'll never help you," said the rebel. "He blames you for the death of his parents."

Peck grimaced. "Well—" he said, suddenly at a loss for words. "Where's your camp?"

"The old hunting lodge by Lake Mansfield."

This was a lie. Peck had seen the rebels retreating up the trail toward Smuggler's Notch, scrambling towards a cave. The stories must have been true. He had memorized the location of the entrance, even as his plane had dropped out of the sky.

The rebel became chatty. "Why don't you release the woman," he said, "and have her bring him a message? Make him your offer. I never liked the guy anyway. Spoiled rich kid, hanging around, expecting everyone to do everything for him. He's useless. If he's all you want, then take him!"

Peck eased his grip on the boy, who ran over and hid behind Dickins.

The captain headed for the door and jerked his head for Dickins to join him. On the way out, he threw a command over his shoulder. "Get him some water and try to keep him alive."

The two of them walked out and the boy ran off.

"I'm sorry, Captain," said Dickins, red-faced.

Peck ignored the apology. "We're going to send a message to Amariah Wales. Give him a chance to turn himself in. Write it up. Make it sound pretty."

Peck had something else to send Amariah. His men had found a watch in the ruins. It bore an inscription from Amariah's parents. He would include the watch as a token of good faith.

"Okay," said Dickins. "So we let the woman go?"

"No. Apparently, she's important. I want to get to know her better. We'll give the message to the one with one arm, the traitor. Bring him up as far as you can. Make sure he gets through their lines. See to it personally."

Dickins headed for the door.

"And Dickins! Find that goddamned doctor!"

Peck walked down the hall to the officers' quarters and closed the door. Hand shaking, he poured some whiskey into a glass and downed the contents all at once.

The interrogation had gone well. He had finally located Amariah Wales. He was hiding with the rebels in a cave in Smuggler's Notch. Who would have imagined it? An aristocrat being sheltered by the poor. It was laughable.

CHAPTER FIFTEEN

Fifteen coffins streamed out of the cavern, carried on the shoulders of the dwindling ranks of able-bodied men, each pine box trailed by the family and friends of the deceased. Wrapped in the darkest clothing they could muster, the mourners stepped over the rocks and stones, down out of the ravine and into the forest, their weeping breath rising in the dampness of the early morning.

Amariah supported a corner of the coffin that belonged to the young man whose life he had tried to save. His name, he had learned, was Zebah. Dead at the age of fourteen.

When the column reached a flat spot at the bottom of the cliff, Amariah helped nestle the box alongside the others, then wiped the sticky pine sap from his hands.

Nurse Isabelle came forward, her mangy black hair streaked with grey. She peeled open a page in an ancient pocket Bible and said, "Let us pray."

The mourners bowed their heads and the simple service commenced, the ancient cliff wall their altar, the forest behind them their church.

Amariah wondered what his own parents' funeral had been like. Did his mother even resemble a human being in her last minutes above the earth? Or was she just a pile of burned bones and hair, tangled in the charred fabric of her evening gown?

Nurse Isabelle droned on about the glories of the afterlife as Amariah tried to remember his parents as they were in life: fully engaged in what they were doing, cheerful in the face of despair, smiling at him, encouraging him, his best friends in the world. As was usually the case when his anger faded, he felt terribly and utterly alone.

Nurse Isabelle finished reading, and the crowd said, "Amen."

In small groups, the relatives of each of the dead lifted stones from a pile of rocks and placed them on top of the coffins. The ground too frozen for digging, this was necessary to protect the bodies from wild animals and observation by Peck's planes. A team would return in a few weeks to bury the bodies properly once the ground had thawed—that was, if there was still anyone left to do so.

When the coffins were indistinguishable from the earth around them, the procession trudged back up the trail toward the ravine, shoulders slumped in the manner of the bereaved. As the sun began to rise, some nervously scanned the brightening sky.

Someone screamed.

Amariah tensed, prepared to duck or run, but the crowd surged forward. There in the center of the trail was Joshua, pale and broken. A resurrected corpse. A ghost.

Nurse Isabelle reached him first. "My God, Josh," she gasped, touching him with her fingertips. "Are you all right?"

The mourners surged around him, peering farther up the trail for any sign of Anne or Daniel, peppering him with questions.

"Let him speak!" cried Isabelle.

But Joshua's eyes rolled back into his head, and he collapsed in her arms.

"Help me get him inside!"

The crowd hustled Joshua back up the trail, through the ravine and into the main cavern, where they sat him down at a table. He regained consciousness, and after a few sips of water and some apple slices, he regained enough strength to speak. In a cracked and weak voice, he told the story of his capture at the church, of being thrown into the back of a wagon, and his interrogation at the barracks.

"Did they hurt you?" asked Rebecca.

Joshua opened his shirt to reveal his thin torso, purple with bruises. His red-rimmed eyes spoke of further horrors in the hands of the NVM.

"How did you escape?" asked Rebecca, pressing him.

"They let me go."

"They what? What about Anne and Daniel?"

"They're alive."

"You saw them?"

"We were separated, but I could hear them."

Rebecca put her hand to her mouth. "Hear them? Were you followed?"

"Worse. They brought me up here, under a white flag, right to the first sniper station."

"You mean you led them to us?"

"No, Peck knows where we are."

The crowd stirred, their worst fears confirmed; their hideout had been discovered.

"He sent me up with a message." Joshua reached with trembling hands into a pocket and pulled out a piece of folded paper. "It's for Amariah."

Amariah groaned—not again. He reached out and took the piece of paper, his name written clumsily across it. He broke the wax seal and unfolded the letter to read its contents, an ingratiating missive punctuated with a direct threat.

"It's from Peck," said Amariah. "He's 'inviting' me to come down off the mountain and return to work in the refinery. He says if I give myself up, he'll let Anne and Daniel go."

There was momentary silence as the people around him took it in.

Miriam Bowman spoke first. "You should go," she said.

"What?" said Rebecca.

"If Peck wants him to work in the refinery then he should go," she said, grasping at this last straw. "We need food. We need Anne back. We can't stay here. The children— we can't live like this!"

"Peck wants Amariah for one reason," said Joshua. "To make more fuel so he can finish us off."

"That doesn't matter anymore," Miriam screeched. "Face it. You rebels have lost. We can't live without food."

"We are not going to give in to Peck, for God's sake!" thundered Rebecca. "He's a liar and a murderer. Do you really think he's going to just let them go?"

Amariah held up his hand to stop her. "She's right," he said. "We can't live like this. We shouldn't live like this."

Rebecca scoffed. "So you're going to give yourself up? Just walk down there and help them start making fuel? Why don't you just kill us all now and get it over with!"

Amariah kept his cool. "As long as Peck is alive and in charge of the NVM, we'll never be safe. We have to stop him once and for all."

"And how do you propose we do that?"

"We attack Pleasant Valley. Take back control of the refinery. Starve the NVM of fuel."

A groan went through the crowd.

"We have to eliminate the NVM as a fighting force," Amariah continued. "As long as they have fuel, they will always have the advantage. So we have to remove that advantage. Without fuel they can't fly."

"No kidding!" exclaimed Rebecca, exasperated. "What the hell do you think we've been trying to do for the past ten years? There's no way to get through the wall, you said so yourself."

The crowd regarded him silently. Amariah's father had designed the barrier. If anyone knew a weakness in the fortifications, through the sharp wooden picket and over its forbidding walls, it would be him.

But there wasn't. If the rebels were going to get in, it would have to be some other way.

He thought of his last visit to the barrier, on Charlemagne, and had an idea.

"Have any of you ever heard the story of the Trojan Horse?" asked Amariah.

None of them had. So he stepped up onto a bench, reached back into his memory, and improvised the tale as best as he could remember it.

ଔ

Joshua sent for Amariah later that afternoon. Amariah felt sick. He had not spoken to his former friend in months; not an easy thing to do in the confines of the cavern. The man had taken a bullet for him, and Amariah had left him there to be captured and tortured.

Joshua lay on a narrow cot in his grotto, attended by Nurse Isabelle. An oil heater kept the damp at bay.

"How's he doing?" whispered Amariah.

"He's dying," replied Isabelle. "I have nothing left to treat him."

Face shrunken behind his beard, Joshua appeared to be in the last hours of his life. While it was true that the watchman had misled him for all of those years, Amariah had learned that few things in this world could be taken at face value.

Joshua stirred and opened his eyes. "Amariah?"

Isabelle reluctantly let him past.

He knelt beside the man. "How are you feeling?"

"Eh. Not good." Joshua motioned weakly to Isabelle. "Bring me my coat, Belle."

"Why? You're not going anywhere."

Joshua waved for her to bring it over from where it lay, then searched through the pockets until he found what he was looking for. "Here."

Amariah stretched out his hand and received a gold watch on a chain. He recognized it immediately, a birthday gift from his parents. He cradled it in his cupped palms, speechless. Except for some char around the winding mechanism, it was undamaged. He flipped open the cover with his thumb and examined the inscription he knew by heart:

To Amariah, our cherished son.
"Soar, and be free."
With love, Mother and Father

For a fleeting moment he was home, on his sixteenth birthday, parents at his side, chatting away, the household staff enjoying cake, one big extended family. The blackened watch was all that was left. Tears swelled in his eyes.

"Peck had it," said Joshua. "He sent it up as a token of his good faith." He smiled weakly.

The dream vanished. Amariah was back in the cold, dark cave, kneeling on the stone floor next to a dying man. He closed the watch. "I'm sorry I left you."

"What? No. I got shot. Believe me, it wasn't intentional."

"Well then, I'm sorry anyway. For the way I've treated you," said Amariah. "I understand now, why you did what you did."

Joshua nodded the barest of nods. Apology accepted.

"If it means anything to you, I'm going to help them destroy the refinery."

Joshua exhaled and sank further into his bed. "That would be a mistake."

"What? You think I should let them do it on their own? Joshua, the fuel is being used to murder people from the sky. I saw it with my own eyes. We buried fifteen innocent people today. I have to help."

"Amariah," said Joshua, his voice weak but firm, "a lot of people are depending on the refinery for their survival. It's all we have left."

"I thought everyone here wanted the refinery destroyed? I mean, don't you?"

"The problem isn't the refinery. It's how it's being used."

"Yes, Joshua, it's being used to kill and enslave people. It's the reason these people were driven from their farms. Why their soil is being ruined, and why there isn't enough to eat."

"Your father had a dream for something better."

"My father was living in a world of his own. He didn't even own the refinery in the first place. It belonged to the

190

farmers' cooperative. He stole it. If it wasn't for him none of this would have happened."

"If it wasn't for your father, it would have been just another ruin."

"Yes, but then he ignored the suffering it caused. We need to destroy it, so no one else gets hurt."

Joshua touched his leg. "But Amariah, you'll destroy the only positive thing your parents left behind. Is that what you want?"

Amariah stood and paced the small dark space, flipping the watch over in his hand.

"Look," said Joshua, rising on his elbow, "your parents may have made some bad decisions, but only after years of making a lot of good ones. If you destroy the refinery, you'll add to the misery of many thousands of people. The Wales name will be tarnished forever."

"But why did they do it? They weren't dumb. They must have known what was going on."

"You left me behind to die, but you had a good reason," said Joshua. "Maybe your parents found themselves in a similar situation. Did you ever think of that?"

Amariah opened and closed the watch, turning its smooth surface over in his hands.

"There are a lot of people who want more fuel," Joshua continued, "and there are a lot of people who want there to be no fuel at all. The problem is that there are too few people making decisions for too many. Solve that and you will have restored your family's good name. Solve that, and maybe you can go home again."

"I don't have a home anymore."

"Amariah, the refinery may have belonged to the cooperative, but Pleasant Valley belongs to your family, fair and

191

square. That's your property down there. Your parents' graves are down there. Charlemagne is down there—he's waiting for you. You have to take back what was stolen from you. Do it now, before it's too late."

Amariah looked down at the ground. He didn't know what to say. A hand settled on his shoulder.

"Joshua has to rest now," said Isabelle.

Joshua's head had fallen to the pillow—unconscious.

Amariah spread the chain and raised the gold watch over his head. The heft of it dangled against his chest like a medallion. He opened his shirt and dropped the watch against his bare skin to keep it out of sight.

ℰ

As the afternoon turned to evening, Amariah wandered to the upper chamber and out onto the ledge. A warm, blustery wind whipped up the cliff, causing small wildflowers in the moss to tremble. Amariah lay down on the carpet of green and pulled out his binoculars.

As he suspected, the NVM and Yorkers patrolled the top of the barrier wall, clustering near Joshua's watchtower. The NVM held rifles, the Yorkers machine guns. At the base of the formidable walls, sharpened wooden stakes bristled at the forest in front of a field of barbed wire. A forward assault would indeed be suicidal; there was no doubt about it.

He lay on the ledge, the very spot where he had planned to make his escape, the air holding the barest fragrance of an awakening earth.

Anne and Daniel needed to be rescued soon. But how? The Trojan Horse had worked for the ancient Greeks, but in his heart, Amariah doubted it would work now. Even if they could get a horse to pull an apparently driverless wagon up to the main gate with two fighters hidden inside, somehow avoiding detection until nightfall, opening the gate from the inside would be no easy task. In fact, it would be nearly impossible. He had to face it: his plan wasn't a good one. It wasn't going to work.

The breeze stiffened. Amariah put the binoculars aside and took a deep breath, hoping the oxygen would clear his brain. He turned over on his back and stared at the endless sky, trying to think of a way through the wall. Was there any weak spot he could remember? Any flaw? A secluded spot they could tunnel under?

Above him, a hawk rode in the air currents, eyes fierce, hovering motionless under a cushion of rushing air. It was a large red-tailed hawk, a denizen of the valley. The magnificent creature soared on the breeze, wings outstretched, making only slight adjustments to hold its position. Suddenly it swooped down, snatched a rodent from the hillside, and sailed out over the valley, gliding out of sight.

Amariah leapt to his feet. He knew what he had to do.

He dashed inside the cavern, down to the grotto that Hannah's parents had made into their living quarters. The Bowman family sat aimless and glum. Their heads turned in unison as Amariah ran up, stumbled, and nearly sprawled at their feet.

"Where do you keep the books?" he asked, gasping for breath.

"Uh, hello," said Hannah, indicating her parents.

"Hello," said Amariah, nodding perfunctorily. "The books?"

Hannah knelt down beside her bed and pulled out the box with her teaching materials. *"Voila,"* she said.

Amariah slid the books onto Hannah's bed. He quickly scanned each cover, tossing them aside as he searched for the one he wanted.

"What are you doing?"

He found what he was looking for and held the book up for her to see. Hannah shook her head and shrugged, uncomprehending.

Miriam Bowman intervened. "Put those back."

"I need Hannah's help," said Amariah. "Down in my cave tonight."

"Not likely," said the stepmother with a smirk.

Hannah turned to Miriam. "Amariah saved me—if he needs my help I'm going to help him."

"No, Hannah, I forbid it," said Miriam. She reached out and snatched the book from Amariah's hands.

Hannah violently snatched it back. "You can't forbid anything! You're not my mother!"

Miriam shrank back, surprised.

"Come on, Amariah, let's go," said Hannah.

Mark Bowman opened his mouth to say something, but Hannah was already gone.

CHAPTER SIXTEEN

"**A**re you sure you want to do this?" asked Hannah.

"Yes," said Amariah, "it's time."

"Um, okay, sit in this chair."

Amariah sat, stiff, fingers twitching.

Hannah's long hair, loose and unbraided, brushed against his shoulders. "Just relax," she said.

"Okay, it's just that it's been a while."

"Shush already." Hannah ran her fingers through his hair, playing with it, drawing it out. "I know what I'm doing. Put this on."

Amariah fumbled with the plastic, all thumbs.

Hannah laughed. "Maybe I should do that."

When the fit was snug, she tossed her hair, lifted a pair of old scissors, and snapped them twice. "How much do you want me to cut off?"

"All of it."

Hannah leaned over and snipped at the tip of Amariah's beard, then stepped back and examined the cut. "Um, maybe we should start with the hair first."

"I thought you said you've done this before?"

"I have," she said, running a finger around his ear, "just never with someone so mangy."

She smoothed the plastic cape around his shoulders, then dove into her work, cutting and trimming his hair and beard until nearly all of it lay on the floor at his feet. Using her fingernails as a comb, she brushed at what was left.

An old straight razor, rusty and unsharpened, lay on his workbench. Hannah raised an eyebrow.

"Uh, let's wait," said Amariah.

"All done then." She held up a broken mirror. His wild-man beard and long hair were gone. What was left was trim and closely cropped.

"Wow," he said, running his hand over the soft bristles.

"Okay, sir. Now you're ready." She helped Amariah remove the plastic cape, then took his hand, leading him out of the storage cave and through the tunnel that led to the ravine. For the first time in months, Amariah felt clean, fresh, and renewed.

Outside, they climbed up a steep path through the rocks that led to an overlook. A large flat rock offered a wide view of the forest that ran north to south along the spine of the mountaintop, completely hidden from their enemies occupying Pleasant Valley.

Rebecca sat waiting for them, shoulders slumped. Behind her, out in the forest, the bodies of the dead had recently been buried.

She took in the sight of them. "Finally."

"I told you I would cut it eventually," said Amariah, running his hand across his trimmed chin.

"No," said Rebecca. "Finally, you're back. The crowd is getting restless."

She gestured to the throng below, assembled at Amariah's request. A few dozen people sat among the rocks, shielding their eyes from the sun. He had promised them a solution, a way to end their diaspora, and they were here to see it.

Rebecca placed her hands on Amariah's shoulders, then scrutinized both sides of his head. "You do look better, I have to say." She turned to Hannah. "He cleans up pretty good, doesn't he?"

Amariah grinned, then dropped down onto his hands and knees. Inching forward under the contraption that he and Hannah had worked on for the past few days, he fastened the straps around his body, mentally rehearsing what he was about to do, his heart and hands fluttering just a bit.

Although he had practiced on an easier slope earlier that morning, the drop below the overlook was steep and unforgiving. He had only one chance to prove his plan would work. If it didn't—well, it was a long way down.

Once the harness was tight, he gripped the control bar and rose to his feet, the hair and beard that had bothered him during practice no longer in his way.

"Okay," he said. "I'm ready."

The women took hold of each wingtip, and the three of them walked forward until Amariah emerged into the view of the crowd.

Several people stood, trying to get a better look. The black plastic wings that stretched above Amariah's head, cut from a roll of thick plastic sheeting the rebels had scavenged from an abandoned office park years before, gave him the appearance of a large black crow. For the first time in their lives, they were seeing what used to be known as a hang glider.

A sudden breeze took hold of the wings and pulled the glider upwards, nearly lifting Amariah off his feet. Hannah grabbed hold, then smiled with false bravado.

"Okay, it's now or never," said Amariah. He exhaled, shook his arms and legs, and focused on the rock that sloped down toward the forest. After a moment's pause, he counted out. "One, two, three!"

The women let go of the wings. Amariah gripped the control bar and took long strides down the flat rock, keeping the nose of the wing pointed higher than the angle of the slope. The harness stiffened around his legs and groin, and the wings lifted until his feet no longer touched the ground. The rock disappeared beneath him and he soared out high over the rocks and forest, the hang glider taking to the air like it was meant to.

The air surged around him, whistling in his ears, the few straps the only thing between him and the rocks below. His body swung freely beneath the glider, and he soared into the atmosphere, aware of every cell in his body. This was natural flying, without the noise or vibration of an engine.

He checked the wires and fittings beneath the wings, every piece scavenged from the junk pile. All was taut and tight. He adjusted his grip on the old metal pipe and stretched his legs out behind him, letting the harness adjust to his center of gravity. He slid his hands to the left, and the glider responded, the air itself holding him aloft. He relaxed and let his weight do the work, turning and rising on a warm updraft in front of the cliff.

As he rose, he caught a glimpse of the horizon, stretching for hundreds of miles in every direction. A sense of serenity and peace flooded through him. He wanted to keep flying, to leave everything behind, and sail through the air to the farthest peak.

Just then, he caught a glimpse of Pleasant Valley and the top of the refinery smokestack. He had risen too high. Quickly, he turned back east and out of sight of the valley, but the error was enough to bring him back to reality. Anne and Daniel were down there, suffering, awaiting a rescue. It was time to come back to earth.

Amariah sailed back to the launch point, over the crowd looking up at him, then turned toward the hidden forest. He began to shed altitude, heading for an open field he had chosen in advance. He widened his grip, hoping that the author of Hannah's book had accurately explained how to land. As he slipped air, the wind rushed around him, and the ground rose up to meet him. At the precise moment, he lowered his feet and stepped down onto the grass, a soft landing.

All was suddenly still and silent. Usually, after a flight in his father's plane, his ears would be ringing from the noise of the engine. It was a remarkable change.

He unfastened himself from the harness and let the glider slip to the ground. He glanced back at the ridge from which he had flown, now too far away to see if anyone was still watching. Scanning the woods, he realized that for the first time, he was alone and away from the cavern. If he wanted to, he could just walk away and vanish, leaving everyone behind.

He cast the thought out of his mind, removed a small wrench from a buttoned pocket, and began disassembling the glider for the long hike back up.

∓

Two hours later, burdened with the packed glider on his back, Amariah finally made it to the bottom of the ravine.

Only Hannah still waited, waving to him from the top of the overlook.

She scrambled down and greeted him with a kiss. "You made it," she said. "I was getting worried."

"Where is everyone?" he asked, slipping the pack from his sore shoulders. He would have to add some padding to the straps next time; if there was a next time.

"Inside," she said, nervously.

"What is it?"

"You need to talk to them."

Amariah rested the pack against the wall of the ravine and went inside, following Hannah up to the great room of the main cavern. Free from the weight of the pack, he felt light, as if he was still flying.

A sense of accomplishment filled him. Had they planned a special surprise to congratulate him? As far as he was concerned, this feat was more of an accomplishment than installing the lighting system. He came around the corner, expecting a crowd.

There was none. Instead, Rebecca waited with a small cluster of people at a table, consulting with one another, voices low.

Amariah approached, smiling, expecting praise. Their faces however, were somber, and the reception decidedly cool.

Mark Bowman spoke first. "We don't understand, Amariah," he said. "How is your hang glider supposed to save us?"

Amariah's moment faded. He had thought his point was clear. "We fly over the wall. At night."

Blank stares.

"We have enough material for maybe twenty of these. We attack the garrison from inside the barrier, not the outside. It'll be a surprise attack. In World War II, the Germans took an impregnable castle this way."

Even Rebecca avoided eye contact, her hands occupied with an empty earthen cup.

Mark Bowman made a face. "Well, there's no way I'm going to strap on one of those things and jump off a cliff."

"There's nothing to it," said Amariah. "I'll teach you."

"Look, it's a great idea in theory. I'll give you that," said Bowman, "but even if we got twenty volunteers to go down into the valley on hang gliders, there aren't enough of us to take on the entire NVM. We've lost too many people."

Miriam Bowman let out a snort. "Oh come on already. Admit it. This is even crazier than his giant horse idea." She tossed her short curls. "Why are we wasting time even talking about it?"

"So, what's your suggestion then?" said Amariah, exasperated. "We sit here and wait for Peck to knock on the door?"

"We *leave*," she said, as if he was the dumbest person she ever met. "Tonight. The snow is gone. We make a run for it, south, and get away from here while we can."

"And what about the wounded? We just leave them here?" asked Amariah. "Look, even if we stuck to the trails and stayed off the roads, we would still be exposed to the elements, and to gangs. Once we make it to a town, they're not going to have enough food to take care of all four hundred of us. We'll have to carry everything with us. The trees haven't filled in yet, so Peck will be able to follow us in his planes. We'll be killed on the trail."

201

"He can't see us in the dark," Miriam retorted. "We've got to go now!"

"Anne and Daniel are down there. Your homes are down there," urged Amariah. "If we fight, we might just get them back. If we run, we'll never see them again. I'm certain of it. We have a chance to win this. We should take it!"

Amariah took the cup from Rebecca, then grabbed another, holding them both above the table. "Look," he said. "We sail over the wall. Some of us split off and take the refinery buildings, others attack the barracks and keep them pinned down. Two fighters shoot a grenade up into Joshua's tower, then we open the gates and let everyone else in."

No reaction.

"I say we take our chances on the trail," said Miriam. "That includes you, Hannah."

Hannah sat by her father, dejected.

Rebecca spoke up, finally. "You can do what you please, Miriam. But I'm not going to leave Anne and Daniel behind."

The farmer's wife threw up her hands, exasperated.

Rebecca erupted out of her seat and leaned across the table. "For God's sake, woman, Anne took you in! How can you just leave her down there to be tortured?"

Miriam looked away, and Amariah finally realized that the Bowmans had already made up their minds. They were leaving, whatever the group decided, and they were taking Hannah with them.

Rebecca's voice rose. "I believe everything happens for a reason," she said. "Amariah came to us for a reason. We have this one chance to save Anne and Daniel and destroy the NVM, and maybe even kill Peck."

She lifted a finger and pointed squarely at Amariah. "But you listen to me, wonder boy. I'll help you make your hang gliders, and we'll get enough volunteers to attack the garrison. But I want the refinery destroyed, including that new contraption of yours that makes fuel out of trees. And if it looks like we're losing, I want enough explosives to blow it up myself, you understand?"

Amariah nodded, distracted by the possibility of Hannah suddenly leaving.

Rebecca got a faraway look. "I will strap myself with explosives, and turn myself into a human bomb."

೨

On the far wall of the storage cave, light from the lantern combined with the pile to create an undulating shadow. Its peaks and valleys resembled a darkened skyline of an unknown city somewhere out in the fallen world, a world Amariah had never seen except in old photographs, a world he realized he may now never see at all.

It was only a week ago that he had first fired a weapon in combat. Now, he was advocating for an all-out assault against the NVM and the Yorkers. People on both sides would surely die. He would likely die. But if the assault succeeded, Anne and Daniel would be saved, the refugees returned to their homes, and the reputation of the Wales family restored. Each of these things alone was worth fighting for— the three of them together were worth dying for.

The Bowmans hadn't persuaded enough people to join them, and were apparently too chicken to do it on their own. Rebecca's resolve, meanwhile, had convinced enough people to join the attack. Amariah's plan had to work, or he might never see Hannah again.

He was nearly asleep when he heard footsteps approaching. Silently, he reached under the cot and grabbed a long piece of pipe he kept hidden there, gripping it tightly, prepared to defend himself.

A figure appeared in the doorway of the dimly lit tunnel. Hannah.

Without a word, she approached his bed and stood before him, wearing only her nightgown, the fragrance of rose petals rising from her freshly washed skin. She put a finger to her lips, then loosened the string around her neck to let the gown fall off her shoulders. She smiled and stood before him naked.

Long black hair draped over her shoulders, framing her upturned breasts. He gently reached up and caressed her firm, trim body with his fingertips.

Hannah shivered. He took her hand and led her down on to the bed, stroking her hair, her shoulders, her waist. Then he cupped her breasts, bringing his lips and tongue to her nipples, which he sucked, tenderly. Hannah pushed him back, then climbed onto the bed on top of him, her long hair brushing against his bare chest.

Gently they explored each other's bodies. Hands and tongues, stroking and probing. Hannah placed her body below his, guiding him along, and they made love, Amariah for the first time.

For a long while they lay together, until Amariah drifted off to sleep. For the first time in nine months, he had happy dreams.

CHAPTER SEVENTEEN

Captain Peck stood with his soldiers by the shore of Lake Champlain, watching impatiently as the flotilla carrying military men and equipment crept into Mallet's Bay. It had taken more than a week to get the Northern Army's tanks, artillery, and ATVs transported from the outpost at St. John's down the Richelieu River. The delay had been excruciating.

In a letter, the outpost's commanding officer, Jack Mac-Donald, had been apologetic. He was being extremely cautious about the conditions on the lake, he wrote, which in spring could turn from flat calm to dangerous whitecaps with little warning.

MacDonald's greatest concern lay with his cargo. The tanks and artillery pieces were more than fifty years old, some little more than functioning antiques. If the barges foundered, the equipment would be lost forever in the depths of the lake, and the Northern Army reduced to nothing more than horseback, light arms, and infantry.

"All the boats are accounted for," said Lieutenant Dickins, tallying off the odd assortment of galleys, schooners, and bateau as they approached the shore.

"And three days late," said Peck, grudgingly. He turned and lowered his voice. "If anyone asks about Amariah, he's a hostage, got it?"

Dickins nodded. They had called for the troops under the pretext of protecting the fuel supply. For now, that's all anyone needed to know.

Out in the bay, the small fleet fanned out, backed up by the majestic, square-sailed brig, the *Ethan Allen*, which remained offshore. The smaller boats, which had formed a cordon around the barges, now opened up to allow them to motor in, diesel engines growling. They drove right up onto the beach, followed by exhausted infantry rowing their bateau. The rest of the flotilla weighed anchor as men and equipment prepared to move ashore.

A small skiff approached from the *Ethan Allen*, rowed by a team of smart-looking military men. In it, Jack MacDonald sat with two subordinates, two oarsmen, and two armed guards. Peck hadn't seen MacDonald since the general's funeral. The man was a professional soldier, and his aides an impressive sight. Peck sucked in his gut and tried to stand as tall as he could.

MacDonald strode up the beach, saluted smartly, then broke into a wide smile. "Captain Jack MacDonald, reporting as ordered, sir."

He dropped the salute and gave Peck a firm handshake. Since he and Peck were both of the same rank, his greeting was delivered with a bit of cheek.

"Glad you could make it, Captain," said Peck. Disappointedly, he was still a head shorter than the war hero who had beaten the Canadians.

MacDonald introduced his two aides—a chief warrant officer and a sergeant major. They made small talk about the voyage for a minute.

"With your permission, we'll bring the equipment ashore," said MacDonald.

"Permission granted," said Peck. It was important Mac-Donald understood he was in charge. The chain of command had been a matter of dispute since the general's assassination, an irksome issue that would have to be cleared up, and soon.

The sergeant major whistled to the men on the barge, and one by one, the tanks started their engines. The deep vibration rattled Peck's very bones, the sound shocking to anyone who hadn't heard industrial machinery before. The tanks came down the ramp onto the beach with a rumble and drove up onto the road.

"Care to ride in the lead tank with me?" shouted Mac-Donald over the noise.

Peck grinned and limped along behind the captain. He had only been in a tank once before, so he followed Mac-Donald's lead and climbed in through a hatch in the rear. He nodded to the men inside and emerged from the turret, feeling like a great conqueror before battle. MacDonald gave an order to the driver below, and the tank lurched forward up the road towards Pleasant Valley.

In the distance, the peak of Mount Mansfield rose between the pines. He had received no response from Amariah Wales, despite the return of his watch, so Peck was going to go and get him. Once the Wales progeny was in custody and back to work, the NVM would blast the entrances and seal off the caves forever.

Then he would start to cut down trees. He would order Amariah to design a bigger biomass processor by the shore of the lake, and then be on the move, cutting trees as they went, shipping logs back by barge to make even more fuel. Every tree felled, every stand of forest cleared, would add to his power and his reach. He would take control of the entire North Country, including all of the Adirondacks, and appoint himself governor of a vastly expanded territory, answerable to no one.

The tank rumbled along the road, Peck standing in the turret, with the power to crush anything before him. He felt himself attached to the machine, a part of it. In fact, he had never felt this powerful in his entire life.

ꝏ

Amariah checked and rechecked the equipment, making final preparations for the assault. The test run of the hang gliders had taken place that morning, on a gentle slope down in the hidden valley, although only ten men had committed to the hang gliding mission instead of the twenty for which he had hoped.

The remaining gliders would go unused. Each empty space glared at Amariah like the missing nail in the proverbial horseshoe. There simply weren't enough volunteers.

"How's it coming?" asked Hannah, giving his shoulder a squeeze.

Amariah smiled. "The birds are ready to fly."

The women had made belly packs for each member of the team. She handed him one and helped him try it on.

"It's a little tight on you," said Hannah. "But look, I made a pouch for your binoculars—"

Amariah held up his hand. There was a faint rumbling in the distance. Thunder? A thunderstorm would bring their plans to a halt. The murmur of conversation ceased as others heard it too. It was a clear afternoon outside, a beautiful

208

spring day. The cavern doors had been left open to allow in the fresh air. How could there be thunder?

The rumbling grew louder. There was something unnatural about the sound, seeming to originate from within the ground itself. A few people headed up the passageway toward the ledge to take a look. Amariah and Hannah went with them.

They emerged into a beautiful, clear afternoon. All eyes turned to the sky. Not a cloud in sight.

"Look!" shouted Hannah.

Entering the valley through the main gate was a vast military force: tanks, artillery pieces, and riders on ATVs, followed by uniformed troops marching in columns. The thunder of the engines and the clanking of metal combined into a horrific grinding sound unlike anything Amariah had ever heard. A large cloud of dust and smoke rose into the sky behind the army like the exhalations of an expanding wildfire.

Mouths fell open and Amariah's heart sank. Peck had brought down the entire Northern Army from the Canadian border. There could be little doubt as to what he had in mind—a direct assault on the mountain.

"What are those?" asked Hannah. "Are those *tanks*?"

The men and equipment took up positions in the bare oilseed fields, then the hardware erupted into a deafening roar—a hellish concert of revving diesel engines.

Miriam Bowman ran up beside Hannah and grabbed her by the arm and screamed, "We've got to get out of here now!" She pulled her stepdaughter back into the cave.

Amariah stayed behind, counting their numbers, fear growing as he tallied the firepower. His plan had stood a good chance of working against the personal firearms of the NVM and the Yorkers, but not a mechanized army.

Rebecca approached, the courage drained from her face. "What are we going to do?"

A dozen faces turned to Amariah, desperate for salvation.

Amariah took a long look through the binoculars as the army took up positions in the valley. He had no answer.

They were trapped.

৯১

"Gun it again!" shouted Peck.

The engine of the tank roared, and the captain laughed. He hoped that the rebels up on the mountain would be shitting themselves by now. He wanted there to be no doubt about his intentions.

"Driver!" he said, tapping the man with the toe of his boot. "Take us down there, to the refinery." He wanted Malinger to see him in the turret of this tank, to recognize the power of the Northern Army, and to deliver the fuel that would keep it running.

MacDonald nodded his consent, and the driver complied.

Malinger stood slack jawed with his son and the other Yorkers in front of the administration building. The driver brought the tank right up to them and cut the engine down to an idle. The Yorkers stared at Captain MacDonald, looking every inch like a field commander from one of the great wars.

Peck rested his elbows on the turret. "Fill 'er up."

Malinger glanced at the sad bunch around him. "Uh, this is a refinery, Captain, not a gas station. We have to fill up the tankers first and then pump the fuel by hand."

"Well, get on with it then," said Peck. He glanced over at MacDonald and rolled his eyes.

MacDonald sized up the Yorkers, his face revealing nothing. He turned his attention to the looming mountain and raised his binoculars.

Peck climbed down from the turret, exited through the hatch in the rear, and leaned against the tank to take the weight off his leg. Although he kept changing the bandages, it had not improved. The damn doctor had gone AWOL.

Malinger approached him, subdued. "Filling up all of this equipment is going to deplete the reserve fuel in the refinery tanks, Captain. Just so you know."

"Soon we'll have the enzyme, and we'll have all the fuel we need. Won't we, Glen?"

The Yorker shrugged. "This is going to take a while."

Peck relaxed. He had everything he needed. He stretched his arms and arched his back.

MacDonald approached, having inspected the undulating ridges that piled up towards the top of the mountain. "You know," he said, "anyone looking at us from up there can see everything we're doing."

"Yup," said Peck. "I know."

He was hoping the rebels would make a run for it. It would be a lot less trouble than digging them out. He had already sealed off the escape routes out of Smuggler's Notch. If they tried to head down any of the trails, they would be captured. They could climb over the hillsides, but that would be difficult, and he would soon have his planes in the air if they tried. They wouldn't get far in any case.

He reclined against the cold hard steel of the tank. "Let's see them use their bows and arrows against these!" he said to MacDonald, patting the metal monster. He smirked at the mountain and had a good laugh.

"Get your things!" screamed Miriam Bowman. "We've got to make a run for it!"

In every corner of the cave people scrambled, grabbing everything they could carry. Ella ran past Amariah with Emily in her arms.

"Wait, wait!" said Amariah, reaching out to stop her. "Where will you go?"

Ella recoiled and kept moving.

Miriam Bowman marched over to Amariah, neck veins throbbing, nostrils flaring, and slapped him hard across the face. "We never should have listened to you!" she shouted, loud enough for everyone to hear. "We could have been miles away by now!"

Face burning, surrounded by stares, Amariah turned his back and resumed checking the equipment. The pieces of the hang gliders were neatly arranged on the floor, ready to be assembled, but no one remained in the staging area. Automatically, he picked up the belly packs left on the floor and put them aside. It seemed his hands were not his own. A warning sign—panic.

He stopped what he was doing and took deep breaths to calm his mind.

Hannah touched his shoulder. "Amariah, what are you doing?"

His thoughts cleared. "Sticking with the plan."

"What?"

"The tanks look intimidating, but they're useless without fuel," he said. "We don't have to destroy them. We just have to destroy the refinery."

"Oh, is that all? You're not going to make a run for it?"

"I can't. My family restored the refinery. We built the biomass processor. I have to fix this."

Miriam Bowman pulled at Hannah's arm. "Come on," she said, dragging her away.

"Let go of me!"

"Are you crazy, girl? Are you blind? There's an entire army down there! You can't fight *them*! We've got to get out of here before we all get killed!"

Hannah's eyes implored Amariah for a rebuttal, some reassurance, anything to convince her that what Miriam said wasn't true. But Amariah had nothing to offer. Crestfallen, Hannah followed her stepmother back to her father.

Miriam shouted instructions and the mob divided in two—those who would flee, and those who would remain behind; mostly those too old, too sick, or too wounded to make a run for it. They would await whatever fate the NVM had in store for them.

Rebecca came up behind him. "I'll go with you, Amariah."

A few others also gave their consent.

Amariah thought on his feet. "We still have the element of surprise. I'll need some help planting the explosives. Since there's only a few of us, I say we destroy the refinery while we have the chance. When that's done, we attempt the rescue."

Rebecca managed a grin. "Leave that part to us."

Amariah completed his check of one glider and moved on to the next. Each would have to be dismantled and reassembled on the ledge. He got back to work, trying to ignore the tears and hurried goodbyes of the people preparing to leave.

Mark Bowman approached, face solemn, and offered his hand. Amariah stood and shook it.

"Good luck," said the farmer.

"And to you," said Amariah. "Where will you go?"

"South. The Long Trail. My wife has family in Spring-field. That's where we're headed."

Amariah grimaced. Springfield was more than a hundred miles away. It would take at least a week of hard walking to get there. The refugees were neither equipped nor physically prepared for such a journey. Hannah's life would be in danger. Yet he had no alternative to offer.

"Stay off the ridge as you leave," offered Amariah. "You'll want to be out of sight of Peck and the troops down in the valley. And watch out, he may already have men out on the trail."

Bowman nodded and went off to join his wife and daughter. Amariah caught one last glimpse of Hannah, looking longingly over her shoulder as she was led away with the rest of the crowd, down the tunnel toward the ravine.

Rebecca gave him a nudge, indicating that he should follow, which he did, trailing behind the crowd until they reached the ravine. More sad faces appeared, and he stood aside to let the people pass. Most ignored him, focused intensely on their own concerns. Some mumbled apologies. Others glared at him.

Ella walked past, carrying little Emily, who was crying.

"Thanks for nothing," snarled the widow.

Amariah turned away. The woman was right. He had provided nothing of real value to these people. For all he knew, the few creature comforts he provided had only prevented them from trying to make an escape earlier in the season. He had tried to fill the void left by Anne and Daniel—to be a leader—and had failed.

The crowd merged into the bright green buds of the forest, and Amariah climbed to the top of the overlook where he had launched his hang glider just a few days before, Rebecca

214

behind him. Together they watched as nearly four hundred men, women, and children filed down the trail heading south, wearing as many of their clothes as they could manage and carrying whatever they could in their arms. Wheeled carts portaged children too small to walk.

"Do you think they'll be all right?" asked Rebecca.

"I really don't know."

"Well, it's not going to be safe here for much longer either," she said, looking around.

"I'm going to destroy the refinery tonight, Rebecca. What happens after that, I don't know. Nowhere is safe. Maybe we can make it to Massachusetts, get on a ship, and sail somewhere far away. The islands, perhaps."

Rebecca regarded him slyly. "Huh. You want to sail with me into the sunset? I didn't think I was your type."

Amariah glanced over at her and smiled. "Actually, it would be the sunrise."

"Oh."

The refugee column had crossed the hidden valley and were about to climb over the southern ridge. Amariah reached into the belly pack that Hannah had given him and pulled out the binoculars, trying to discern Hannah among the crowd, but the budding trees made it difficult to see. This was it. He would never see her again. He moved the binoculars up ahead along the trail to the top of the ridge and froze.

A large group of armed men approached down the trail in the opposite direction, directly toward the refugees. Neither group had yet seen the other.

"Oh no," said Amariah.

"What now?"

He handed Rebecca the binoculars.

"Oh God." She handed the binoculars back. "I can't watch."

Amariah's gaze darted back and forth between the column of refugees and the approaching armed men. What happened next unfolded silently through the lens.

The leaders of each group saw one another at exactly the same time, stopping dead in their tracks. Neither moved. Then one of the rebels raised a rifle and shot at the armed men, but missed. The sound of the gunshot was delayed by the distance, and by the time Amariah heard it, the refugee column had stopped. Miriam Bowman, waving her arms wildly, turned and ran in the opposite direction, a pantomime without sound. The refugees dropped what they were carrying, turned, and stampeded back down the trail.

Amariah's stomach turned. It would only be a moment before the armed men started shooting the civilians in the back.

But they didn't. Instead, they cautiously peered around the rocks and held their fire.

What are they doing? he wondered.

The people with children in the wagons stopped. The trail was too narrow to turn around, and there were too many children to carry. Ella picked up Emily and ran, but tripped over a tree root and fell hard onto the ground. Emily stood, apparently unhurt, and pulled at her mother's sleeve.

The armed men emerged from their hiding places. A tall man in the lead cautiously approached the woman and the girl. Amariah watched little Emily reach high above her head in surrender.

Oh no.

The man reached for Ella. As he touched her, she raised her arms and tried to beat the man away. He stopped and

216

spoke to her for a few moments. Then, she slowly lifted her elbow, and he helped her back to the wagon. Another man picked up Emily and handed her to her mother.

The man in the lead spoke with Ella for a moment. She pointed up toward the cavern. The man turned and looked up in Amariah's direction, as if he was looking right into his eyes. Amariah nearly fell backwards. The bald head was un-mistakable. These men weren't NVM. It was the entire Wales Guard. More than thirty armed men!

"It's Hodgkins!"

Rebecca reached out to steady him. He had nearly fallen off the cliff.

Amariah had assumed that Hodgkins and his men had fled to one of the townships after the fire. But here they were, coming from the direction of Stowe. He scanned the rest of the men, recognizing them all.

The refugees, however, were now in a full blown retreat, running in terror down the trail, casting off their belongings along the way. The first of them had reached a fork down below Amariah. One path led up to the ravine and back to the cavern, the other over the ridge toward Jeffersonville. The people at the head of the column stopped running and hesi-tated. Amariah could see the Bowmans with them.

"Stop, stop! They're not the NVM!"

Amariah and Rebecca waved their arms, both shouting at the Bowmans to stop.

Through his binoculars Amariah saw Mark Bowman look up at him. He seemed to hesitate, then his wife shoved him in the center of the back, urging him down the other trail. Han-nah stood there, forlorn, staring up at Amariah. For a mo-ment, he looked right into her brilliant blue eyes, before she too was yanked along.

217

"Come back!" cried Rebecca, in vain.

It was too late—the Bowmans and the others disappeared over the ridge.

Amariah surveyed the rest of the column. Some men lingered behind, taking up positions to protect the fleeing refugees. Someone was about to get shot.

Amariah handed the binoculars to Rebecca, and then dashed from the overlook down the trail. He leapt over the rocks and stones, running as fast as he could, until he encountered the next group of desperate, winded people.

"Stop!" said Amariah. "That's not the NVM! I know those men. Go back up to the cavern and wait!"

The people slowed and cowered on the side of the trail, checking behind them, certain they were being pursued. Tom, the old man who had helped him with the lightbulbs, brought up the rear.

"Are you crazy?" said the old man.

"Tom! Just stay here for a moment. Please?"

Amariah ran along the trail as quickly as he could, telling everyone he encountered to stop running. He came across a fighter with his rifle aimed down the trail. "They're not NVM, don't shoot!"

"Get out of the way you idiot!" snarled the man.

Amariah ignored him, ripped off his white shirt and ran toward the Wales Guard position, waving it over his head like a white flag.

"Don't shoot! Don't shoot!" he continued to yell. He ran right up into the line of fire between the two groups and stopped, hands raised in the air, weapons trained on his heaving, bare chest. "Everyone, hold your fire!"

A bald head peered around from behind a tree. Slowly, Hodgkins emerged, ramrod straight. He had lost some weight but seemed as solid as ever. The two of them stood there for a moment on the trail, taking one another in. His old friend reached out and shook his hand.

"Man, am I glad to see you!" Amariah finally managed to say.

"Likewise," said Hodgkins, grinning.

From both sides of the trail, people emerged from hiding.

"Where have you been?" said Amariah.

"We overwintered in Stowe. I'll tell you about it later. Right now, you better get these people off the trail. There are NVM troops all around you. Wherever you folks have been hiding, I suggest you go back."

"We're in the Notch," said Amariah. "There are caves up there. It's safe, but we ran out of food. Then the Northern Army showed up yesterday, and everyone panicked."

"Northern Army?"

"They're camped in the valley."

"Well, we have plenty of food, enough to spare." He gave orders to his men. "You two! Get that wagon turned around."

Ella made a move to get out of the wagon, too embarrassed to look Amariah in the eye.

"No, no, miss, stay there!" said Hodgkins. "We'll manage." He turned to his other men. "Go back and get out as much food as we can spare. We're going to need nearly all of it, the entire reserve. Start bringing it up to the Notch."

Hodgkins turned to Amariah. "You'd better go on ahead," he said. "And tell everyone with a gun to stop shooting. I don't want anyone to get shot today. Especially me."

CHAPTER EIGHTEEN

On the floor of Pleasant Valley, Peck huddled with Mac-Donald over a hand-drawn map. Their respective staff eyed each other as the two captains discussed the plan for the assault.

Lieutenant Dickins, standing off to the side, scanned the mountain with a pair of binoculars. "Movement!"

"What is it?" asked Peck, taking the binoculars.

"Way up there, along the top of the ridge. I saw some movement."

Peck scanned the ridge. A small crowd hurried north along the trail, exposed on a rocky outcrop. "Rebels! They're making a run for it! Let's see what that artillery can do."

MacDonald gave an order to two of his men. "Get a bearing on that location and bring around one of the guns."

The soldiers ran over to one of the motorized artillery and started up the engine. The truck bounced out of the formation and turned its large gun barrel to point up at the ridge. One soldier took a bearing with a small handheld instrument, while two others loaded a shell. Peck marveled at their discipline and efficiency.

"Ready, sir," said one of the men.

MacDonald took out his own binoculars and scrutinized the mountain. "I see them," he said. He turned to Peck. "How do you know they're rebels?"

"Anyone up on that mountain is a rebel. Look, they're making a run for it. We've been waiting for this. Let's hit them!"

MacDonald looked through his binoculars again. "Okay, Captain, I see several men, and they appear to be armed." He gave an order to his men. "Fire when ready."

The soldiers covered their ears with their hands. Peck's men shuffled in place, glancing at one another, uncertain.

"If you want to keep your eardrums I suggest you cover your ears," said MacDonald, covering his own.

Peck and his men did so just in time. The barrel of the artillery piece erupted in flame and smoke, and Peck and his men recoiled at the shock. Within a few seconds, there was a puff of an explosion on top of the ridge.

Peck lifted his binoculars. The rebel crowd was unharmed, running for their lives. "Missed!" he said, disappointed.

"Adjust your bearings and fire another round," said MacDonald.

The gun blasted away again. This time Peck saw an explosion right in the middle of the group. Bodies tossed into the air.

"Hit!" said Peck, thrilled by the power of the long-distance killing machine "Ha! Shoot another one!"

"Hang on," said MacDonald, adjusting his own binoculars. "There are women and children up there!"

"So what?"

"Cease fire!" MacDonald yelled.

"It doesn't matter," said Peck. "They're rebels, all of them. Blast them before they get away!"

"On whose authority?"

Peck straightened. "I am my own authority."

"Professional soldiers do not kill civilians, Captain!"

"Those are enemy combatants, Jack. We can't get to know each and every one of them before we kill them."

MacDonald scanned the mountain again then turned on Peck. "The priority of this mission is to ensure and protect the fuel supply—period. If there is a rebel force that threatens that supply, we will eliminate it. But civilian casualties are to be kept to a minimum, and we are certainly *not* going to participate in a massacre of women and children. Is that understood?"

Peck didn't budge. "Need I remind you of the chain of command?"

"I don't take orders from you," said MacDonald. He raised his voice so that all the men around him could hear. "We'll begin the assault first thing tomorrow morning. My troops will be in the lead, and this operation will be under my command."

"Now, see here—"

"No, you see here," MacDonald snapped. "You and your men are to stay in the rear and act as advisors only. I will call you as needed. And if needed."

MacDonald's men closed ranks around their captain, squaring off against Peck and his men, faces hard.

"We've heard as much as we need to from you today," said MacDonald, turning back to the map. "Dismissed."

❧

A loud boom shook the cavern. Pebbles and dust fell from the top of the cave, and everyone cowered in unison.

"That sounded like artillery," said Hodgkins.

"Come on!" said Amariah. He led Hodgkins and his men through the cavern and up to the ledge, emerging on their hands and knees, leveraging the safety of a large rock.

Hodgkins whistled as he scanned the view. "What are they shooting at?"

Amariah searched for the refugees who had ignored his advice and crossed the ridge, including the Bowmans. "There," he said, pointing down to the right.

Nearly a mile away, two dozen men, women, and children scurried down the trail.

On the floor of the valley, a puff of smoke erupted from an artillery piece, sending a shell tearing through the air. The blast obliterated the small crowd in a plume of fire and smoke.

"Oh no," gasped Amariah.

"The bastards!"

Hannah! As the smoke cleared, Amariah nearly vomited at the sight of body parts strewn among the rocks. He tensed up, anticipating the final shell that would finish them off. But none came.

Hodgkins turned to one of his men. "Get down there right now and see what you can do."

"I'm going too," said Amariah. He stood and turned, ready to help although fearing the worst, when standing at the entrance to the ledge, he saw Hannah, uninjured, her hands cradling her head, tears in her eyes.

"I was coming back," she sobbed. "I didn't want to leave you here. No one else was following us, so I wanted to come

223

back and see what—" She pointed down the trail. "My father!"

She collapsed, gasping for breath between crying spasms, a drowning woman. Amariah held her close.

In the distance, like a swarm of approaching bees, came the growl of NVM planes. A half dozen small dots appeared from the direction of Burlington, flying in formation.

Amariah led the weeping Hannah over to the rock to hide beside Hodgkins. There they hid while the aircraft flew overhead—dark green biplanes bristling with weaponry. The planes circled over the site of his former home and came in for a landing on the grass airstrip.

The summer killing season had begun.

Hodgkins quietly observed the troops and heavy equipment in the valley, then put the binoculars down and contemplated Hannah, head in her hands.

He turned to Amariah.

"Tell me more about those hang gliders."

&

In the barracks by the main gate, Peck toyed with his rabbit stew, the meat dry and tough. He wondered what Mac-Donald and his soldiers were eating in the tents they had pitched out in the field. Probably salted beef or fish. Unlike his internal security forces, those men were real soldiers, with true logistical skills. They weren't eating goddamned rabbits.

He was still smarting over his humiliation. Okay, perhaps he had overplayed his hand a bit, but that was no reason for MacDonald to be so harsh. To make a fellow officer look bad like that in front of his men; it wasn't fair.

He spit a piece of bone onto his plate. At the very least, he would insist that he be given total control over the prisoners. Anyone not killed outright would be interrogated, and after MacDonald left, any girls above the age of fourteen would be passed around for his men to do what they pleased.

Through the barred door of the detention area, the male prisoner, Daniel, lay in his tiny cell, leg amputated above the knee, the final act of the doctor who had apparently fled for good. The formerly burly man, traumatized by an amputation performed without painkillers, spent his days staring weakly at the ceiling.

"We're going to go and get your friends tomorrow," Peck taunted. "Maybe you can have a little reunion. Let us know which of the girls are worth having." He egged his men on, and they chuckled.

The female prisoner turned and glared at him. She hadn't said a single word despite the waterboarding.

"What are you looking at, bitch?" He stood and flung his plate at her cell, shattering it against the bars.

The woman turned away. He would break her, given time.

The door opened. It was one of the new young guardsmen, stationed at the front gate. "Er, excuse me, Captain. Can I speak to you for a moment?"

Peck drew his sleeve across his mouth and limped out of the room.

"There's a woman down at the gate," the young man said, hesitantly. "In an automobile. She says she's Malinger's wife. I told her we're under lockdown, but she won't leave. She insists on seeing you."

Peck followed the guard to the gate. Outside the barred window, a Range Rover waited, engine running, headlights burning bright. Madeline Malinger sat in the back, illuminated by a small lamp, all hat and mascara.

"Looks like someone got lonely in Albany all by herself," said Peck. He picked a piece of food out of his teeth, opened the heavy door, and warily approached the car.

The Yorker woman lowered her window. "Captain, how nice to see you!" she cooed.

"Madeline. What can I do for you?"

"I've come for my husband and son."

"They're a little busy right now."

"Yes, I can see that. You've got yourself an entire army now, Captain. I'm impressed." The blonde Yorker shifted in the car seat, revealing her ample bosom.

"We're on lockdown. No one comes in or out. I'm sorry, but that's the way it is."

"But Captain, I came all the way across the lake. I couldn't get here any sooner. It was frozen the entire winter—we were only able to get our boat up again now."

"If you'd like to leave a message, I'll see that they get it."

"Captain, I realize that your time is valuable. So, let me be completely frank. I want my husband and son to come home. Surely with all of these men under your command, there must be someone else who can run the refinery?" She leaned forward, making an obvious display of cleavage.

Peck took a moment to appreciate the view, resting his arms on the car door. "Madeline, to be completely frank with *you*, your husband screwed up, royally. But we've given him the opportunity to make things right. Once the growing season is over, I will entertain other suggestions," he paused, and took another good look, "but for now they will stay here until I'm done with them."

"Isn't there anything I can do?"

Peck hesitated. The woman wasn't bad looking, but this was neither the time nor the place. Besides, who knew what kind of tricks she had up her sleeve.

"Not right now."

The woman sat back. "I hear that you are on the verge of a great victory, Captain. I brought along something to celebrate." She addressed her driver. "Jason, open the trunk."

The driver got out and walked to the rear of the vehicle and opened it. Peck gripped his sidearm, glancing quickly around the back of the car. Inside the trunk were baskets of food, wine, whiskey, and brandy.

He walked back to the window. The sight of the liquor loosened his tongue. "As I said, Madeline, we're on lockdown tonight, so no guests. But stop by tomorrow and I'll see what I can do."

"I understand, Captain. Now is not a good time. But please, take some brandy for you and your men. It's from my father's own vineyard. The kind you like. I'll come back in a few days and we can have a proper celebration after your victory."

Peck went back to the trunk and helped himself to a case of the brandy. She knew his taste well. While he was at it, he helped himself to some wine and food, piling each box onto the young guard, who tottered off.

"Captain, please understand that when I leave, I expect to take my husband and son with me."

Peck limped toward the gate. "Well, you'd better find a place to stay then. Because they're not going anywhere until the storage tanks are filled to the top."

CHAPTER NINETEEN

On the ledge above Pleasant Valley, illuminated only by the vast and starlit sky, Amariah contemplated the dark expanse between himself and his former home. Somewhere down there lay the remains of his parents, their lives over, beyond saving. However, everything they had worked for—the refinery, the oilseed fields, the stables and sheds, the hope that they offered for a reborn world—remained. And now, their only son was about to end it all in one final conflagration.

Behind him, working in silence, Hodgkins and his men labored side-by-side with their former enemies, warily cooperating in the shared perplexity of assembling the hang gliders. They had spent a couple of hours before sunset practicing outside of the ravine, and had learned the basics of unpowered flight. No fancy aerial acrobatics were required, they were simply going to launch the gliders, make a turn, sail over the wall and drop down as close as possible to their objective.

Amariah was already strapped into his harness and stood ready to go, the wings light and easy in the stillness of the night.

Hannah checked his glider over one final time, tugging at his straps more than necessary.

"Do you think they're there by now?" she asked.

Amariah reached for the pocket watch that hung around his neck and flipped it open, squinting at it in the starlight. "Yes, it's time."

Down by Joshua's tower, nearly a hundred men and women, led by Rebecca, awaited the explosion in the tower that would precede the opening of the secondary gate. Nearly every able-bodied adult had agreed to participate in the attack, emboldened by the unexpected arrival of Hodgkins and his men.

Hannah touched his forearm. "Amariah, I've changed my mind. I don't want to run away anymore. I want us to be together, to make a home together, right down there in Pleasant Valley. I want us to be a family. Promise you'll come back to me?"

Her uplifted face shone in the light, her eyes a brilliant blue, her brown hair loose down to her waist. She was undoubtedly the most beautiful woman he had ever seen.

He leaned in to embrace her, but the glider nearly knocked her over. He reached out to steady her, and she squirmed through the wires and gave him a quick kiss.

"I love you," he said.

She smiled and kissed him again, then stepped back to give the men room for the launch.

Hodgkins watched from a polite distance. "See you on the ground," he said.

Amariah focused on the objective that he and Hodgkins would take—the refinery. Ironically, the square necklace of sparkling security lights would serve as an unintended beacon for their attack. To the right, the Northern Army's tanks, artillery, and support vehicles, parked closely together in the fields in the classic mistake of an overconfident opponent, would be the target of the men behind him.

He took a deep breath, exhaled, then strode quickly off the ledge and out over the void. The night air struck him at once, colder than his last flight. He shot forward, the glider seeming to travel faster than before, the drop below deep and terrifying. He clutched the control bar tightly, as if holding on would make any difference, then clumsily shifted his weight. The glider responded, and he steered left toward the lights of the refinery, giving the men behind him as simple an approach as possible.

He hadn't counted on the cold. The chill went right through his clothing, causing a cramp he couldn't shake. It took everything he had to resist the urge to shed altitude. If he landed short, he would crash into the barrier wall, or worse, be impaled on the sharpened spikes of the no-man's-land.

At last, he sailed over the wall. The seed silos, from which his father had once fired upon Yorker militias, grew closer. He veered to the left and spilled air as quickly as he could, fearing that at any moment a bullet would penetrate his soft belly. Another tight turn brought him in behind the storage tanks. The ground rushed up to meet him and his feet hit the ground hard. He tripped and stumbled, falling flat.

He raised himself up, unbuckled the glider, and darted toward the maze of pipes behind the refinery. In the corner of his eye, he caught a glimpse of the next few gliders as they slid from the sky, black wings lit from below by the security lights, the approaches fast and clumsy, landings rough and scattered.

Sneaking through the infrastructure he knew so well, he reached the first pumping station, removed a charge from his belly pack, and slipped it into a darkened recess. A signal from a transmitter he carried would ignite the charge.

He moved quietly through the rest of the mechanical equipment, recalling moments in the sunshine when he and his father had worked together to install or fix the irreplaceable pumps, sensors, and electrical equipment he was now about to destroy. When his belly pack was nearly empty, he hustled over within sight of the loading dock, anxiously awaiting Hodgkins and the Wales Guard.

Shadowy figures scurried toward his position. Hodgkins reached him first, his bald head hidden under a black cap. He gave the thumbs-up, the signal for having successfully planted explosives around the biomass processor.

Hodgkins grabbed his arm and motioned for him to wait. Then he and the Wales Guard entered the refinery, silently, stealthily.

Amariah waited, expecting to hear muffled gunshots. Finally, fearing the worst, he grabbed a charge in one hand, and the detonator in the other, preparing to storm inside, when the door opened, and one of the guardsmen casually waved him inside.

Amariah entered the cavernous processing room. It hummed with power, ablaze with electric lights. A different world. It was his first time back in the building since the morning of the fire, a lifetime ago. But the past was the past.

Covered by Hodgkins, he went directly to the enormous mixing tanks and attached the last of his explosives to the central cylinder, catching a glimpse of himself in the brushed steel.

"I'm sorry, Father," he whispered.

231

၈၃

Unconscious, deep in a drunken sleep, Peck lay snoring, oblivious to the world. The deep thump of an explosion shook him awake.

Groggily, he pushed himself up from the cot in the back of the barracks. An orange glow flickered through the barred window. Was he dreaming?

He reached for the lantern on his nightstand, but knocked over a half-empty bottle of Madeline's brandy instead. Cursing, he rose, woozy and thick-headed. He had passed out in his clothes. His uniform was a wrinkled mess, his boot laces half-untied. The room spun.

He tried to recall the evening. He hadn't had that much to drink. He stumbled over to the tiny window, nauseous. The nearest watchtower burned like a giant torch in the night.

Pounding rattled his door. Peck staggered over and opened it.

"What's going on?"

Dickins stood in his underwear. "There's been an explosion, in one of the watchtowers," he stammered. "It's on fire!"

Peck stumbled into the main bunkroom. His men appeared just as groggy as he was, falling out of their beds, awkwardly climbing into their clothes.

"The bitch drugged us!"

Another explosion shook the air, followed by another, and another. Through the windows, fireballs erupted in the field.

"The planes! We've got to get to the planes!"

All around him, men fumbled for their weapons. Peck hurried to his room to retrieve his sidearm. When he emerged, he saw the rebel Daniel standing upright on his one leg, a smirk across his dirty face.

Peck un-holstered his gun, intending to shoot the rebel dead on the spot. Another explosion rocked the night, this one much louder than the ones before. The entire building shook.

The rebel ducked to the ground and rolled underneath his cot.

"Let's go! Move!" said Peck. The rebel could wait.

His men swung open the door. The first one to exit fell dead. Bullets slammed into the door frame and the others threw themselves back into the room.

"Out the back!" yelled Peck.

Heads low, they moved toward the rear door. Dickins un-latched it and gently inched it open, peering outside.

"Go on!" urged Peck, shoving his lieutenant into the darkness.

Dickins cowered, expecting to be shot, then dashed pell-mell for the bushes, pants falling around his ankles. Peck lingered for a moment, then hobbled through the door, zigzagging until he reached the trees.

He tried to get his bearings. The watchtower smoldered red; the orange flames of equipment burning in the fields illuminated the valley. A trail led into the woods, behind where the mansion used to stand, and he scrambled up it and into the thickening underbrush. Branches pulled at his clothes and scraped his face. The deeper he went into the trees, the more they seemed to grab at him. He moved faster, trying to break through the clawing branches. Nettles caught his pants and dug into his legs and hands. In a growing frenzy, he fought back against the branches as he ran, causing them to whip at him even more.

He dashed into a small clearing. Halfway across, he tripped over a fallen piece of wood and went sprawling, feeling blood seep out of his wound.

"Dammit, dammit, dammit!" he cried, the pain in his leg bringing tears to his eyes. He gripped his leg and rolled over onto his back, his shoulder brushing against the object that had tripped him—a white cross, tipped onto its side, dislodged by the thawed earth. Peck sat up with a start. He lay directly on top of the graves of Kenan and Sarah Wales. His hands sank into the moist dirt as if he was being pulled into the ground.

He screamed, jumped to his feet, and ran blindly into the woods. He sobbed as he fled, half-expecting the cold dead hand of Kenan Wales to fall on his shoulder.

ॐ

"That's it," said Amariah, holding up the small radio trigger. "When I flip this switch, the whole place blows sky high—if it comes to it."

Hodgkins twitched. "Be careful with that thing."

The ground below them shook, and the largest explosion of the night sent a shockwave that Amariah could feel in the center of his chest. Dust fell from the brick walls, and Amariah fumbled with the trigger, nearly dropping it.

Hodgkins noticed the save, and swallowed. "That was the ammo."

Amariah nodded. All was going according to plan. So far, the only thing that had not gone well was the intended arrest of the Malingers. The Wales Guards had searched the facility from top to bottom, but the Yorkers could not be found. Bunks empty, living quarters abandoned, it appeared as if they had left in a hurry, leaving everything behind.

"Phoenix!" called a voice from outside the door.

234

Hodgkins lowered his weapon. "Phoenix" was the code name assigned to the mission. A guardsman poked his head around the door and entered the room with several others, their faces dirty, eyes intensely alert.

"We followed footprints to the wall," said the guardsman. "There was a ladder on the other side and tire tracks in the road."

"They're halfway down the lake by now," growled Hodgkins.

"We'll get them another day," said Amariah. "They're not that important."

"They're important to me."

Amariah took in the scene before him as if it were the last thing he would ever see. Right there in the room, the fate of the known world hung in the balance. The refinery, the source of all liquid fuel in Northern Vermont, was primed with explosives, and Amariah held the trigger. If he flipped the switch there would be no more fuel: no more lighting oil for lamps, heating oil for space heaters, stovetop oil for boiling water and cooking food, no powered flight, no mechanized agriculture, and no electricity in the big manor houses of the Stakeholders. Their little world, the last bastion of known civilization, would fall back to pre-industrialized times, and starvation would be always at the door.

A commotion down at the entrance of the administrative building echoed through the halls. Hodgkins motioned for Amariah to take cover as he and his men took up firing positions.

"Phoenix!" came the call.

"Come forward!" shouted Hodgkins.

A squad of Wales Guards entered the room, escorting three prisoners in the uniforms of the Northern Army.

"Bring them here," ordered Hodgkins.

The squad had been given a special task: to take Captain Jack MacDonald alive. They had succeeded.

Amariah emerged from behind the steel mixing tank. "Captain MacDonald," he said.

The professional soldier carried himself with an easy poise, even under arrest. His eyes widened. "Amariah Wales? What the—I thought you were dead!"

"I'm very much alive, thank you, Captain," said Amariah. "But perhaps you would care to explain why you have tanks and artillery in my fields, and why you are vandalizing my farm?"

MacDonald stood dumbfounded. Whatever fate he had expected, explaining himself to Amariah Wales had probably been the last thing he expected.

He straightened. "We were told that the refinery was under attack by rebel forces, so we came down from the border to help protect it," he said, glancing over at his two men. "But things are not exactly as they were described."

"Is that your artillery out there?"

"You know it is."

"So then you are the person responsible for the murder of a dozen civilians, including women and children, on the ridge yesterday afternoon."

MacDonald's jaw stiffened. "Yes, I am responsible."

Amariah examined the man closely. His father had always spoken highly of MacDonald. He had integrity.

"Captain MacDonald, the people around here have been terrorized by the NVM for years. When my parents were still alive, we turned a blind eye to their worst excesses. My parents are dead, and there's nothing they can do to make up for it, but I can, and I will." Amariah motioned to the guards-men. "Untie them, please."

The Wales Guard did so, respectfully. The captives rubbed their sore wrists.

"Let me tell you what is going to happen here, Captain," said Amariah. "Peck and his NVM are going to be held ac-countable for their crimes. There will be a public trial, and the worst offenders will be punished." A great deal depended on this moment, Amariah knew. It would be ironic if his sweaty hands somehow activated the trigger he held behind his back. He shifted hands and continued. "This refinery, however, is going to stay in operation, providing fuel for the people, for tractors, for electric generators, and for civilian aircraft. It will also continue to provide you and your troops with fuel for the defense of our borders."

Hodgkins looked at him, surprised.

"The people you call rebels are farmers," said Amariah. "They only became rebels because of the brutality they en-dured under Peck's militarized police. They will return to their farms, and their rights will be restored. There will be elections, civilian oversight of the military, and accountabil-ity, starting today."

MacDonald regarded him with a tilt of his head. "So that's what this is all about?"

Amariah nodded. "That's what it's all about, Captain. The NVM will be disbanded permanently, but I would like to see you and your men keep your positions, and whatever of your equipment you can salvage. You can be a part of this, but I need your commitment right here and now."

Outside, small arms fire echoed in the night. MacDonald contemplated the floor, apparently reluctant to agree under duress.

"One thing is certain, Captain," said Amariah. "Things will not continue the way they are."

He held the trigger out before him. "If I throw this switch, some very powerful explosives will blow these tanks apart, destroy critical infrastructure outside, and render this refinery inoperable. That will be the end of the fuel for your military, and the world as you know it, whether you like it or not. But if you help me, help me restore the rule of law, we can leave this facility intact."

Amariah lifted the trigger higher. "I do not intend to kill you all—you are free to go if you wish. But if you do, the rebels outside will consider you their enemy, and you will have to fight your way back to your troops." Amariah felt the world closing in. "If your answer is no, I would not linger. In fact, I suggest that you leave right now, and run for your lives."

The soldiers glanced at the door, and at one another.

MacDonald loosened up. "All right, dammit. You'll have my support."

Amariah lowered the trigger, and nodded. "Thank you. Hodgkins, is the flag ready?"

"Ready."

"We are going to raise a white flag, Captain," said Amariah. "Not a flag of surrender, but a flag of truce. We are also going to sound a siren. It is a signal to the men and women out there to stop fighting. We expect your troops to do the same, and to put all the NVM you see under arrest."

"I'll have to tell them first," said MacDonald.

"You may send your men to spread the word, Captain, but I'd like you to stay here with us. At dawn, I expect to see your troops assembled on the west side of the creek. Tell them to place their weapons in piles, and then stand in formation as a sign of their compliance. If your men decide to make a run for it, let them be reminded that the barrier can keep people in, as well as out."

MacDonald turned to his men. "Do as he says."

Eight months of watching Anne handle difficult situations had taught Amariah much about handling delicate situations in confined quarters. "Why don't you join us up top, Captain, and we'll watch together?" he offered.

He waved over one of the guardsmen and gently handed the man the trigger.

"Stay here and hold onto this," said Amariah. "Don't touch anything, just hold onto it."

The man took it gingerly.

"This will keep everyone honest, I trust?" said Amariah. He gestured for MacDonald to precede him up the stairs. Before they went more than a few steps, Amariah stopped, turned around, and hurried back to the man with the trigger.

"That one," he said, pointing to a toggle switch with a metal thumb guard over the top. "Whatever you do, do not throw that switch while we're all still in here, understand?"

The man nodded, eyes wide. Another guardsman got him a chair. He eased down into it.

Hodgkins led the way up the circular steel staircase and the three of them strode out onto the roof, the valley spread out before them. Artillery, trucks, and other equipment blazed in the fields like haystacks on fire. Thick black smoke poured into a brightening sky.

"Oh geez," said MacDonald, taking stock of the ruined equipment. "I hope you guys speak French. You're going to need it."

Hodgkins waved his hand with a flourish. *"Ce'st la vie."*

Amariah chuckled. "You're going to have to work on the accent."

He walked over to a panel on the wall. Years ago, the facility had been equipped with a siren to call the fire brigade in case of emergency. Amariah hoped it would still work. He pulled open the small metal door and pushed the button.

Above their heads, a slow, mournful siren wailed over the valley. Amariah took the flag from Hodgkins, attached it to the rope on the flagpole, and raised it hand over hand, the signal for the rebels to stop fighting.

A distant cheer went up from the barrier walls, and Amariah smiled.

The battle was over. The rebels had won.

CHAPTER TWENTY

The sun crept over the ridge of Mount Mansfield, bringing with it the light and warmth of a bright spring morning. Escorted by Hodgkins and his men, Amariah walked up the road he had traveled so often with Charlemagne, past the smoldering remains of artillery pieces, tanks, and aircraft, the smoke acrid and harsh.

While the Northern Army had suffered very few casualties, the same could not be said for the NVM. Around the barracks, dead bodies littered the ground, taken down by sniper fire and Rebecca's assault team. Those who had not been shot or clubbed to death had been rounded up and roped into circles on the ground, hands tied behind their backs.

Lieutenant Dickins dropped his head as Amariah walked by, his formerly pristine uniform stained with blood. The lieutenant was never far from his master, but as far as Amariah could tell, Peck wasn't among the prisoners; nor the dead.

From the front door of the barracks, Anne and Daniel emerged, helped along by Rebecca and her team. Anne stood erect, moving stiffly, her swollen and haggard face suggesting mistreatment. Daniel, however, had to be carried out.

Amariah gasped at his appearance: grey and weak, his right leg amputated above the knee.

But when he saw Amariah, he broke out into a smile. "It seems our Master Wales has saved the day," he said, voice hoarse. "And you found time for a haircut too. How nice."

Amariah pretended not to notice his friend's condition. "I had some help," he said, looking over at Hodgkins.

"His girlfriend cut it, not me," the guardsman dead-panned.

Daniel smiled, and his helpers eased him down onto a bench in the yard.

Anne had disappeared in Rebecca's embrace. Amid the tangle of hugs and kisses, it was unclear who was consoling whom. After a few moments, Anne detached herself and approached her nephew, beaming.

"Nice work," she said. "I'm—"

The roar of an aircraft engine shattered the moment. All heads turned to the runway as an NVM plane bolted out of the hangar at the far end of the valley and accelerated wildly down the airfield.

"Hodgkins!" said Amariah, alarmed. "I thought you took out all the planes?"

"We took out the ones we saw land. You didn't tell us there were more in the hangar!"

Everyone ducked as the dark green biplane roared over their heads. It circled, gained altitude, and then dove toward the barrier wall by Joshua's tower. The flashing light of the machine-gun fire reached them before the sound of the chattering guns.

"It's Peck!" shouted Amariah.

The plane pulled up sharply, circled around the burned-out tower, and headed straight for them.

"Get back inside!"

Amariah grabbed Anne around the waist and pulled her up the wooden stairs. "Everyone under the table! Stay away from the windows!"

Rebecca screamed. "Daniel! He's still outside!"

Amariah dashed back over to the door and saw Daniel crawling toward the door, stump dragging. Two lines of bullets raced along the ground and cut right across his back. He arched one final time, then dropped and lay motionless.

Rebecca screamed, "No!"

Amariah held her back. "Stay here!"

"What are we going to do?"

"Stay inside!"

Amariah dashed out of the door and ran up the hill toward the site of his former home, sprinting up the driveway under the scorched trees, past the stone staircase that led to empty air. Up ahead, the doors to the stable were wide open, and he ran right in. Urgently, he checked the stalls until he found his beloved friend.

"Charlemagne!"

His horse lifted his head and nodded up and down, excited to see him. There was no time to tack up. Amariah opened the stall and jumped on his back.

"Master Wales!" exclaimed the stable master, looking as if he had just seen a ghost.

"Stay out of sight, Mr. Tipton!" shouted Amariah as he barreled past.

Above the barrier wall, Peck's plane picked off its defenders. Amariah took off down the road as fast as he could, reunited at last with Charlemagne, holding on with his legs, his fingers in the horse's mane, the two friends complete again. Memories flooded through him, thousands of trips back and forth through his valley, his mother and father waiting for him at either end, the faces of the dead urging him on faster and faster.

In front of the hangar, a small crowd stood watching open-mouthed as Peck attacked. Among them, amazingly, was Caleb, appearing exactly as he did the last time Amariah saw him. The man turned and stared at him as he ran up, his face contorted, as if trying to solve a puzzle. Then his face broke open with the shock of recognition.

"Amariah!" he exclaimed. "You're alive!"

The men around him, servants whose faces Amariah remembered, gasped.

Amariah ran right past them, through the hangar doors, and up to his father's golden plane. He checked the cockpit. The fuel gauge showed a third of a tank. He yanked the blocks out from the wheels.

"Caleb, get Charlemagne out of here and take care of him!" shouted Amariah. "You," he commanded, "throw the prop!" There was no time for them to push the plane outside. "No, no, right here!"

The engine caught and let loose a belch of smoke. Amariah quickly buckled himself into his father's seat. He opened the glove compartment and found his father's cloth helmet and goggles, the same ones Kenan had worn the fateful day he flew in with Glen Malinger. Amariah strapped them on. They still bore his father's scent.

Amariah increased the throttle to a deafening roar and steered the plane out of the hangar, praying that Peck wouldn't notice him until he was airborne. He raced down the runway until he reached twice the speed of his galloping horse, then pulled back on the stick and rose sharply into the air, pressed back into his seat by the uncompromising g-forces.

Higher and higher he climbed, gaining altitude, while Peck's plane continued to fire at the base of Joshua's watch-tower, like a fisher cat trying to pry out its prey. Amariah suddenly realized that he was going up against Peck un-armed—his father's plane was designed for transport, not armed combat.

Too late now!

Acting instinctively, with the memory of the hang glider flight still in his veins, he pushed the stick forward, zeroing in on Peck's plane. Diving as close as he dared, he swept over the green military craft at high speed, trying to knock it out of the sky.

Peck's plane wobbled. Amariah circled in tight for anoth-er pass and flew past it again, nearly clipping the captain's wings. Peck narrowly missed the stone watchtower, then banked hard and peeled away.

Amariah no longer had the advantage. He throttled up and tried to gain altitude, the force of the acceleration weigh-ing on his chest. Peck closed the distance and opened up his machine guns. Amariah threw the plane into a barrel roll, avoiding the spray of gunfire.

The two planes danced around one another in a deadly ballet—Amariah flying as fast as he could, trying to outrace and outmaneuver Peck, while the murderer in uniform took every opportunity to shoot him to pieces.

Amariah looked for an advantage but had none. Peck grew bolder, closing in, the predator against his prey. Then the more experienced Peck found his target, and bullets tore into Amariah's canvas, just missing the cockpit.

He had one last chance. Remembering something his father had told him long ago about desperate pilots facing no-win situations, he pulled back hard on the stick and gained as much altitude as he could, turning his father's plane upside down in a giant loop. For a moment, the entire earth was above his head, as if he was flying beneath it. Peck had broken off, and now Amariah raced down on his six o'clock.

Pushing forward with everything he had, he inched his plane up behind the green NVM attack plane and drove his propeller into its tail. The back of the plane shattered into thousands of pieces, fragments flying. Suddenly rudderless, Peck's plane flipped onto its nose and dove straight down, gaining speed until it smashed into the parapets along the top of the barrier wall, ejecting Peck directly into the field of sharp wooden pickets, skewering him on the sharp spikes.

There was no time to celebrate. Somewhere out there Hannah was watching, praying for his safe return.

The stick shuddered violently in his hands. The impact had damaged his propeller and thrown the plane off-kilter. With all his strength, he pulled the plane around over the landing strip, hitting the ground diagonally across the runway before lurching to a stop, engine smoking. He unbuckled himself and scrambled out of the cockpit.

Ears ringing, he staggered to a safe distance and pulled off the helmet and goggles. He fell to his knees, drove his hands into the cool, moist earth, and raised the loamy soil in his cupped hands.

He was home.

ৎও

The smoke of the battle cleared during the course of the afternoon, hastened away by a warm spring breeze. Above Amariah's head, fresh green leaves, newly emerged from the trees left undamaged by the house fire, rustled in their eternal way, just as they had on thousands of warm afternoons before. He had watched these same trees from his window as a boy, cycling through each season of life, loss, dormancy, and rebirth.

Around the empty perimeter of his former home, however, a dozen dead, scorched trees would not be coming back to life—the magnificent hard rock maples that had trembled in the stiffening wind on the last day he had spent with his mother. Their broken branches rose into the air as if frozen in horror by the conflagration that had killed them. But now, these victims of the crime would also bear witness to the testimony.

The heir to Pleasant Valley sat in the center of the circular driveway that had once graced the front of his mansion, at one of two tables brought up from the barracks. Quietly, unobtrusively, he took even, steady breaths, preparing for the final confrontation of the momentous day. Hodgkins sat to his left, leg jumping with impatient anticipation, Rebecca and Anne to his right, consoling one another, eyes red, faces distraught over Daniel's horrific death.

Around the perimeter of the driveway, the battle's victors had assembled at Amariah's request. The rebel fighters and their unlikely allies, the Wales Guard, stood uneasily on one side of the driveway, MacDonald's troops on the other. No NVM were present; every one of Peck's men had been killed, beaten, or arrested.

Jack MacDonald, seated on the stone staircase, rose to his feet. "They're here."

Coming up the main drive, the Stakeholders' carriages and automobiles approached between armed escorts. As the vehicles slowed to a stop, the faces of the Stakeholders fell at the sight of the crowd. Some balked and tried to pull away, but MacDonald's men opened their doors and threatened to drag the occupants to the table if they didn't come willingly.

An awkward silence hung over the scene as each Stakeholder took a seat facing the young master, framed by the empty space where his home once stood. Craggs sat first, Dotty Labreche last, but all of them were tense, unaccustomed to being surrounded by more than a hundred armed men and women.

Amariah opened his watch and checked the time, brushing his thumb over the inscription. Had his parents been watching over him during his travails? He thought so. And he hoped they were still watching now.

At precisely five o'clock, the same hour at which the Stakeholders had arrived for the banquet, Amariah rose to his feet and raised his voice to full strength.

"Today, at great peril to themselves, and with considerable loss of life and suffering, the people of Northern Vermont took back what had been stolen from them—their freedom and their dignity."

He focused on the Stakeholders. "Each of you, either through your actions or your inaction, caused many innocent lives to be lost or ruined. Board of Stakeholders of the Territory of Northern Vermont—it is time for an accounting of misdeeds."

Craggs made every effort to appear unimpressed. "May I speak?" he asked, in his distinctive gravelly voice.

"You may," replied Amariah.

"Well, first of all, it is wonderful to see you alive, Amariah. Welcome home. We were all very worried about you. As for the rest of your comments, and all of this," he waved dismissively at the armed throng, "I'm not sure where it's coming from. No one stole your property. The fact is, you disappeared, leaving the rest of us to clean up after the disaster here. Not only that, you abandoned your responsibilities at the refinery, and failed to fulfill your family's obligation to the people of this community, leaving all of us here in a rather difficult position."

Rebecca nearly spoke, but Amariah placed his hand on her arm.

Craggs scanned his opponents with contempt. "Now you have returned, and in rather poor company I might add, inflicting additional damage to your fellow citizens in the process."

"Ha!" exclaimed Rebecca.

Amariah leveled his gaze at Craggs. "You are the one most responsible for what happened here, Craggs. When my father wouldn't go along with your plans to clear cut the forest, you arranged to have him removed."

Craggs shook his head. "Amariah, out of respect for the memory of your esteemed parents, I agreed to come here today in a spirit of mutual cooperation. But, frankly, I think they would both be appalled at this performance. I had nothing to do with what happened here. As you may recall, it was the Yorkers working with Peck that caused your house to burn down, aided by your trigger-happy guardsmen."

Hodgkins remained silent, glaring at Craggs, leg jumping.

Amariah reached into his jacket and pulled out a folded piece of paper he had found that morning among Malinger's possessions, after he had returned to the refinery to relieve the nervous soldier of the remote-controlled trigger.

"This is a letter from you, Craggs, to Malinger," said Amariah. "In it, you go into great detail regarding your frustrations with my father's unwillingness to share the secret of the biomass processor. You wanted to start tearing down the forest to make fuel to make up for the declining oilseed output on the farms. You invited Malinger to come up with a way to get what you wanted, then you left everyone else to fight it out while you sat back and watched."

Craggs chuckled. "I wrote no such letter."

"This is your handwriting, Craggs, and your signature," bellowed Amariah. "I've seen many of your letters to my father over the years."

Dotty Labreche spoke up, her voice without its usual politesse. "It's over, Craggs. You went too far, admit it. Take responsibility for once in your life."

"Now, just a moment," said Craggs, businesslike. "These are all lies. This young man has been through a traumatic experience. His judgment has been influenced by his kidnappers here. For all we know, he has been brainwashed."

He turned back to Amariah, conciliatory. "There will be plenty of time for investigations into what happened. When you have recovered from your ordeal you can take the vacant spot left by your father on the Stakeholder Board. Until then, I think it's best that we call this meeting adjourned."

Amariah slammed his fist into the table. "Bullshit, Craggs! I saw you at the banquet the night of the fire. You and your family pushed me aside and stepped right over my father as he lay dying on the floor! You knew what was going to happen that night. Peck and Malinger could never have pulled off what they did without you!"

Angry shouts erupted from the crowd in support of Amariah. Dotty Labreche raised her hand and the shouting subsided.

"What Amariah says is true," admitted Dotty. "I tried to warn Kenan, but he didn't believe me."

Anne leaned over and whispered, "It was Dotty who kept us alive. She and her sister were our main suppliers. Whatever she might have done in the past, she's already made up for it."

Amariah nodded. "Bernard Craggs, I assert my family's right as a founding member of this Board. I move that you be stripped of your title as chairman and dismissed. I nominate Dotty Labreche to be the new Chair. All in favor?"

The rest of the Board saw which way the wind was blowing. "Aye," they mumbled.

"Well, if that's the way it's going to be," said Craggs, "I have one last act as chair, Amariah, and that is to put you under arrest before you can do any more harm. MacDonald ..." He waved to the captain, not bothering to check for his consent.

Jack MacDonald didn't move from his seat on the stairs. "Why don't you do it yourself, Craggs?"

The old man balked, and backed away, looking for a way out. "I'm leaving. Bring my carriage around." He scanned the crowd, looking for anyone to assist him. No one did.

"Oh, you'll be leaving all right," said Amariah. "In fact, you and your entire family will all be leaving. For your crimes, you are herewith banished from the Territory of Northern Vermont. Your lands and property are forfeit. The farmland you stole will be returned to the rightful owners, and you will leave here as you left them: penniless and poor."

From the direction of the stables, a green prison wagon drawn by four horses drove up. On top sat two fresh-faced young soldiers. MacDonald's men.

"You and your family will be brought to the Connecticut River and deposited on the other side. If any of you are ever seen in this territory again, you will be shot on sight. Consider yourself warned."

MacDonald's soldiers gripped the corpulent man by the arms and dragged him to the wagon. They shoved him into the back and threw the bolt shut, and the wagon drove away toward the gate.

"As for the rest of you," said Amariah. "All of the land that you've taken from the people will be returned to their rightful owners. Furthermore, all indentured farmhands are to be released and allowed to go free, effective immediately."

Dotty nodded. "Is there anything else, Amariah?"

"Yes, there is. Town Hall meetings are to be restored. The Board of Stakeholders will become an advisory body only. Power is being transferred back to the people. And if any of you don't like it, you can resign and run for election. They will be held this fall."

With great dignity, Dotty stood, walked over to the center chair that had been occupied by Craggs and sat down.

"Amariah," she said, "on behalf of this Board, I apologize for the suffering that has been visited upon you and your family. I know it is small compensation, but I move that your home be rebuilt, exactly as it was, and that it be paid for by the Board. There will be a Wales mansion again, and there will be a Wales family in it, as there should be."

Applause broke out. Amariah put a stop to it. "That's very kind of you, Dotty, but no. This land will remain the way it is, in memory of what happened here. The grounds will be restored, and the fields repaired, but this site will be a memorial and a park for the living to enjoy."

Dotty nodded. "Very well," she said. "I'd like to assure you, then, that this Board is committed to the responsible use of your biomass processor for the common good. I look forward to you taking over the refinery and increasing the output—responsibly—as your father desired."

Amariah checked his watch again, carefully noting the minute hand.

"No, Dotty," he said, snapping the watch shut. "What you are suggesting is impossible. The temptation will always be there to take more from the land than it can provide. My father saw that danger, and so do I."

Dotty's eyebrows furrowed. She had been following a script, and suddenly it had changed. "I don't understand," she said, glancing at Anne.

"The refinery shall remain, but control will be returned to the farmers' cooperative," said Amariah. "This facility will only produce as much fuel as the land can support, and no more. As for the biomass processor, the trees of the forest cannot restore the world that was lost. The secret of the enzyme will remain with me until the day I die, and the processor will be destroyed to remove the temptation to use it."

"Well, now," said Dotty. "Let's not be too hasty—"

Amariah glanced over at MacDonald, and then at Hodgkins, who both nodded.

"What's going on?" asked Dotty.

"It's the end of the world as we know it, Dotty, and the beginning of the new."

Hodgkins produced the radio-controlled trigger, flipped open the protective guard, and pushed the toggle switch over. There was a flash of light down at the other end of the valley as the biomass processor blew apart. A large cloud of black smoke rose into the sky as the shockwave reached them.

"Oh my God!" exclaimed Dotty, hands over her ears. "What did you just do?"

Amariah watched the last bits of debris from his father's invention come falling to the ground. The biomass processor had been completely destroyed.

Anne leapt up and gripped his arm, her face pleading. She pointed down the valley. "Amariah, the refinery, it's still standing!"

He put his hand over hers and gave it a reassuring squeeze.

"Yes, Anne, it is. And so it shall remain."

CHAPTER TWENTY-ONE

A strong summer sun pounded on the rooftop as Amariah Wales, proud owner of a small village home, drove the final nails into his recently milled cedar shingles. He put down his hammer and brushed the last specks of sawdust from the peak of the roof, releasing the wood's sweet perfume.

Wynant had done a fine job as usual; each shingle had been cut clean and sharp, each surface sanded smooth and bright.

Turning on his hands and knees, Amariah sat up against the incline and wiped the sweat from his brow. The morning sun had just crept over the mountain, revealing the valley in its full green splendor. He took a sip of cool water from an earthen jar he kept in his toolbox, idly observing the villagers as they planted, harvested, and weeded food crops beside the patchwork of ripening oilseed. From the way things were growing, there would be plenty of both food and fuel by the end of the season.

"Are you nearly done up there?" called Hannah from the yard. Three months pregnant, surrounded by her tidy vegetable garden, Amariah's wife beamed up at him, a picture of fertility.

"Yup. Just finished!"

"Well, you'd better come down then. You don't want to be late!" She shook her finger in a mock scolding, and Amariah laughed.

He climbed down the ladder, the sound of hammering echoing down the narrow street. He wasn't the only one working on his home this morning. Throughout the former workers' village, men and women mended roofs, rehung doors, and replaced broken windows. While the entire village had once belonged to his family, Amariah had divested ownership and split the homes up among the refugees, although everyone had insisted that Amariah and Hannah retain the finest residence for themselves.

Right on time, the steady clip-clop of a newly shooed horse announced the arrival of Charlemagne and Joshua at the curb, the one-armed delivery man in control of a small covered wagon. Amariah gave them a wave, and placed the ladder carefully beside Hannah's garden.

His wife waited for him in the walkway. "Make sure you bring the other books back," she said. "Another family has them on reserve."

Amariah smiled. Hannah took her new role as librarian very seriously, keeping close tabs on every book she lent.

"I'm sure Ella will have them waiting," he said, giving his wife a kiss. Just a brief peck, since behind her, Mrs. McGrath stood watching.

His housekeeper, who had a small apartment of her own on the first floor, handed him a small package, fragrant with the smell of freshly baked cookies.

"Hmm, hmm—smells good."

"Don't you go eating those on the way," she said. "Those are for Emily. But here, I made these for you."

Amariah took the small towel with two fresh cookies wrapped inside. "Thanks, Margaret."

256

Mrs. McGrath carried a larger package for the pregnant Hannah, and placed it into the back of the wagon. Since her return to Pleasant Valley two months earlier, she had insisted that he call her by her first name, something he still hadn't quite gotten used to.

Hannah kissed him goodbye again. "Be careful."

"Always am." Amariah smiled and headed to the wagon. He greeted Charlemagne with both hands, climbed into the passenger's seat, and waved goodbye.

The two old friends rode down through the village, past the bakery and new Town Hall, and then headed for the airfield. On the runway, Amariah's golden plane stood ready and waiting, a new inscription emblazoned on the side in bold black lettering: "Territory of Northern Vermont – Air Mail Service – Amariah Wales, Proprietor."

Caleb approached the wagon. "Good morning, Amariah." He took the packages and sack of mail from the back of Joshua's wagon and loaded them into the plane.

Amariah offered Joshua one of Margaret McGrath's cookies, and they sat there for a moment, munching, watching the crew prepare the plane for flight.

"Books for Emily?" asked Joshua.

"Yup," said Amariah. "She's coming right along, apparently. Even Ella's learning to read now."

Joshua took another bite. "Hmm. Why don't you fly a bit farther someday? See the world like you wanted to?"

"Well, everything I want is right here. Besides, Paris is a bit out of range. I can only fly as far as one tank will take me, and that's once around Vermont and back. Just enough to make a profit."

"Delivering mail."

"Air mail," said Amariah. He finished his cookie then got out of the carriage and buttoned his coat. "It's the hallmark of modern civilization, you know."

With a grin, Amariah patted Charlemagne on the neck, then turned and walked toward his plane.

Joshua called out to him. "There's fuel in Albany."

"That's one place I won't be visiting soon!"

"Let's hope that none of us will ever have to," muttered Joshua.

Amariah checked over the manifest with Caleb, then climbed into the cockpit, giving the patches over the repaired bullet holes a quick inspection. He donned his goggles, helmet, and gloves, and then gave the ground crew a thumbs-up.

Caleb threw the prop until the engine coughed to life. After a quick check of the gauges, Amariah pulled onto the runway, opened up the throttle, and roared down the runway up into the sky, the plane heavy with its parcels, tools, and seeds.

Engine humming, wind in his face, he circled once over the village, glancing down into his own yard where Hannah and Margaret stood waving. He wiggled the wings, then headed over his parents' new granite tombstones, a tribute he made at the beginning of every trip.

He banked and turned south, passing the peak of Mount Mansfield, its eastern side bright in the morning sun, then turned east to follow the Winooski River toward Montpelier, his first stop of the day.

All alone, he flew his plane, surrounded on either side by a vast expanse of undulating forest, steering his craft into the morning sun.

Just like a sailor on a rolling sea.

ABOUT THE AUTHOR

Upon graduating from New York University's Gallatin Division in 1984, George R. Fehling moved to Tokyo, Japan to teach English, write instruction manuals, and act in television commercials, until a chance meeting landed him a job as a writer and editor at a local English-language magazine. Two years later, George left Japan to journey through Asia and Europe as a freelance writer, eventually ending up in Amsterdam. A well-timed ad in a local newspaper led to a career in corporate communications at a large professional services firm, which enabled him to return to the US with his Dutch bride and buy a home on 10 acres in Underhill, Vermont. Accompanied by his yellow lab Jack, George began exploring the woods around Pleasant Valley where his first novel, DARK PEAK, is based. He now lives with his wife and daughter in a 250-year-old farmhouse in the Hudson Valley of New York, working as a writer and consultant.

CPSIA information can be obtained at www.ICGtesting.com
Printed in the USA
LVOW07s0020190116

471173LV00002B/328/P

9 780692 554296